PORPOISE IN QUICKSILVER

To Gayle and Roger
Best Wishes
W.J. Munro

PORPOISE IN QUICKSILVER

Chronicles of a High-liners Wife

M J Munro

© 2015 M J Munro
All rights reserved.

ISBN: 1515364410
ISBN 13: 9781515364412
Library of Congress Control Number: 2015912623
CreateSpace Independent Publishing Platform
North Charleston, South Carolina

For Sandy

Good enough for who it's for.

—Cap'n Munro

To my ever-patient family go thanks from my heart. Without the support, encouragement, remembered events, and technical input from each and every one of them, this book might never have been written. Special thanks go to daughter Jan for her patience and editing skills, to son Tam for actually writing one of the "tales" in the book, and artist son-in-law Steve for the truly beautiful cover painting.

There are people who will say that this whole account is a lie, but a thing isn't necessarily a lie even if it didn't necessarily happen.

—JOHN STEINBECK, *SWEET THURSDAY*

TABLE OF CONTENTS

Introduction

Since the advent of print, tales of the sea have captured readers' imaginations. The best are now classics, as popular today as when written. Almost without exception they are books about men, written by men. This is a less conventional sea story, one written by a woman about a woman.

Porpoise in Quicksilver: Chronicles of a Highliner's Wife, tells of America's West Coast commercial fishing industry as it existed over thirty-five years of the mid-twentieth century. It is told through the often graceless, usually querulous voice of a woman struggling to cope with her husband's leap from the security of an established career into a lifestyle affecting every aspect of her life and the lives of their five children. From the trials of household adjustment to hard work and high adventure at sea, she lives a life experienced by few women of her generation.

The book is a work of fiction. The characters are fictional. The incidents described, though inspired by reality, are fictionalized.

While the work is colored by imagination, it is authentic; it is an echo of the life I lived.

M. J. Munro

1

HARD DISCOVERY

World War II was at an end. It was the mid-twentieth century, an era of freedom and confidence, a time when babes, boobs, and booze were a given in the language of hardworking men, and women discouraged unwelcome advances with a laugh or a slap. Anything was possible, and men home from the wars were eager to prove it. Peace seemed sure. Optimism was the tone of the time. Wives and lovers rejoiced at the prospect of normalcy.

Ty and I were no different from the rest. Like other veterans, he came home with a need to make up for lost time, and he went at it with determination wrought by the hard-won wisdom of wartime navy service. I shared in the collective sigh of thousands of women hunkering down in no-longer-empty nests, happy to cast aside independent habits developed during those awful years of waiting.

Life for Ty and me rumbled along in this vein without much variation over the first years following the war's end. Our world was secure, our path into the future well defined, adjustments made, danger and worries bred of separation long past—or so I thought. I didn't recognize the mists of change creeping toward us, and it was a hard discovery to find that I must sink or swim in the wake of my husband's ambition.

It all began on a windy day in May when he slammed through the door, calling out, "I found her! I found my boat!"

The uneasiness I always felt when he'd been down at the docks grew. I knew the harbor was filled with the commercial fishing fleet waiting out an offshore storm, but that happened often. In the past, I'd managed to temper Ty's love affair with the sea by a recitation of the realities of our family life. The controlled chaos of the waterfront fascinated him, and he never failed to come home with wild talk about buying a boat and getting away from the desk job that left him increasingly frustrated.

No doubt it was tedious, humdrum work, but it paid well. I was certain, as all sensible adults should be, that with our growing children, we needed the financial security it provided. Ty ought to know it was time to settle down and accept the mundane bits and pieces of life as everyone else we knew had done. I hated those times when he made his restless forays among the fishermen.

Forcing a laugh, I said, "You ought to take a look at this month's bills before you set sail. What we pay for the kids' milk alone competes with the national debt."

"Yeah" was his indifferent response.

I knew he'd chosen not to hear me.

"She's a real beauty, exactly what I want to start. Proven in big seas, Jimmy 471 war-surplus diesel engine in good shape, fourteen ton refrigerated hold, even a loran. She has a great catch record, and the fellow who owns her has decided to move on to something bigger. He says he'll take me on as a puller, teach me what I need

2

to know, and then let me take over at the end of this season. Man, I can't believe my luck." He hardly took a breath during this outburst, and his azure eyes were glazed with what looked to me like delirium.

"Ty!" I snapped. "Don't be ridiculous. You've got a bunch of kids to feed and clothe. Grow up and face your responsibilities!" I knew all about the often-poor and always-uncertain markets as well as the seasonal stints at sea for weeks, even months, that were part of the business. "No. I won't hear of it!"

He whirled to face me with a look of disbelief. "Since when haven't I taken care of my family?" He glowered as the joyful glow faded from his eyes. "You've known for years that this was coming. I've considered the business from every angle. It's going to grow, and it's going to be profitable. You and I have talked about it over and over again."

He continued to stare for long moments. "Can't you see I'm sick of feeling half alive? You know I want to work for myself; I can make a better life for us!" With a snort, he turned to go. "What are you afraid of?"

With a new set to his chin, he stomped from the room. My heart banged in my throat while a thousand unspoken arguments exploded in my ears: *He's wrong!* I ranted to myself. Only *he* talked about it over and over again! No, I hadn't known for years that it was coming! How could I seriously believe an intelligent, well-educated family man would make such a decision? Join a band of roughnecks? Better life, indeed!

I didn't speak to Ty again during that long and strained afternoon. Through a haze of tears, I fixed dinner while he rustled papers holding our financial records. The boys, sensing trouble, made themselves scarce. Baby Jenny followed me around the kitchen with big, questioning eyes.

During dinner, Ty outlined his plan to the whole family. The boys were ecstatic. Chance, the oldest, yelped, "That's slick, Dad! You'll outfish 'em all." He had friends who'd already sailed on family boats, and had a fair idea of what was in the offing. His younger brothers had fuzzier notions.

Only a year younger than their brother, and a team as always, twins Cord and Chase echoed Chance's sentiment with rousing cheers: "Yeah!" and "We'll sail the bounding main!"

"You could get shipwrecked on a desert island!" Cole, youngest of the boys, suggested happily. Poor little Jenny, still a year or so from kindergarten, stared worriedly.

The boys' reaction was no surprise. From birth, they'd been indoctrinated with tales of sea and sailors. They were still in toddler's beds when their father first read to them of Robinson Crusoe. Of course they loved it. By this time, they were thoroughly steeped in those action-packed adventures found in the pages of volume after volume of pirate-and-clipper-ship classics. The problem was that they had reached that age of anticipated manhood when adventure beckons, unfettered by experience. I was nervous about what their dad's bewitching madness might encourage.

Over the following days, Ty went methodically forward with his arrangements while I bombarded him with tears and recriminations. I'd never before known him to be so quietly unbending. Nothing I could conjure shook his determination or the arrival of the day when I stood on the dock staring at a gray-trimmed boat of would-be white knocking gently against the wharf, its soaring cedar poles swaying against a sky swept blue in a northwest breeze.

Beside me, my entranced husband murmured, "Isn't she a beauty, Bailey? Just look at those lines."

I looked down the docks where dozens of white boats trimmed in various shades of gray, black, or green were tied. Sullenly, I retorted, "Looks just like all the others."

"No! No, she's not the same. Look how she settles down in the water with her bow high. Now, look over there." He pointed to a nearby boat. "See how that one is all straight lines and bounces with every eddy?"

"You're nuts." I was disgusted at his besotted stare, though I looked. There might have been a little difference in the boats, but I pulled my hat over my ears, refusing to acknowledge it. "I'm cold. Do we have to stand here?"

With a cheerful "Nope," Ty urged me forward. "Come on. I want you to meet my shipmate, my new boss. You'll like him, and you can check out our boat."

The reference to "our" boat made me wince, but I kept quiet until I caught sight of the boat's name painted on its bow in large black letters. I couldn't keep a sarcastic sniff to myself. "*River Run?* I thought it was a seagoing boat."

Ty grinned. "*River Run*'s been her name from the start. The old-timers say it's bad luck to change a boat's name, and I don't plan to test the theory."

He ran an affectionate hand over the boat's hull as he walked by. Frustrated and furious, I opened my mouth to hurl hostile words about childish superstitions, but that caress told me they'd be wasted.

"Her name's because she was built up Washington way, near the Columbia River," he explained. "This old girl's had a string of owners that made good, and none of them saw fit to call her anything else. I'm not going to be the one to jinx her."

I muttered a heartfelt curse under my breath that had little to do with boats or fishermen. Boat names and their owners' beliefs were nothing to me. All I knew or cared was that the tidy little world I'd created for my family was under siege and that the person I trusted most led the charge.

Through all the feverish preparation for this day, I clung to the thought that time and argument would make my husband see reason. Instead, here I was, standing on a surging dock, staring at the man I married, a stranger with formidable confidence and a jaunty swing to his step. He looked years younger than he had only weeks before, and a quirky grin that I'd forgotten shone through uncharacteristic whisker stubble. I had the sudden, jolting suspicion that there wasn't, and never had been, a question about the outcome of our quarrel.

Ty and I were married long before the *River Run* entered our lives. The years had their bumps, but the marriage was a happy one and our skirmishes minor. He fought his battles by ignoring or laughing away arguments. I pecked, but there were few occasions when I didn't accept his decisions.

This fight was different in ways I couldn't comprehend. Everything I cherished was threatened. Awash in doubt and fear, I was now forced to the realization that I might have no choice but to find a way to live with both. In a daze of anger and uncertainty, I followed down the shifting dock ramp.

As luck would have it, my first unsteady steps on the boat's rocking deck sent me reeling toward a low side rail and the cold waters of the bay. Only Ty's last-minute grab saved me. In a strained mutter, he said, "I should have let you go over the side. That might cool you off."

For a second I felt blistering resentment. Then, in a piercing stab of insight, I let it go. I'd given the battle my all, and lost. Tiredly, I leaned into his protective arm.

"Okay, Ty, you win. I give up."

It was done. There would be no turning back.

2

WALLY AND THE RIVER RUN

It was only days after my capitulation that the *River Run* set sail with Ty aboard on his first working trip. After watching the last of the groceries disappear into the hold, the children and I climbed into the station wagon and followed the boat on its slow journey all the way down the bay, past the waterfront restaurants, past the PG&E stacks puffing their white billows of steam, around the massive primordial rock marking the entrance to the harbor, and all the way to the end of the breakwater. The boys tumbled jubilantly out of the car to race to the highest vantage point where they danced, screaming their good-byes. I stood with tears streaming down my cheeks, waving my man out of sight while Jenny clung quietly to my jacket.

There's no use in dwelling on the beginning. Suffice to say that the first year was a horror of adjustment. Jenny had nightmares, and the boys were quick to challenge my authority. Household maintenance, from paying the bills to fixing leaky faucets, was now my responsibility. Important decisions had to be made without support. Already thin, I lost even more weight. Worst of all, my family was scandalized by Ty's defection, my parents quietly, my sister far too vocally.

"Why are you putting up with this, Bailey? Think what you are doing to your children. First thing you know they'll turn into bums, too!" My big sister always had felt it her duty to point out my failings.

"What would you have me do, Kayla? He's determined, and it's done. Besides, Ty is not a bum, and none of the fishermen I've met are bums." I wished my beautiful sister a little less perfect and less compelled to lend her "moral support." I wished with all my heart that she was back in her perfect home with her perfect family, a thousand miles away.

With a sigh of relief, I watched her go at last, leaving me to stew over her baleful predictions. Fortunately, coping with my new circumstance didn't allow much time for dwelling on them. Necessity soon demanded that I forget her blather and set myself to the serious business of putting new routines in place.

From the first, Ty's trips kept him away from home for much of the time. When we were no longer a reliable twosome in our social circle, old friends drifted away. In the turmoil, I hardly noticed. Other friends filled the void as the seasoned wives of local fishermen welcomed me into their close-knit community. It was a comfort to know I was not alone with my problems, though I was sure I could never find the trusting, optimistic serenity in this new life that these spirited women displayed. They saw me through that dismal time, and I eventually came to understand that they were of the same hardy breed as their colorful husbands.

My real introduction to the type began on the night of my surrender to Ty's decision. We were still standing on the deck of the *River Run*, in deep study of one another after he had saved me from a chilly swim, when a cheery greeting startled us. We had not yet come to terms with my giving in to his senseless wishes, but at the sound of the oddly pitched voice, Ty abandoned me and fairly leaped across the deck to pump the hand of the leather-faced man who leaned over the open upper half of the boat cabin's Dutch door.

Still numb with defeat and still hoping, I suppose, for a reprieve, I watched with sinking heart.

It was clear that Ty and Wally, as his name proved to be, were firmly bonded in friendship despite their few weeks of close acquaintance. Even in my state of denial, I could see that Wally was a man of intelligence, energy, and good nature. I was all but ignored as they launched into an animated discussion thick with technical terms beyond my ken. Introductions were offhand and vaguely acknowledged despite Wally's courtly handshake. In a silent funk, I allowed myself to be guided into the interior of the boat I dreaded to see and immediately found myself seated at a small table, listening to the drone of gibberish while a cup of coffee strong enough to curl hair steamed in front of me.

That entire evening is a fog surrounding odd incidents that remain crystallized in my memory. I don't remember much more than heat and the vague smell of diesel from my first introduction to the *River Run*'s interior, but somehow I've kept a vision of going off to a local restaurant where Wally neatly packed an astounding quantity of food into his wiry body. The greasy cap he'd worn was now snow white; I hadn't seen him change it.

I remember a stream of other white-capped men stopping for a friendly handshake and an insider's joke of one kind or another. Most vivid, though, is the picture of Ty and Wally chattering happily together like kids on a picnic. Ty, tall, blue-eyed, well pro-portioned, and always quietly controlled, made a striking contrast to his new business partner.

Wally was a study in contradictions. His gentlemanly manner disagreed with his outward appearance. Neither handsome nor plain and average in height, he was an unusually energetic man, never still. His legs, disproportionately long in comparison to his compact torso, matched thin arms that ended in incredibly large and work-worn hands. Most striking were his intelligent brown eyes that missed little. He invariably wore the white fisherman's cap dubbed a "Norwegian Stetson," usually covered in engine grease and often doffed in the manner of a gallant.

In time I came to know him as a fascinating, paradoxical man, but my only thought then was of an accomplice in the ruin of my world.

Indeed, I held an unreasonable grudge against Wally, and he was far more generous in ignoring my pettish behavior than I de-served. How shaming to remember those early days, because it was Wally who taught me first and most of what I needed to know if I was to make the best of Ty's eccentric switch in careers.

A first glimmering into the breed he represented came on the day Wally's warm and immaculately groomed wife, Martha, teased about a seagoing run-in with the government. Her story was that Wally had been ordered away from an area of naval missile-launch practice maneuvers. He'd been having unusually good fishing there, so he went on about his business, ignoring radio demands and the small naval cutter sent to warn him away.

"It was idiotic to ignore the warnings, Wally, and you know it. Those people were only doing their job. They were trying to keep you safe," she chided.

Wally grinned. "I didn't ignore them. I let them know I was sailing outside their jurisdiction and that it wasn't too long ago I was being paid twenty-two dollars a month by the United States Army to get shot at by people who were aiming at me! I told them they were welcome to go ahead with all the target practice they wanted. For the dollars I stood to make in staying there on the fish, I didn't mind taking my chances."

I blurted, "Surely you didn't talk like that to the authorities! What on earth did they say?"

"I don't know. I turned off my radios. I was glad when the cutter left, though. It was interfering with my tack."

I laughed then, admiring Wally's independence, and thought how like Ty's his attitude was. Though I knew, of course, that Ty would never endanger himself so foolishly!

3

SOMETIMES TOOLS ARE NOWHERE

Before Ty's learning curve as Wally's puller ended, I managed to concoct a workable routine, which included listening patiently to my husband's growing litany of the foibles of his mentor. Apparently, all was not caviar aboard the *River Run*.

"How can a man as successful as Wally ignore some of this stuff?" Ty stopped pacing long enough to poke the air with his finger. "That gap between the deck and the smokestack is wide enough for a whale to fall through! Everything loose goes straight down to the bilge. He would never let it go if it was outside of the cabin and open to the weather. Something's always rolling around on the inside deck, just begging to slip down into the bilge. He's terrible about dumping stuff just anywhere!" He sighed heavily. "One of these days, we're going to have a serious gum-up from junk that's fallen through."

The pleasure of having my husband at home for a day or two kept me from stirring trouble by reminding him that he hadn't needed to join forces with Wally. Instead, I murmured sweetly, "Can't you do something about it yourself? Anyway, you ought to forget the business for a little while."

"Uh-huh," he mumbled vacantly. "I've got what I need to fix things. It'll be done before we leave port." He glanced at me, his mind clearly engaged elsewhere. "Damned if I can figure what makes the man tick. Wally is smart, the best small-boat troller on the West Coast, the first to find fish and stay on top of them, and farsighted enough to try every piece of new equipment that comes out. He's an ace at troubleshooting anything and everything— engines, electronics, and right down to a frayed line. I think he spends half his time hoping something will give out just so he can fix it." Light returned to Ty's eyes, along with his usual grin. "Oh well, Wally's a great guy. But, geez, he sure is a careless slob."

"Well, why don't you pick up stuff if he doesn't? It seems like that would be easier than tripping over it."

"Oh, I pick it up all right but he's oblivious. He's a stickler for keeping anything to do with the engine or fishing gear in top shape, but that's where it ends."

As the weeks passed, the complaints grew and my antagonism built. The inevitable explosion took place in San Francisco, where I was spending a couple of days while the latest catch was unloaded. We were relaxing in a waterfront inn a few blocks from the docks when he began repeating the same complaints that had battered my ears for weeks. Resentful at my darling's failure to recognize that I also had hardships to air, I could stand to hear no more of his.

"Stop it, Ty!" I couldn't restrain the months of bottled bile. "You said you liked him. You made him out to be downright saintly before you bought his boat. I told you this was a bad decision. Now you're in the middle of a big mistake, stuck with something you can't do anything about."

With a disbelieving look, Ty slammed back, "Who said I didn't like him? Who says I made a bad decision? Wally has done a lot more for me than all those years of school did." His cheeks were ruddy with pique. "And there's plenty I can do about it. I can try to be as good at this game as he is, if he can put up with me long enough to teach me how to do it." He glared for a long moment and then grinned sheepishly. "But I wish he'd put the tools back where they belong. Nothing is ever in the same place twice. Sometimes it's nowhere!"

This exchange silenced me on the subject of Wally's peccadilloes and let me know that any criticism of the man was best kept to myself. It was a lesson that served me well over the months that the two worked together on the *River Run*, for Wally's idiosyncrasies remained.

As Ty's education continued, I discovered that it brought more lessons to me, too. One of the first began with a sunrise call telling me that they were in Half Moon Bay delivering the few fish they had. Ty's prediction was on target—their trip was cut short because of a jammed pump.

"One of Wally's socks got sucked up with the bilgewater and stuck in the intake valve. It burned out the motor. What a stink!"

"Uh-oh! What did Wally have to say about it?"

"Never crossed his mind that he had anything to do with it. All he said was, 'I wondered where that sock went.'" Ty chuckled, his admiration palpable. "That man is the best baling-wire mechanic afloat. He had us jury-rigged in nothing flat. We hardly used the hand pump at all."

After listening to another word or so of worship, I relaxed, anticipating our usual prolonged phone chat. Instead, his next words brought me bolt upright. "I want you to bring a new pump up to us. The old one isn't salvageable. Martha can't make the drive, so it's up to you. We've already called Dom down at the marine store. He'll have it ready for you to pick up on your way out of town. If you start right away, you should have it here by this afternoon."

Of course I did as directed, wondering the whole two hundred miles up to Half Moon, and the whole two hundred miles back, how I had become involved in this unpredictable, irrational, and thoroughly irritating business.

4

DOM'S MARINE STORE

Marine equipment stores were an essential to the business, and there was sure to be one in any given port, large or small. They varied widely in size and merchandise as well as personnel. Dom's Marine Store offered as good a selection of boating supplies as any such establishment on the West Coast and far better than most. My acquaintance with it began during the earliest stages of Ty's adventures with the *River Run*. It was there that the needed replacement pump waited.

The building itself was a large barnlike metal-and-glass structure situated a few blocks above the harbor, with its back to the bay. The dim interior boasted a methodically displayed mélange of boating necessities for both commercial and pleasure craft, and a few not-so-necessary gewgaws attractive to wives and yacht owners. On this occasion, when I arrived to retrieve the ordered pump, there were the usual half dozen customers inside, including a clearly stressed fisherman.

"Hey, Dom, got any more of them new hoochies? I don't see 'em here in the bins." The agitated sailor pointed to an empty spot in the midst of a large collection of containers holding lures in a wide variety of colors and shapes.

Dom's dark eyes sparkled with kind good humor touched with sympathy. "Sorry, Sil. Those new jigs went out like lightning. The replacements should be here in a couple of days."

"Aw, Dom, you know I can't wait. I hear the fish are begging to get aboard with those lures. Don't you have a couple of 'em stashed somewhere?"

"No, none left, Sil, but Ray on the *Albatross* bought quite a batch of them. Maybe he'd let you have what you need."

Muttering hard words about that "stingy so-and-so not likely to do diddly-squat for nobody," Sil took his worried frown out the door and headed toward the dock where Ray's boat was tied.

Dom turned to me with a shake of his head. "Poor guy's been tied up too long with a bent propeller. Ray will help him out if he can, and if he can't, Sil will be all right. They're both good men."

I nodded, only vaguely aware of Dom's concern and only minimally interested in either Sil's or Ray's problems. "Sure. Ty said you would have ready something he called about this morning. A pump, I think?"

Suddenly all business, Dom strode over to a nearby counter, calling out, "George! Come carry the *River Run*'s order out to Bailey's car, will you?"

"Can I write a check, Dom?" I cautiously asked.

Looking surprised, Dom answered, "Charges will go down in the *River Run* book with the rest of their stuff. They can settle up when it's convenient."

With a sigh of relief, I watched as he pulled a small account book from a stack and methodically filled a line with scribbled numbers. "Thanks, Dom. It's a lot easier on me if the boat account takes care of it."

"Wally and Ty are good customers, always Johnny-on-the-spot when it's time to pay up." Dom patted my shoulder in kindly reminder. "You should be on your way. I see George has the pump in your car." With a smile and a wave, he turned and hurried off in response to an urgent call from the other end of the building.

"Dom! Where the heck is the weasel pee?"

"It's on the shelf, next aisle over, Charlie! Hang on, I'll be right there."

Shaking my head, I turned to go, remembering the first time I'd been sent to pick up this particular item and been hesitant to use the term. The reference was to WD-40, a popular and widely used aerosol lubricant with water-dispersant properties, hardly ever referred to as anything other than weasel pee!

I reached the door in time to meet Sil pushing noisily through in high good spirits. "Let's get this show on the road! Hey, Dom! Where are you?"

Even before I reached the main highway, I was in deep assay of Dom and the esteem in which he was held by anyone who knew him. The stories were legion, and my own observations during the endless string of errands I'd run while the boat underwent out-fitting and repairs were making inroads on my prejudice against anything associated with commercial fishing.

Dom was one of those singularly attractive Italian men whose swarthy features settled early into character that aged enviably. His persona was upbeat, he had a smile for everyone, and his dark-brown eyes seemed to reflect inner warmth. He was kind and trust-ing, but he was also shrewd and thoughtful enough to maintain a thriving establishment that depended on the fruits of a volatile business with men and boats in constant flux.

On one particularly hectic day, when the store was filled with men preparing for a big push, I watched Ty catch Dom's eye by holding an item high. To my surprise, Dom nodded and pointed to the account books. It was even more surprising to see Ty walk over, pull out one of the books, enter his purchase, and then leave with no more than a wave and a nod.

Outside, I questioned, "How will Dom know that everything you wrote down is right? Isn't he afraid of being cheated?"

"I'd wager Dom knows exactly who can be trusted, and I'm dead certain he knows who can't be. On a day like today, he'd be glad of the help. You saw he had only two clerks on the floor. He carries most of the locals on his books—it's kept more than one from having to choose between an expensive bank loan and going broke. I know it hasn't always been easy for him, either."

I also remembered Wally singing his praises: "I had an engine breakdown way up north, near one of those doghole anchorages, where I patched things together enough to limp into Brookings, but I couldn't find the one part I needed anywhere. Do you know what Dom did? Nothing in it for him, but he went out of his way to find that part and then talk a supply rep into delivering it. The rep was headed in the right direction, and I had it a day later. Imagine! That fellow was all right, too. He wouldn't take a dime for his trouble, so I gave him my biggest salmon. Without Dom looking out for me, I could have been sitting on the dock for weeks."

Dom had come to his marine supply store well prepared. He began life as a member of a well-established Oregon seafaring family. By the time he touched our lives, a good portion of his fifty-plus years had seen experience in almost every aspect of commercial fishing. He understood not only the industry but the aches and pains, physical and mental, that went with it. A dedicated family man with an ailing wife and two teenagers still at home, as well as grandchildren from older offspring, he was civic-minded and active in community affairs. He made an excellent spokesman for the industry.

Chewing on these thoughts made the miles fly, but at the end of my journey, Dom, boats, and fishermen were no less a mystery.

5

WALLY QUITS SMOKING

Toward the end of that first season, during one of the rare occasions when the boat made home port, Ty and I sat hashing over the events of his months away. By then, he was speaking less of Wally's bad habits, and when the subject did come up, it was more often than not with a shrug, if not a laugh.

"Wally decided to quit smoking." Ty grinned. "First thing I knew about it was when he came aboard with the announcement. We made the trip okay, if you don't take into account the effects of too much coffee. That stuff he calls coffee is black enough to pass for anchor paint, and he drinks quarts." He grimaced. "I felt sorry for him. Can't say I know what he was going through, never having been a smoker, but it was easy to see that he was in a bad way. Once we had our full catch and were pulling up to the buyer's dock, he was off like a shot. Didn't even wait to tie up and wasn't back until half the load was already out of the hold. Can you believe it? All that time looking for a place to buy a pack while he left me flat! I was busy as a shark in a bait ball, taking care of his job and mine, but he came back with his smokes and the first smile I'd seen in weeks."

"I guess that was the end of that experiment."

"Oh no. Wally doesn't give up that easy. When we left port again, it was without cigarettes. Next delivery, same story. We weren't even tied up before he jumped ship to go looking for his poison." Ty chuckled. "I wised up after that and hid a pack on the boat before we started the new trip. Next time we made port, the minute I spotted the first harbor buoy, I gave him his blasted weeds. It worked like a charm. He was happy as a clam by the time we docked. Now I hide a pack every time we go out."

"Oh good! Problem solved."

"Not quite. Once he realized what I was doing, he started looking for them every time I left the cabin. It's gotten to be a regular game of hide-and-seek." Ty laughed. "So far, I'm ahead two to one."

I laughed with him, wondering at the hijinks, but I guess their nonsense meant something because Wally did eventually quit smoking.

6

LONG SWIM

It was in the last month of Ty's sojourn on the *River Run* with Wally calling the shots. They were on the way to San Pedro with a delivery and would be sailing the Santa Barbara Islands channel that runs the length of Southern California. When morning news broadcasters reported that a couple of shipwrecked fishermen had dragged themselves ashore below homes perched on the cliffs of Pacific Palisades, not far from San Pedro, my heart plummeted. I was convinced from the sketchy descriptions that the two could be no other than Ty and Wally. When there was no answer to my anxious ship-to-shore call, I was near panic. I wasted no time in getting to Martha's doorstep.

"The boat doesn't answer the radio, Martha." I stood before her, trying to look unconcerned.

"When did you call, dear?" I could see no hint of worry in Martha's eyes.

"As soon as I heard the local radio news report about those two men. They didn't give names."

"Well, I wouldn't be too alarmed. Wally and Ty are probably busy unloading and can't hear the radio, or they may not have turned it on at all. From the information I had, those two men were discovered at daylight. If it were our boys, they would call home right away, count on it. Now, do sit down and have coffee."

Reluctantly, I did as bid and was there when Wally's reassuring call came through. After Martha returned from her kitchen "radio command center" to rejoin me, she patted my hand while relaying the welcome news.

"Wally said Ty called home a short time ago and was concerned at not getting an answer, but not to worry, he'll call again after they get the boat cleaned up."

"Well, don't I feel silly!" And I did, fervently hoping that Ty would never learn of my foolishness. I avoided Martha's sympathetic glance. "I wish I could be as sensible as you are. I should have thought of all that," I said.

"Don't worry, dear. That will come with time."

The two men who had given me such a scare turned out to be Bart and his crewman, Jiggs, a respected team from a neighboring port. I happened to be standing with a waterfront bunch gathered on the docks near Casper's electronics shop when the two dropped by to discuss new boat possibilities. I heard their story firsthand.

Bart ran his big square hands repeatedly over the front of his fresh blue chambray shirt. His brow, usually smooth above firm Scandinavian features and a stocky body, furrowed as he spoke.

"It was late, near midnight, and everything seemed normal under a clear sky, no moon. The shore lights stood out but did us no good where we sailed, far enough offshore to make the night black as ink. An occasional boat passed by, and the lights of one or two could be made out at a distance, but there was no heavy traffic. We saw nothing close enough to be a worry."

Slumped next to Bart, Jiggs, long legged and rumpled, shifted in his seat to reveal a boney profile with a clump of shaggy red chin whiskers. "The sea was calm, barely breezy enough to let us know we were on salt. As sweet sailing as you could want."

"Exactly," Bart agreed. "We were moving along smooth as silk, when, wham! Out of the blue, we were in the water, and the boat was on its way down. There was no time to do a thing."

To the general demand for an explanation of how such an accident could happen, Bart obliged in detail. "I have a hunch the wreck was caused by a barge with an unlighted tow or a tow on an extra-long cable hidden in the dark. If we hit something adrift, things would likely happen slowly enough to at least get out a Mayday call, but a snagged tug towline would drag a boat down instantly. Nobody knows anything about that possibility, though. It seems there wasn't a single barge-and-tow out that night." The remark was made with irony and met with sly smiles.

Jiggs gave a little chuckle. "Yeah, we were dumped in the middle of the channel, in pitch dark with no vests, no raft, nothing. I thought I was a goner. Luckily, that Bart there is one lollapalooza of a coach. I didn't know how fast I could learn to be a champion swimmer."

"It doesn't take long for your brain to rev up when you realize that the only chance you have is the one you give yourself. Well, maybe with a good bit of help from above. And don't let Jiggs kid you; he was thinking as fast as I was. We paddled around for a minute or two, getting our bearings and making sure we'd both made it into the water in one piece, but pretty quick, we decided on a plan and agreed to stick to it.

"We knew the important thing was to conserve strength. There was no waving our arms or hollering. Without a light to show, we'd never be seen, and yelling couldn't be heard over engine noise. We figured it was no good to try breaking any speed records, either. Slow and easy was the way to go. Any unnecessarily spent energy could make the difference between sand under our feet or ending up crab bait. Believe me, we thanked our lucky stars that this happened in calm, warm water. If we'd been off the Columbia River, we wouldn't have had a chance.

"We decided that no matter what, we'd stick together. That turned out to be the toughest part, but probably the most important. We kind of kept each other going." He shook his head. "Seemed a long time before those shore lights looked any closer."

"At least you could see them." Jiggs grinned wryly. "That was more than I could do."

"That's right! Somehow I managed to keep my glasses on when we went in the water. Sure glad I had them on the string I always use at sea. If I'd lost them, maybe neither of us would be here now. That constant saltwater splash got to Jiggs's eyes about halfway in and blinded him, bad. These glasses kept mine clear." Bart grinned widely. "Sort of makes up for being called 'frog' and 'four-eyes' when I was a kid!"

After a general laugh, someone in the crowd asked, "How did you stay together if Jiggs couldn't see? Those currents can part anything not tied together."

"Noise, that's how! Jiggs recited little ditties, and the good Lord must have a sense of humor if he let him get away with some of them. I sang a little."

"Hymns, if you can believe it. Pretty bad, too—way off-key," Jiggs interjected with a wink.

Bart saluted, as if acknowledging praise. "I also told out a couple of nonsense rhymes and sometimes the times tables when we drifted apart. We kept it up, back and forth, until we were side by side again. Mostly, we listened for the other guy's splashes. We kept our energy for moving ahead, resting and talking only when necessary."

By the time the two hit the rocks at the base of the cliff, Bart had just about had it. He remembered a man coming down to meet him, but almost everything else was a blur. The man was sitting out on his terrace with morning coffee when he spotted Bart. At first he had a little trouble accepting such a bedraggled visitor rising from the sea, but as soon as he knew Bart was a legitimate beached sailor, he couldn't help him enough. Meanwhile, Jiggs was caught in the surf and carried about a quarter of a mile down the coast. He was found with the surf breaking over his legs and had to be pulled in.

"Sure did," Jiggs concluded. "I have no idea who found me, me being blind and him disappearing as soon as I connected with Bart.

But thank God, he was a good-sized guy. Had to be to get my pretty-near dead weight all the way up on land. I couldn't hardly even crawl."

The pair was soon back in the business of catching fish. My recovery from their story took longer.

7

THE CASTAWAYS

Despite determined resistance, the business began to interest me. I found we were not reduced to poverty after Ty took charge of the boat. Money came in as plentifully as it always had. In fact, our income increased, bringing with it another set of lessons. In my past, salaries were paid at regular intervals, expenses were predictable, and budgets were counted as meaningful. I learned that this process is not universal.

Ty's first payload brought a sizeable check and a dose of reality. "We've never had this much money in our account all at once!" I was ecstatic. "It won't be long before we can get a bigger house with a room for each of the kids."

"Not so fast! Just because the money comes in chunks instead of dribbles doesn't mean we have more. What I bring in has to last. Maybe the price won't hold, and there's a lot of expense coming. We have to pay for boat insurance, mooring fees, licenses, taxes, engine maintenance, fuel, and electronics—then, of course, there's haul out."

"Oh." My dreams exploded. It was a few seconds before I could go on. "I guess I forgot about some of that stuff. Is haul out, whatever that is, expensive?"

"What's the matter with you?" Ty was annoyed. "You know what haul out is. You've seen the boat in dry dock. Of course it's expensive, but cost isn't relevant. A working boat has to be taken out of the water for maintenance if it's going to be safe and efficient. We have to plan for the expense." He stared dubiously at me. "You'll have to begin paying attention to what you spend."

The dressing down smarted, and I bristled from it, but after a bit of seething, I vowed to myself that if we were to have money problems, they wouldn't originate with me.

As it turned out, prices remained stable that year. Fishing was good, there were no unexpected emergencies either at home or on the boat, and I kept my expenses firmly in hand. However, another, more worrisome aspect of the business was introduced.

Martha and I had long since established a practice of making daily calls to chat and review the scuttlebutt that kept those of us on the beach informed of what was happening with our men at sea. Though Ty and I continued to rely on ship-to-shore phone communication and had not set up a citizens-band radio for the house, many of the fishing families had. News from sea was quickly spread.

On this day, most of the fleet had already "hung it up" for the season, though there were still boats out hoping for a final bite, including the *River Run* and Wally's new boat, *Mariner.* When Martha's call came, it contained far more than fish scores and weather reports.

"The *Sarah Ann* hasn't been heard from in three days. Bess is terribly worried. Joe has missed every appointed time on their CB schedule. She's afraid he might be having trouble because of all the heavy weather south of us. She put the word out, but not one of the fishermen still on the grounds has seen the boat." Martha's voice was tense. "That nice-looking kid, Elmer, is with him."

This unexpected news was chilling. Joe and Bess were among the best-liked fishing families. Their boat, the *Sarah Ann*, smaller than most in the fleet, generally day fished for local markets in waters close to home. Joe had this time chosen to venture farther in response to reports of a good albacore run not far offshore. Elmer was one of the usual parade of young men looking for adventure and a little money by hiring out as a puller, the helper who worked the deck and fishing lines. His easygoing attitude made him a fleet-wide favorite.

"Oh, Martha! Is there anything we can do?"

"Pray," was her only suggestion.

We had a weary time while friends and the coast guard scoured coastal waters, but the fruitless search was called off after several heartbreaking days. Bess was inconsolable, insisting that Joe was sure to be out there somewhere. The wives' network continued to add casseroles, cookies, and comforting shoulders. There was nothing more we could do.

I knew with the others that a time would come when each of us would accept what had to be and move on with our lives, but the sour lump residing in my belly through the whole miserable episode expanded each time I thought of Ty roaming the Pacific in a cockleshell. During all this, he fought a refrigeration malfunction that finally forced him to give up the season and bring the boat home. Wally, true to character, continued to hunt for more fish.

Joe and Elmer were determinedly tucked away in a dark corner of my mind. Life had moved on, so it was disturbing to receive a call from Martha babbling senseless words about the lost pair.

"Why, Martha, what on earth do you mean?" I gently objected. "You know they weren't found."

"Yes! Yes, they were! Wally found them! They're alive! I couldn't make much out of what he said, though. I swear it sounded like he was talking about a cat!"

Ty came running from the docks soon after, beaming relief, to confirm the news now spread across the waterfront. All anyone knew then was that Wally found the two men on San Miguel Island, the westernmost and one of the least visited of California's Channel Islands, and that he was on his way home with Joe and Elmer aboard.

We had another anxious vigil, but with lighter hearts. By the time the *Mariner* came through the harbor entrance in late afternoon of the next day, it seemed like the entire population of the town was on hand to greet it. Wally, with a big white grin splitting his face, steered from the flying bridge. The two castaways, wrapped in blankets, waved from the deck below, where Wally's puller, Tony, scurried around preparing to dock.

Martha, Ty, and I stood with Bess, watching the little knot of local reporters with their popping camera lights surround the rescued men and their saviors. None of the four looked pleased with the attention, but we did learn from insistent questioning that bad winds had forced Joe to look for a place to ride out the weather. He'd headed for the nearest island, found a likely spot, dropped anchor in one of its coves, and then decided to kill time by exploring ashore. When the pair returned a few hours later, everything they'd left was gone. Their boat was on the bottom of the bay, their dinghy shattered in the surf.

Eventually, Joe and Elmer were spirited away and safely deposited in their homes. The rest of us retired to Wally's and Martha's cozy fireside, eager for details of the rescue. Wally was hamming up his part, claiming he'd been sent "a message from above" to sail out of his way and check San Miguel on the way home from his last San Pedro cannery delivery.

"Yeah, yeah," Ty finally challenged Wally, "now tell us what your *passengers* had to say about their boat going out from under them. And what's this rumor I hear that Tony mistook a *cat* for a walrus?"

The challenge was met with hooted laughter, and it was some time before our performers settled down to something approaching seriousness, but once they did, the quiet remained.

"About the only thing they could come up with is that the anchor didn't hold," Wally said. "They figured that with the high tide and an unusually strong surge in an unfamiliar anchorage, the boat was pushed by those heavy wind gusts that San Miguel Island is famous for, into underwater rocks that punched a plank open. The bilge pump just couldn't keep up."

Our narrator was silent for some time, then straightened abruptly with amusement brightening his eyes. "And you betcha there was a cat, and it sure didn't look like any walrus I've seen." He gleefully pointed at Tony. "I thought it was a bundle of sea-weed on driftwood sticking up through the wash. This joker here was looking through binoculars, all the time insisting it was a mast crosstree with something alive hanging to it."

"A pretty sorry-looking thing it was, too," Tony put in.

Wally grinned. "It looked more like a wad of kelp than anything alive. When we got close, we heard it howling and could see its tail going to beat the band. If Tony hadn't spotted that poor, miser-able thing, we'd have gone on by. He was right; what I thought was driftwood was the *Sarah Ann*'s mast. That poor little creature must have hung on for who knows how long. No food, no water—it's a miracle it survived. I figure the cabin roof was above water at first, giving the kitty a place to hide, but the boat gradually shifted deeper, forcing her up into the rigging."

"Poor little kitten," Martha crooned.

"I set Tony off in our skiff to check the situation, and when he got close, that cat made a leap to remember. She stayed attached to him until we pried her off, you betcha!" Wally concluded.

Serious discussion about Joe's and Elmer's ordeal was nearly lost in the euphoria of the rescue, but eventually the question ev-eryone had was asked: How could a thing like that happen to a man as seasoned as Joe in the ways of the sea?

Wally shook his head. "Joe's punishing himself with that same question. He says he made sure the anchor was well-set, with plenty of scope. He'd expected to be away from the boat only a short while, not the several hours the two of them were lured into. Mostly, he didn't count on a high tide combining with a big swell and heavy wind gusts before they got back. I suspect it'll be a while before he can forgive himself."

After that, we mulled their harrowing time as castaways, knowing now the hard conditions they faced. Still, there was a spring with plenty of water to drink and, to eat, there was an abundance of shellfish along the shore. They might yearn for steak and coffee, but what they had could keep them alive indefinitely. Joe was a smoker with matches in his pocket, so they had fire as long as matches, embers, and fuel held out. For the first few days, they kept a lookout and a pile of tinder on the highest point, the idea being to set off a signal if someone sailed close. But that plan was abandoned when they realized it was too late in the year to expect to see another fish boat or vacationer's yacht anytime soon.

"Why, they might have had to wait for months," Martha softly murmured. "Poor boys, what dreadful thoughts they must have had. I know Joe would worry himself sick about Bessie, and they must have been so hungry and cold! All they had were the clothes on their backs, neither of them wearing so much as a warm shirt."

Wally stared pensively into the fire for some time. "The cat was the real savior. If it hadn't survived, we would have sailed away without a suspicion they were there. They didn't see us pull in because they were huddled around a driftwood campfire in a protected spot well above the high tide line."

Tony nodded. "Yeah, it was lucky they were close enough to hear Wally's whistle. They sure come on a run, yelling like a couple of banshees. It was good they were camped close by. Otherwise we'd have had to stay and comb the island until we figured out what happened to whoever belonged to that poor cat."

We sat late that night, basking in the warmth of miracles and dying embers. The *Sarah Ann II* replaced the *Sarah Ann* within months. On its maiden voyage, Bess quietly waved her husband out to sea. The cat, now called Angel, sailed with it.

8

PROMISES, PROMISES

Time began to fly. We'd been in the business long enough for me to plan on Ty being at home by Thanksgiving, more or less, the date always determined by the strength of the albacore run during the season's waning days. Likewise, I knew he would be ready to leave on April 1, opening day of salmon season.

Salmon and albacore were his two main fisheries, and he promised that those months between seasons' ends and beginnings would be dedicated family time. No doubt he thought he lived up to the promise.

"Hey, men, who wants to help scrape barnacles?" Ty hollered in from the back porch one morning and was immediately rewarded by an enthusiastic scramble of boys.

The *River Run* was in the boatyard awaiting repairs and paint. It had been a tedious time getting it there, but at last the weather calmed, tides were right, and the appointment kept. I wasn't happy about any part of it. Even now, after having been through this ritual often enough to expect glitches, I continued to chafe at the delays and the whole boring nuisance of seasonal preparations.

"Can't you at least let them finish their breakfast? Hire some-one else to do that dirty work! Besides, here it is January, and we still haven't taken the kids up to San Francisco." The promised trip was a sore spot with me, and I reminded him often of his declared intention to take the family to that favorite city for a visit to its zoo and a ride on its famous cable cars.

Ty stopped tussling with his "men" long enough to lift a quizzi-cal eyebrow at me. "How long do you think I'd last in this business if I hired out everything that needed doing? You're talking some mighty big bucks, there. And how else would I know what's hap-pening below the boat's waterline if I didn't look for myself?" He winked at the boys. "Besides, I like working on the old girl, and so do they."

It was true. The boys had taken wholeheartedly to the lifestyle. Chance, now an actual teen of a month or two, had already gone along on a couple of trips with his dad, and his brothers were hard in his wake. Even Jenny had learned to watch with composure each time her daddy sailed away. With a grudging sigh, I decided to make the best of it.

"Shall I make lunch for everyone? Jenny and I could bring it down, and you wouldn't have to eat junk food again."

Surprised, Ty quickly accepted my offer. "A picnic is a great idea. It's a good day for it, too—no fog, no wind. Maybe you and Jenny would like to help with the work."

"Fat chance," I muttered as I headed for the kitchen.

As it turned out, it was one of those balmy midwinter days of California sunshine. When Jenny and I arrived unnoticed at dockside with our food basket, there was just enough breeze to fan the fresh smells of the sea and ruffle the bay's surface with glitter. The *River Run*, up on scaffolding, was lifted high in silhouette, her sleek cabin newly white above the fresh primer red of her bulbous hull. Ty and the boys worked shirtless around her, their bodies glistening in the warmth.

How beautiful it was! And how startling was the sudden realization that Chance, Chase, and Cord were now flirting with manhood. Even Cole had lost the look of a child. So much like their dad they all were, tanned and muscular, with his same blue eyes and curls.

"Mommy"—Jenny tugged me back to Earth—"can we carry the basket down now?"

"Sure thing, sweetie! Our men must be pretty hungry." I smiled at my daughter, grateful to have at least one child remaining, though even she had lost the look of babyhood.

Later, we lounged amid the lunch debris, enjoying the antics of seagulls intent on snatching up the crusts Jenny tossed. Ty leaned sleepily against the wooden scaffolding that held the boat while I curled against his shoulder. "It's a really pretty day, isn't it?"

He grinned and opened one eye. "It sure is better than being up on a windy hill in San Francisco, fighting cable car crowds."

I gave him a poke in the ribs before settling back on his arm.

Before that afternoon was done, I found myself beside my boys, brush in hand, coating the boat's bottom with algae-retardant copper paint as Ty fastened electrolysis-dampening zinc bars in place. Everyone's cheerfulness despite the hard work made me ashamed of my own sour attitude. Even Jenny had made a good attempt with a brush and now gazed intently up at the hull from a perch beneath its bulging sides.

With the approach of late afternoon, I packed the remains of our picnic in the basket, leaving the boat work in the hands of others. As I dragged Jenny away from her spot under the boat, I asked, "What were you thinking about, sweetie? Are you tired?" Her long, thoughtful repose beneath the boat seemed uncharacteristic.

"I had fun, Mommy. I was only watching how the boat is fat where it's in the water. I'm glad it's fat, 'cause now I know Daddy and Chance are okay riding on top." The blue of her eyes deepened. "I'm glad I helped make it so the water can't come in. Every night when Daddy is fishing, I ask God to keep the water out and let the fish come in."

Like her brothers, Jenny was taught the usual "Now I Lay Me Down to Sleep" children's prayer, but I was astounded at her childish insight as she went on. "I like to talk to God. I want him to take good care of Daddy's boat. Do you think He likes it if I help to keep it on top of the water?"

With a lump in my throat, I gave my last baby a hug. "Oh, sweetheart! I'll bet He's really glad for every single bit of your help."

41

The memory of that day, especially of my pride in our children, stayed with me until finally, weeks later, I said something of it to Ty.

"I thought the fishing business was going to ruin them," he teased, and then in a more serious tone, "They're okay. Looks like all four of your boys are turning into some pretty independent little bozos. Hard workers, too. Yeah, I think they'll all do just fine."

"Kayla doesn't think so." My sister had troubled me on her last visit. "She says she doesn't think boys should get too independent, that it's already hard enough to control them." She had spoken with authority, as always, and in the habit of years, I had gone along. "Maybe she's right. Her boys never give her a bad time. She sure had conniptions when someone let the cat out of the bag about her boys going surfing with ours, using borrowed wet suits and boards. They didn't give her any guff at all when she told them they were not to go surfing again!" I snickered. "Actually, I have it on authority that they went anyway, when she wasn't looking."

Kayla and I had discussed the matter roundly and with heat after she learned that her teenagers, Jeff and Jake, had gone off with their cousins to surf in that "awful ocean" while she spent an afternoon shopping. She was even more horrified, despite the fact that her boys had been declared excellent swimmers by their gym coach, when she discovered it was done without my personal watchful eye.

I'd had to confess that I wouldn't have been the smallest help to any of them even if I had been there. I also told her, and immediately regretted it, that when conditions were right, our boys were commonly up and in the water before classes in the morning, and back at it again as soon as school let out in the afternoon. Reliable, and strong swimmers familiar with the sea as they were, it hadn't occurred to me to curtail their fun or to police them. Of course, she felt it necessary to rail interminably about my irresponsibility.

Ty snorted. "Why do you listen to that uptight woman? I know she's your sister, and you think she's great, but look at her! Does she ever smile? Those kids had probably never been out from under her thumb for as much as an hour before that day. She'd better be careful, or they'll end up inept misfits," he scoffed in disgust. "I'll take a little 'wild' anytime."

I couldn't bring myself to think Kayla entirely wrong, but Ty's reaction gave me new confidence. I thought about how our life, our family, and especially our personal relationship had changed.

Everything was better.

One thing and another kept us all busy. The San Francisco trip was postponed so often that finally, one afternoon as we dawdled over a late lunch, Ty volunteered, "It isn't right, my not getting everyone up to the city. After all, I made the promise."

He had been unusually quiet of late. I had chalked it up to the stress of preparing for the opening of salmon season. Surprised, I hastened to reassure him. "Don't be silly. The kids have been too busy to be disappointed."

Ty's guilty response to this casually made promise brought me to an uncomfortable truth. It wasn't the kids who were dead set on making the trip. It was their mother. My words of intended comfort to Ty were exactly right: the children were too busy and content for disappointment. The dissatisfaction was mine, as was the original suggestion and all the nagging that followed.

One evening soon after, as we lounged before the fireplace catching up on the day's doings, I found myself confessing, "It was only because of me the San Francisco trip was promised." I felt so ashamed. "The kids don't care a bit about not going, and anyway, it doesn't have to be right now. Next time you deliver fish in San Francisco, they can go to the zoo on the trolley instead of hanging around the docks. They'd love the adventure of going alone."

Ty gazed quietly at me for a moment before breaking into a comic leer. "Good idea, but if they're so happy without the trip, maybe you should leave them at home and come alone. You know how nice those hotel rooms can be when it's just you and me."

These light moments from a man who shied from usual terms of affection were treasure to me, and they came far more frequent- ly now than they had in years, an undeniable boon in our new lifestyle.

I first noticed this welcome change when I agreed to meet Ty in a tiny port in Oregon shortly after he'd taken over running the boat. Weather had driven the fleet from the fishing grounds, and he asked me to leave the children with a sitter and drive up the coast with an urgently needed piece of machinery for the *River Run*. To my surprise, it was a memorable time, a thrilling rush of new friends, music, and dancing, things that had all but disappeared from the life I so desperately tried to keep. The honeymoon aspects of those few days were a revelation. I never again found it a hardship to join Ty at the end of his trips, trysts that were a renewal of everything fresh and young between us.

9

SAL BATTLES A SEAGULL

E ven after a few years in the business, I was still a novice despite daily exposure to its volatility in both the gritty end of the business and in dealing with the folks that made it work. I had long since adapted to the fact that routine seldom remained routine. Unusual ideas and salty individuals I had come to expect, but each could still jolt my embedded pedestrian outlook.

At the beginning of each albacore trip, the *River Run* was outfitted for thirty days, and it sometimes happened that Ty didn't make port for that entire time. More often, he made land again within two to three weeks. Usually, time ashore was brief, lasting only long enough to unload the catch, refuel, and take on water and groceries. Occasionally, equipment needing repair or a particularly vicious storm kept him ashore longer. Following the Pacific "bite" from Ketchikan, Alaska, to Guadalupe Island, Mexico, he might show up at any one of the dozens of ports dotting the western coastline. I was there to greet him whenever and wherever possible.

Fishing villages have a charm acknowledged the world over, and those who know them best make no argument. Our own unique West Coast ports played a major role in the gradual disappearance of my early antagonism toward Ty's choice. These places brought not only new attitudes but many of my new friends.

It was in one such quaint Northern California port that I first met Sal. At the time, she was in profane battle with a seagull that had taken up residence on the *Pisces*'s mast. That day she wore cherry-red tennis shoes, jeans, and a sweatshirt with its sleeves cut away. A faded blue heart tattooed at the point where shirt and shoulder met seemed to pump with the action of her sinewy arm. Outside of a circus, I had never before seen a tattooed female. Even more startling was her glass eye, slightly out of sync with her good one.

"Get offa there. I'm tired of cleanin' up your crap!" Sal yelled while shaking a fist at the gull that lifted gracefully upward in token acknowledgment before settling back in the same spot.

The *Pisces* was tied up next to the *River Run*, both driven into port by a storm. Sal, fishing partner with her husband, Jim, was busily taking advantage of harbor time to give their boat a major freshwater cleaning. Fascinated, I watched the minor war. Sal's language missed true obscenity; rather, its vulgarity had a sweetly amusing quality, coming as it did from lips painted in a purple cupid's bow that reached almost to the nose. Somehow, even with her brilliantly hennaed hair, she missed clownishness.

I immediately liked Sal, and was told by those who knew that she was a true beauty in those days before a fishing line parted, snapping back to destroy her eye, and that she had the proverbial heart of gold, a designation I would never argue. She was smart, too. It was Sal who kept their borderline business solvent and Jim mostly out of trouble.

Since the *Pisces* frequently tagged along with the *River Run* in the casual partnership practiced by sensible boat owners as a safety precaution, it was natural that Sal and I would periodically find ourselves thrown together. This proximity led to an unlikely friendship, loosely including our husbands, and over the measure of seasons, the four of us spent many shore-bound days in company. Jim and Ty always had plenty of business to hash over—meaning that they spent time comparing the results of their last trips while Sal and I traded trivia. Even though Jim and Sal didn't have much in common with Ty and me outside of fishing, we did have great times ashore. What I saw in the two of them was that they did everything together, seemed to be friends, and were happy enough.

One day when our two boats were again teamed up and in yet another strange port, Sal and I sat in the sun catching up on the latest gossip.

"How come you don't sail with Ty?" Sal had been studying me as she perched on the rail of the *River Run* while I sorted fish lures.

The question was abrupt, and so was my answer. "Why would I want to do that? I have kids at home." Feeling a little pettish at the inquiry, I countered with, "Anyway, why on earth do you go along with Jim?"

Her response was as quick as mine. "I don't have kids. Besides, that big galoot wouldn't catch one single bloomin' fish without me." She laughed her big laugh. "Hasn't Ty ever asked you to go along?"

"He knows I have to stay home." I squirmed. In fact, Ty did invite me to come along almost every time he started a new trip.

"Sometimes men have funny ideas we don't know anything about." Sal paused thoughtfully, then persisted. "Don't you have folks who'd like to stay with the kids for a couple of weeks?"

"I couldn't. The kids are still in school."

"What's that got to do with it? You gotta police their homework? Anyway, summer's almost here. What about then?"

She just wouldn't let it go. "You and Ty'd make the best team in the fleet," she urged. "You got a nice boat, he's a real good man, and you're a hardworking gal. You'd have a helluva good time!"

"Good time, my foot!" I exploded. "I couldn't swim ten feet."

Sal threw her head back with a raucous bray. "Scared. You are just plain scared!"

"I am not!" I objected while she continued to hoot.

To her amusement and my discomfort, the issue was revisited each time we met.

10

LEX THE GREEK AND OTHERS

We were still early in the business the year the markets for both salmon and albacore took a serious dive, leaving a noticeable gap between income and expense. It was just days into the off-season, and I'd been juggling accounts, looking for ways to cut corners, and had reached a point where I was forced to recognize that resources looked precariously thin.

"How much will you need for the boat, Ty?"

"More than we have. At least, not without tapping too deep into what's left of our fallback account."

From our earliest days together, saving was a priority, and the habit served us well over the years. Not only could we count on being able to handle unexpected bills associated with broken bones or treats like new bikes for Christmas, we could buy a boat with confidence. Just now, however, the account was suffering the effects of the troubled markets and an expensive engine repair.

I glanced again at my notes. "I don't know how we can juggle much more. I'm afraid we're at the point of either breaking into our investments or taking out a bank loan."

Unnecessary expense and robbing Peter to pay Paul were things we both fought to avoid. The added interest outgo in a bank loan, and the loss of interest income in retirement investments were equally troublesome options. The thought of the hours of careful analysis needed to determine which would do the least damage did not sit well, especially since we still had a house mortgage and final payments on the *River Run* added into the equation.

"Damned if I'm going to do either one," he said without heat, and continued to sit looking vaguely off into the distance while fiddling with a corner of my numbers sheet. For some five or ten minutes he mused, then slapped his hand against the table, making me jump. He grabbed his cap and headed for the door, saying, "I'll be back in a while."

It was a long while before he returned. Dinner was ready, and it was becoming hard to keep the kids away from snacks, but when he at last blew in, he was smiling.

"All set. I'm going to line tend on the Greek's abalone boat. He suggested it about a month ago, but I wasn't interested then."

"You can't be serious. You don't know anything about abalone diving!"

"I know some, and I can learn the rest. If the Greek trusts me to do the job, that's recommendation enough. He is one of the top divers, you know."

"I don't like it. It's dangerous, Ty."

His rolling eyes and muttered "Here we go again" brought me quickly to my senses. Of course there was no point in my making an objection. The matter was settled. I had only to make peace with it.

My acquaintance with the "ab" community began in earnest with Alexio Klemes, the Greek, who was classically Grecian in appearance, a forty-some Adonis with black waves above a chiseled profile. The silver that teased through curls falling to his brow brought an intriguing hint of mystery.

Immigrating with his parents to the United States as a youth, he grew to manhood in Florida, where his father, following the family's old-world tradition, set up business as a sponge diver. Young Lex followed in his father's footsteps until modern technology begat a synthetic sponge that proved cheaper and more adaptable than the original. It was the end for the family's hitherto flourishing business.

Eager to use the skills he'd gained over his lifetime, the Greek settled in our town. Its draw was a well-established multimillion-dollar industry requiring his particular skills: underwater harvest of the wild abalone growing in abundance on our coastal rocks and reefs. He folded his considerable talent seamlessly into the local scene.

Ty had no trouble adapting to this new commitment. "Nothing to it, Bailey, it's a piece of cake. All I have to do is keep the air hose free of kinks, keep kelp out of the way, and pull the abalone baskets aboard."

I knew it couldn't be quite that simple. How could it be with another man's life in the balance?

Though he began the job ostensibly for the money, and it did help us through our thankfully temporary financial squeeze, it was clear that Ty's real pay was in his love of the work. For me, it was an introduction to another incredible facet of commercial fishing and the discovery of a whole new dimension in personalities. The professional abalone diver puts his life quite literally "on the line" each time he goes down. This no doubt explains the general air of extreme self-assurance apparent in the majority of them—plain "cocky," some might say.

I'd met Lex on several previous occasions and had listened to his interest in all things epicurean, so was not surprised when Ty called from the dock one midafternoon. "Come on down, Bailey. Lex has invited you to come try one of his delicacies. I think you'll find it interesting."

I arrived to find six large sea urchins, a loaf of French bread, and a dish of olive oil lined up on a dockside bench while Lex stood aside smiling whitely in greeting. "This is a prized delicacy among my people. I thought you might like to taste it. Most Americans find the flavor strong, but you would like to try?" The invitation was offered with warm, manly grace, and the hint of an exotic accent in his words added even more appeal.

In all my life to that point, the familiar sea urchin had never been more than a spiky amethyst curiosity, never an edible. When I comprehended that those darkly globular shapes bristling with calcified spines were the prized delicacy, I swallowed hard and struggled to look enthusiastic. But Lex's old-world charm dazzled me; I found the invitation irresistible.

With little ceremony, our host broke open one of the armored creatures, discarded its inedible parts, and revealed bright-orange flesh formed in sections, much like the familiar citrus fruit. Pinching off a chunk of bread, he quickly dipped it in olive oil and handed it to me with a section of the urchin, repeating the process for Ty and himself. The colorful concoction looked surprisingly appetizing.

Ty, as uninitiated as I in the glories of sea urchin hors d'oeuvres, bit into the orange flesh and recoiled in surprise. "Whoa." He eyed me with a twinkle. "Give it a try. It's tasty."

Mindful of Lex's suggestion to take bread with the shellfish, I nibbled cautiously until I got a mouthful of salted iodine. "Wow. You're right, it is tasty. I'll probably taste it all night long."

Lex laughed good-naturedly, then made short work of the rest of the shelled urchin.

"Americans think it may not be good to eat, but in the world, others find it a prize. Here you have many, many urchins waiting to be picked. Perhaps one day they will make a new business," he said.

While Ty and Lex talked, comparing life stories and dreams of the future, I continued to slowly sample my bit of bread and fish, in the end deciding it was a food that could in time become an acquired taste, even for me.

When Ty first joined Lex, divers were still wearing hard hats attached to heavy canvas body suits weighted at the feet, exactly like characters from any one of the hundreds of sea epics filmed by early moviemakers. A diver fully suited, with hoses and lines attached, dredged up memories of films featuring frightening undersea battles with giant octopuses, or other demons of the deep, in fights that didn't always end well for the divers. Those old adventure pictures were giving me some sleepless nights.

"Ty, do the divers ever have to fight off things like a giant octopus or a man-eating shark?"

After a flash of amusement, he replied, "Maybe so, but I watch them go out every morning, and come back every afternoon, and as far as I can see, they all come back with the same number of arms and legs they had when they left. But who knows? Why don't you ask one of them?"

His teasing tone brought me back to Earth, but it also made me more curious. What *did* happen in that diver's world? I decided to take his advice. I would ask.

Our friend Arno was a tough red-haired firebrand, a diver with a swagger. His ruddy face was usually wreathed in smiles, though he was said to be short fused and occasionally involved in barroom brawls. He was also thoroughly likeable and a firm family man. The combination seemed to make him the logical choice for my questions.

The next time we met on the docks, I eagerly blurted out, "Tell me what exciting things happen when you're underwater, Arno. Have you ever been attacked by a shark or an octopus or anything?"

Taken aback at his incredulous stare, suddenly and uncomfortably aware of how ridiculous the question was, I lamely added, "I just thought you might have some interesting stories to tell."

"Well, Bailey, on most days the only interesting thing that happens to me is realizing that I should have put on an extra pair of long johns. It gets cold down there." He eyed me dubiously before demanding, "Why do you ask? Some days are better than others, but I can't say sharks come much into the picture."

At my crestfallen "Oh," his quizzical expression disappeared in a huge guffaw. "What did you expect? I pick abalone for a living. It's a job like any other."

Despite my embarrassment, I shot back, "Abalone diving isn't 'just a job,' Arno, not by any ordinary standards!" His chuckles doubled at my ferocity, but I forged on. "It's only that I'm curious to know what goes on down there."

Arno's expression softened. "You're right, the job is different from most. Maybe only a fool would go in for it, but it's a job that grows on you. It's—well, all you hear is the hiss of incoming air and the bubbling as it's released. It's peaceful. When you're on the abalone beds, it's kind of like walking through a big forest with light shafting down through treetops. The currents are like the wind making the branches sway back and forth, except you see bull kelp and fish instead of birds and trees." He leaned back in reverie of some remembered underwater seascape. "The kelp is what the abalone feed on. It's actually beautiful—but it'll tangle your air hose if you're not careful. We're more scared of that than we are of sharks or giant squid."

My expression must have been so rueful that he burst out laughing. "Sorry, Bailey," he said, patting my shoulder. "I haven't come up against any seagoing lions or tigers yet, only harmless fish. The octopuses around here are pretty reclusive, and a long way from giant. The few we get close enough to see scoot away quick in an inky cloud. As for monster sharks, they're all off looking for better prey, like fish schools and seals."

I stared for several moments, somewhere between disappointment and relief.

"Gosh, Arno, you make it sound nice," I finally said. "I thought it would be more exciting. In all the old movies, divers are always in danger."

"Well, we don't like excitement underwater," he said grimly. "It usually means trouble. But I admit it is possible to get a buzz when a giant rockfish swims up and glares at you through your face mask."

He eyed me now with open amusement. "Actually, I do remember one exciting day—I looked up from the bottom and saw my boat wafting slowly like a leaf in a breeze, swoop, swoop, swoop, down to meet me. I guess you could say that was exciting."

"Are you telling me your boat sank while you were underwater?" I gasped. "Are you pulling my leg, Arno?"

"Oh, it happened, all right. I managed to drop my weight belt and pop to the surface. I got the attention of another boat's line tender, and he pulled me out. What lousy luck. My best day in weeks, and I lost the whole catch."

I was shocked. "You're nuts, Arno! How could you worry about that when you might have been killed? And what happened to your line tender?"

"I was alone. I set the air compressor going and made the dive as usual. There was never any real danger. I was shallow enough to be safe. A lot of guys go out solo. Anyway, dive boats can usually be replaced or salvaged pretty easily. But you still lose the dough from the catch."

When I repeated this conversation to Ty, he laughed and confirmed it all, including the solo diving. "Lucky for me, the Greek won't dive without a tender. I guess he's had too many close calls to take chances."

"What kind of close calls? What do you mean?"

"I mean he's been diving for years, mostly in deep water. He's gotten cautious. He's had the bends more than once because his hang-off time wasn't calculated right. Or maybe he just got impatient and came up too fast. He lost air one time, too, and was hauled up just in time."

"Hang off? What in the world is that?"

"If a diver breathing compressed air has been down over thirty feet, the drop in atmospheric pressure as he comes to the surface can cause nitrogen 'bubbles' in his blood. See, the air he's breathing has to be compressed because his whole body is compressed under all the weight of that water. The air he's breathing takes up less room in the bloodstream the deeper down he is. When he comes up, there's less pressure, so the same amount of oxygen, which the body converts to nitrogen, takes up more space—basically, it expands. So he has to come up slowly enough for his body to sort of equalize itself for the increased volume. Divers on compressed air have a schedule to periodically 'hang off' on the lifeline at a specified ratio of time to depth, allowing the body to adjust to the change in pressure."

"What happens if he comes up without stopping?"

"Well, it'll make him pretty sick. It's extremely painful, and if it's bad enough, it can even kill him," Ty said.

The degree of danger, he went on, depended on how long and how deep the diver was and how swiftly he rose. Serious decompression sickness could cause convulsions and, sometimes, death.

"That's why big-time deep-sea divers have decompression chambers on site, though nobody ever plans on getting sick enough to need them," Ty added.

"You said Lex lost his air once. How? He had someone watching his equipment, didn't he?"

"He got trapped in a kelp bed, and while he was winding around trying to get out, his hose kinked. Lucky his crew got him up in time. Luckier he didn't pass out and go head down. If he had, his helmet would have filled instantly. He'd have drowned."

Aghast, I breathed, "I guess that's what Arno meant when he talked about scares. How do those guys at all manage to stay alive?"

"That's where men like me come in. Aside from watching the air hoses and lifelines, our job is to keep kelp out of the way by using a cutting tool on a long pole. The kelp can usually be poled aside, but if not, it gets cut back. Sometimes it can be tricky cutting the kelp without hitting the lines or hoses. But by keeping the boat directly over the diver's bubbles, it's easy going most of the time."

I shivered. "I don't like it, Ty. Do you have to keep on with that job?"

Evidently, he did, because he continued working with Lex through that pinch period and stayed with him in the off-seasons whenever Lex called over the next few years, a period of profound change in the business, especially after SCUBA, or Jacques Cousteau's invention, the self-contained underwater breathing apparatus, entered the picture. Legally used for sport and research, its use of air tanks was made illegal for professionals, but other aspects of the gear were soon adapted. Ab diving went from hard hat and canvas to "Hookah-gear" (boat-to-mask air hose, wet suit, and fins), from rope signals to intercom, and from the business's heyday to its veritable extinction.

ABALONE DIVER AND BOAT

11

A DANCING ABALONE

Foy Beebee, one of the primary fish buyers in our port, was another of those darkly handsome men descended from stock associated with Europe's seafaring nations, in this case Portugal. It was known that he spent much of his young manhood as a lightweight boxer and had done well. Despite this rather flamboyant past, he was a quietly friendly, well-liked man with a long and varied history within the industry, having worked from one end of the West Coast to the other. He settled in our little port town after discovering its lucrative abalone business. He soon became a successful diver, acquired prime waterfront property, and there established a buying station and a restaurant.

"That Foy is a gem. He treats us fishermen like royalty," Wally opined as we stood together watching Ty's salmon catch being hoisted up to the dock. "Sure nice that we don't have to worry about the underhanded shenanigans that go on with some of the big-city buyers." After a pensive moment, he looked up with a twinkle and asked, "Did you know he's quite a scientist?"

I eyed my companion with skepticism. "What baloney are you dishing up now, Wally?"

Looking thoroughly pleased, Wally retorted, "Baloney is it? Well, as soon as he's finished with Ty, you ask him what he has in that shed over there." He pointed to a small barnlike building perched on the edge of the dock.

It was a couple of hours before the catch was fully unloaded and business complete, but eventually Foy, smiling broadly, shepherded me through the door of his waterside shed. Inside was a scientist's laboratory, an airy room with long steel vats against a wall directly above the bay. It was scrupulously clean and neatly organized. Foy pointed to the first tank, where miniscule creatures swam or settled on the bottom.

"Abalone," he said, "baby abs. I believe they can be cultivated and farmed like any other crop. It's already being done with shrimp."

"I've never heard of anything like that," I said doubtfully, questioning this titillating suggestion made by a businessman apparently seeking scientific answers in the midst of waterfront bustle. "Do you really believe it can be done?"

"Oh, certainly it can be done. I've been working on it for a few years. They seem to die off at some point beyond this stage." He pointed to the tank. "The die-off times vary, making me think it has something to do with the quality of the bay water that I pump through the tanks. The silt runoff that we get with the rains is a real concern, and the temperature is sure to be wrong. I would like to draw clear water directly from the open sea, but for now the distance is too great to consider it an option. For me, this can't be anything more than an interesting hobby. I doubt I'd live long enough to figure it all out, anyway. But look over here—these are my pets."

He led me to a gurgling tank where a large red abalone clung quietly to a small boulder fully submerged and embedded in sand. The addition of a few delicate fronds of seaweed created a serene saltwater scene. "Pretty," I teased. "But where's the action? It needs a couple of exotic fish."

"Oh! Well!" Foy smiled mysteriously. "If you want action, this should do it."

He reached into a neighboring trough to pull out a starfish with long arms and body suggestive of an athlete, quite unlike the stubbier variety familiar to me. "You'll see some real dancing when I put this fellow in the tank." He dropped the starfish into the middle of the tranquil aquarium, announcing, "He feeds on abalone!"

Instantly, all serenity vanished as the abalone rose up, ruffled its mantle into an undulating tutu, and glided as swiftly and as gracefully as a ballet dancer might do, straight into the farthest corner of the tank. There it immediately climbed up the side and out of reach of the starfish. All this took place in seconds, leaving me mesmerized. I had just witnessed what previous experience said was impossible. Foy laughed as he carefully removed the starfish from the tank.

"You've just seen what is ordinarily reserved to the diving community. But it'll be better known soon enough, now that new underwater inventions are showing up." He shrugged with an air of defeat as he continued, "Then there'll be well-meaning folks thinking they're saving the abalone by hacking up these starfish and leaving the bits underwater. Not a good idea to leave them in the water, where each piece will develop into a new and complete duplicate of the original. Where once there was one of these predators, there'll be several." Foy shook his head and moved on.

"Here, come meet my octopus." In a daze, I followed him to a new tank where he reached into a dark corner and pulled out an octopus some three or more feet long. "Shake his hand. He will be happy to meet you."

Shuddering, I pulled away, put off as much by the huge, almost-human eyes staring at me as by the jumble of suction-cupped tentacles, all of which reinforced long-standing prejudices. At Foy's insistence, however, I finally did grasp a tentacle and found it eerily soft and flexible, almost liquid in retreat from my hand, and completely unthreatening.

"Don't squeeze too hard," Foy instructed. "That will hurt him in the same way it would hurt you."

My host couldn't know how heartfelt my promise to oblige was! Still, I was intrigued and eager to learn more. My host was happy to comply.

"This is one in a long line of octopi I've had. The first ones kept disappearing from tanks I thought it impossible to escape. Then I realized they were getting out through the water-intake pipes, some only an inch and a half in diameter! The creatures are basically made up of water. They simply ooze into and out of confining spaces through whatever aperture is available. Every opening here is now screened tight." Foy's grin deepened. "I keep waiting for one to get through screen!"

It was an afternoon of great interest, though I'm afraid I came away with no more friendly feeling toward the octopus whose hand I shook, or with any less dread of those I might meet in the future. However, I did certainly leave with a far greater appreciation of the kind and gentle Foy, perhaps a genius out of his time, a pioneer looking for answers to questions that would be resolved—someday.

Another highly regarded local fish buyer, Geoff Federsen, first established a series of oyster beds in the shallows of the Back Bay. His history contained nothing as flashy as prizefighting, but he was a veteran Bristol Bay salmon fisherman, and that was enough to draw admiration. His buying station was located beside his oyster-and-abalone-processing plant at the far end of the harbor closest to the oyster beds and in proximity to most of the local fishing fleet's moorage docks, including the *River Run*'s and the *Mariner*'s.

Geoff's wife, June, an attractive woman about my age, helped in the office and the fresh fish market fronting the processing plant and was always a supportive friend in my early trials with the industry. Geoff, honest and friendly, was as often as Foy the buyer for the *River Run*'s local deliveries. Geoff and June also had a family of children whose ages tallied with our own kids'. Four were beautiful girls of great interest to our boys; the youngest was Jenny's special friend.

It was time to admit that my life was comfortably filled with purpose and meaning; moreover, it was among caring friends not possible to know in my stiff and structured past.

12

THEY KEEP THE FLEET AFLOAT

Our home waterfront first developed with a traditional fishing village orientation. From the bay's entrance to its tidelands, space was originally dedicated to the needs of the fleet, with a variety of support businesses dominant. Dom's marine supplies shop and the local fish buyers were only a few of those important to the increasingly thriving commercial fishing industry.

However, the business at the top of the list of those that keep the fleet afloat was not found in a waterfront shop. That business was, and is still, housed in a solidly dignified building several blocks uphill from the embarcadero. It is the local bank, and the man running the show generally wears a suit. In our time, the bank manager made all the decisions concerning bank terms and loans, and bank dealings were often the door to friendship. We dealt with two such friends during our fishing years.

The first was a fine man looking to retirement, a man Ty knew through his previous career, and a man who spent years dealing first with the farming community surrounding our town and then the fisheries as that industry grew. He helped Ty to get started.

The second banker was young when we were young, with children in school with Jenny. He grew to manhood in the area and was no stranger to hard outdoor work, as well as the vagaries of agriculture and the fishing industry. Like Dom, he was not only diplomatic but also a flawless judge of character. No doubt, these gifts contributed to success on all sides of his business dealings and to his stellar reputation. Well liked and actively civic-minded, he was an ideal man for our changing community, and his savvy kept many boats in the right hands through some of the tough years. He remains a man we consider our friend.

Businesses geared to the fisheries' day-to-day needs were first lined up on the bay's edge, with the barnlike shop of Thor Thompson leading. He was the valued machinist and owner-operator of an enterprise nudged by the newly built restaurants and curio shops that were beginning to grace the embarcadero. Thor was especially appreciated by Ty, having once rebuilt the *River Run*'s bent propeller shaft to a condition like new, just one of dozens of boat owners equally well served.

Next door to Thor's shop was the boatyard with its ways and a looming hoist settled on rails bolted to a massive concrete base. There, a fishing boat could nearly always be seen up on scaffolding in any one of several stages of undress as it underwent maintenance. The yard was a particular source of fascination to visitors unfamiliar with harbor life, or for that matter, anyone tempted to ponder the sight of a boat out of water, with gawkers nearly always in attendance. The boatyard, originally established with no other thought than convenience in a working harbor, was, like Thor's machine shop, now becoming increasingly orphaned as shops catering to a burgeoning tourist trade grew up around it. To men trying to get work completed before the next tide, the change was a complex annoyance.

The *River Run* was up on the ways, and Ty came stomping through the door, looking disgruntled.

"I tell you, Bailey, it's near impossible to get any work done. People walk right up on the lot. Today I had a man with two little kids come over while I was using the welder. That's dangerous work! The damned fool wanted me to explain what I was doing for the benefit of his kids and was so insistent that I finally had to be rude, which is too bad. Duke agreed that we're all facing a problem that promises real trouble."

"I'm sorry, Ty, but what can you do? There's already a 'no trespassing' sign up. Anyway, I think it's kind of nice that folks are interested. That won't do the industry any harm."

"True. But their interest can't interfere with what we're doing—it's dangerous! What if a kid was injured or burned running around like they do? We'd all be sued out of the water. Duke worries about that. He plans to put up a fence, but what a nuisance for all our work trucks needing to get in and out!" After a couple of tongue clicks, he went on. "Oh well, maybe none of it matters. The way the bay is filling in, it's getting harder every day to find a tide high enough to make a lift possible. If that dredger doesn't get to work soon, the ways hoist will be useless. We'll just have another knickknack shop in its place."

"And then what will you guys do? You have to take the boats out of the water."

"I hear the folks in the next port down the way are talking about putting in a big hoist with plenty of space. That's close enough for us, and it's sure better than having to run the boats a couple hundred miles away like some of the big draggers are doing now. The plan is for a boatyard where lots of boats can be hauled out and worked on at the same time, and the hoist will handle boats three times the size of ours."

Soon after this particular discussion, Duke sold the boatyard, bought a boat, and joined the fleet. After he left the yard, Alf Hale took over. Luckily for Alf, dredging by the Army Corps of Engineers soon began, and the bay's boat-oriented businesses received a reprieve of a few more years.

Ultimately, however, our little boatyard was forced to give up its space to a seafood restaurant. As boats grew ever larger and delays caused by a never-ending wrangle over distribution of the sand tailings produced with regular dredging continued, pressures became too great. Tourists now have to be content with watching an occasional dockside delivery of a local boat's day catch.

MAINTENANCE

13

PAUL KEEPS THE FAITH

During the off-season, in the slip next to the *River Run*, the *Faith* was regularly moored. One of the smallest vessels in the long-distance fishing fleet, its owner, Paul, lived on board with his wife, Amanda, a pleasant young woman who clearly wished for a more convenient home. The pair's surprisingly good-natured discussions of the matter were frequent and often public, thus providing hours of speculative gossip for their friends.

"Honestly, Paul, you have to start looking for a bigger boat! How long must we eat from paper plates simply because there is no place to store real ones?"

"Think of the dishes you don't have to wash, honey. No dishpan hands! Plenty of gals would love that. Besides, this beautiful little ark is perfect for two."

Their arguments usually ran in this frivolous vein and were soon replaced by good-natured laughter, but sometimes they were followed by the clicking of Amanda's town shoes as she ran off up the dock with Paul's plaintive call lingering in the air: "Aw, c'mon, honey, you know you don't mean it!"

Apparently Amanda did mean it, because one day Paul put out word that he was in the market for a new boat. He spent several months exploring choices, traveling from one port to another, from San Diego, California, to Bellingham, Washington. A few received a second look, and on those occasions, Amanda glowed with good humor. The glow lasted until Paul found an insurmountable flaw and the arguments returned, ending more and more often without laughter.

"Who's going to win, Ty? Do you think Paul will actually trade the *Faith* for a bigger boat? I'm with Amanda. They can hardly turn around in that cabin when they're both in there. I don't see how she can get a meal together." Ty's answer was an indifferent shrug.

Paul was new to the business, with no previous contacts within the fishing industry, arriving quietly in the fleet's midst unmarried and apparently unencumbered. He was a determined man, intelligent, and a hard worker, so it wasn't long before he earned the respect of most of his peers. Fit and handsome, he had two hobbies, beach volleyball and listening to classical music, neither of which were common pastimes among the fishermen, to state it lightly!

This oddity delayed his acceptance in the fishing community's social network, but Amanda's unforeseen arrival as a bride quickly changed that. A lively, witty extrovert, she added much to the waterfront and to her husband's graduation from social limbo into a sort of stardom. Ty and I saw them often. We laughed, dined, and danced together for more than a year.

Then Paul began arriving alone at our gatherings. At first he seemed unchanged, as friendly and amusing as ever, though his conversation sometimes seemed to wander. Amanda bounced in and out, explaining that her aging parents needed help. Paul brightened with her visits, then slumped back into an increasingly apparent shell when she again left

One evening, alone again, Paul had dinner at home with Ty and me. The plates were cleared away as he held his fourth, or perhaps fifth, glass of wine, already nearly empty, when with no preliminaries, he began, "I trained as a musician, a violinist, and was assured that the first violin seat in the most important orchestra in the city would be mine."

Ty and I exchanged disbelieving glances before Ty questioned, "You play the violin? Why have we never heard you?"

"They gave the first violin seat to someone else on the day I was to start. I put my violin in its case and haven't played since. Guess I wasn't as good as everyone told me I was."

"Paul! Are you feeding us a bunch of malarkey?" Ty leaned forward with a half smile and put his hand on Paul's knee.

I suppose Paul had just enough wine to jar loose his demons, because he gave us a puckish grin and rose from his seat.

"Want to hear a concert? Give me time to get my music maker from the boat, and I'll play for you." With that, he leaped out the door and was gone with the roar of his sports car.

He was soon back, despite our betting that he would not return. In his arms he cradled a violin case wrapped in a cotton coverlet. Once the case was unwrapped and open, Paul lovingly lifted the age-glossed instrument and began testing its strings, twisting pegs, tuning until he had sounds clear and mellow. Then he began to play.

The notes dreamed and made to live in centuries past lived again in our living room that night. Tears rolled from beneath Paul's closed lids as his bow flashed and fingers danced across violin strings in obedience to emotion too deep to know another outlet. It was a concert like no other before or since in my experience.

Ty came slowly back from his own private musings, as deeply moved as I. Paul worked quietly, readjusting his violin and putting it lovingly back into its case, again wrapped in the coverlet.

We were all silent until Ty said, "Those people missed the boat, Paul. You should have had the job."

"That's what my professor said. He also said personal politics had no business in the musical world. I suggested that it had most likely been part of that world for too many centuries to go away." Paul tucked the treasured violin securely under his arm and turned to go while ruefully adding, "I'm no good at the politics of it. I just decided I'd stay away from the whole scene."

About two months after our concert, we were giving the *River Run* a fresh coat of paint when Paul motioned from his cabin door for us to come on over. He welcomed us aboard with an odd mixture of amusement and sadness, then stepped quietly aside to let us into the tiny cabin. Every trace of Amanda was gone, even the smell of her perfume.

Replacing the pair's wedding picture, and unavoidably dominant in the close quarters, a document now greeted the eye. Framed in black, the message was printed on thick parchment in large and carefully rendered calligraphy. It read:

I have fought a good fight.

I have finished my course.

AND PAUL KEPT THE FAITH.

 —2 Timothy 4:7

14

SCUTTLEBUTT

I'd met Ty in one of the less interesting ports to the north where he waited out a storm, and it was there that I was first introduced to the jargon of my husband's chosen profession. Whether dining or simply killing time on the docks, clusters of assorted fishermen were sure to be found, and there is this thing about fishermen: they love to talk. Their discussions are rarely dull, even when they cover nothing more than catch numbers, routes, and hazards. From the beginning it was all educational for me.

John, on the *Maybe*, observed one evening at dinner, "The most dangerous time to leave port is early in the morning, especially if a few boats go at the same time."

A big laugh went up at this, and somebody picked up with, "You can believe that! Not everyone's night before has settled down to a clear head. Maybe not even to clear sight."

Immediately, the table came alive with laughter and tale after tale of the alcoholic exploits of certain notorious individuals. Finally, Andy, captain of the *Cornelia*, ended the subject when his observation that Smitty's accidental back dive off the pier was because "he had too much blood in his alcohol system" couldn't be topped.

From there, conversation drifted into a discussion of the hazards associated with certain ports and various locations. Bill on the *Lazy Dee* offered, "I was running with a couple of companion boats when we hit Coos Bay during a fog not long ago. It was bad, heavy enough and wet enough for the coast guard to order us to wait outside the entrance until they could guide us in. That's a good practice. Even without fog, the place is dangerous for boat drivers that don't go in and out real regular."

Someone else put in, "Be a good idea for Columbia River and the Grace Harbor, too. Both those entrances are treacherous."

After this, the discussion turned into a general run of information. "Leaving Port Orford and heading for Cape Blanco, you'd better be there by four a.m. Early morning is your best shot to squeeze through, and sometimes that's the only time."

"Cape Flattery is pretty easy."

"Getting through the Puget Sound is a long and touchy trip. You better know where you're going, and your charts better be up-to-date."

"What about Blount's Reef, below Eureka? That continental shelf drop-off can make for hellish conditions."

"Yeah, and that's one tough passage through Saint George's Reef. It is so bad that they sometimes can't service the lighthouse."

As is usual, the talk drifted from one thought to another. "I was talking to one of the coast guard ensigns the other day"—John grinned at his audience—"and he let me in on a secret. Some of you yahoos might want to know about it. He'd been out responding to a missing person call. This one happened to be a sportsman, but maybe one or two of you professionals could find yourselves in the same fix. Anyway, this coast guard fellow had a call from a woman whose husband said he would be home by eight o'clock that night. It was nine, and she was worried. Would he go look for him?

"This coast guard ensign said that in cases like this, they look first in harbors close to home. He looked, and sure enough, he found the boat tied up real cozy. He located the adventurer, too, but in a situation strongly suggesting that he would not be home before morning."

Bill snorted a laugh. "I feel sorry for that ensign. I sure wouldn't like to report that to some of the wives I know!"

"Not to worry, the coast guard has that situation covered. Policy is that they never say where the man is or what he's doing. Their standard answer is 'We have located the boat. Your husband is safe. He will call home in the morning.'"

The responding laughter was followed by an observation from across the table. "My old lady wouldn't for a minute let them get away with that! She'd raise so much Cain that someone would sure as the devil have to yell, 'Uncle.'"

As must always be in a band of fishermen, the talk turned to accidents and near misses. "Say, did you hear about Axel Lundgrun on the *Eureka* getting run over by a steamer? Happened at night outside Westport, a few weeks ago, even with the *Eureka* well lighted and owning the right-of-way. Axel managed to get off the boat and in the water before it went under. The steamer came back and picked him up, but he was pretty hot under the collar and wasted no time in telling that steamer captain just how he felt."

Again from across the table, "Maybe he should have thanked his lucky stars they came back for him."

"That's exactly what that skipper told him. It didn't make Axel any happier, but it sure shut him up."

Again in the way it goes in such groups, the conversation turned to fish scores, past and present, with numbers multiplying by the minute. Finally, one old fellow stopped the contest by pointing out, "There are only two kinds of scores, those for brag and those for comparison out on the grounds. Okay, fellas, which are these?"

After the obligatory laugh, Ty chimed in, "I had my boy Chance with me, fishing salmon, not too long ago. We pulled into Drakes Bay late and dropped anchor on the outside of others anchored there. Next morning, we were up and making our way to the grounds before the sun rose.

"We were nearing the marker buoy, ready to make the turn for Point Reyes, when I sent Chance out to get the gear ready. He was kind of surprised to see the fellow coming along behind us, who had given a friendly salute from his little sailboat as we passed, but he went ahead with his chores. When he looked up again, the sailboat was still following, but now the man was waving his arm half out of its socket.

"'Come look at this, Pop,' he says, so out I go, and I could see that we had a problem! That sailboat was hung up on our stabilizer, getting towed along at a pretty good clip. I cut the engine and brought him up close enough to disentangle his 'peanut' anchor while kind of hinting that it probably hadn't been well seated on the sandy bay bottom, letting his boat shift toward the channel. His excuse was that he came in late and dropped anchor at the first opening he saw. It was plain that he didn't understand anchoring in a crowded harbor.

"He wasn't much more than a kid, so even though I was dealing with a belly of scare mixed up with not much patience, I tried to let him know how lucky he was without laying it down too hard. Fortunately, we'd been moving slow and easy, getting everything together, but it's still a miracle he wasn't pulled under and the boat swamped.

"The last we saw of that poor kid, he was making his way back into Drakes Bay, probably with sour thoughts about fishing boats and their skippers."

Not much was said after that until the same old fellow heard before brought the conversation to a philosophical close.

"I was going over my logs not long ago, and I made an interesting discovery. I've been fishing for near thirty years, and for three hundred sixty-five days of that time, I sat on the hook, waiting out the weather or for delivery of this essential or that, in one harbor or another." He looked around at listeners grown thoughtful. "Yes, sir. For one year's worth of fishing time, I sat, tied up in some dog-snot port, twiddling my thumbs and wondering why Superman wears his shorts on the outside!"

15

A CHRISTMAS GIFT

I t was in the wee hours of Christmas morning. At home with our children, Ty and I had just gotten to bed. All the gifts were wrapped and piled under the tree, and the cookies left for Santa were mere crumbs, when the jangle of the telephone brought us both upright.

Ty snapped up the receiver with a curt greeting, listened alertly for several seconds, and replied in a low, steady voice, "Okay, Wally, I'll be right there."

With dread I asked, "What happened?" Ty's response to the call had suggested that this Christmas would not be as planned.

Hurrying into warm clothing, he explained, "The *Molly E*, Leo Engel's boat, is on the rocks not far down the coast. He was alone bringing the boat up after coming off the ways, probably tired and pushing too hard to get home for Christmas. Wally said he's not sure what happened, but whatever it was, Leo swam to shore and is pretty worn-out from shock and hypothermia."

"But he made it! Oh, what an awful thing to have happen at Christmas. I don't see what you can do. The boat must be lost, or Leo wouldn't leave it."

"Wally went down to have a look, and he thinks it can be saved."

"You mean he expects to save a crashed boat from that rock-ridden surf?" I was incredulous. Ty glowered blackly as he dressed, and I bit back sharp words while struggling for a reasonable tone. "It has to be too beaten up to salvage. That surf is fierce!"

Nearly snarling, he retorted, "Wally says the ocean is pretty flat, and even if it isn't, when he says the boat can be saved, the odds are good." More calmly he added, "Leo's whole life is in that boat. If there is a possibility of rescuing it, we have to help him. Leo is always on hand in times of trouble, and I don't know of anyone who wouldn't do the same for him."

Grabbing his heaviest jacket, he was out the door while calling back, "Go ahead with Christmas for the kids. There is no telling how long this will take." Then he was gone, clanking down the driveway in his old pickup truck.

Well-liked by all in the local industry, Leo and his wife, Molly, were from families that had been in the business for generations. "Salt of the earth was the well-deserved tag regularly applied to them, and there were dozens of stories of their generosity and willingness to assist in all sorts of situations. When I remembered that Molly had been among the first to welcome me into the circle of fishermen's wives, I blushed at my initial reaction to Wally's phone call. Shamed, I made up my mind to a change in attitude: I would be as helpful as possible during this latest crisis, starting with assuring a happy Christmas for my family.

At earliest light, the children, wreathed in the usual glow of suppressed Christmas excitement, gathered expectantly around the tree and were chattering happily as I stumbled sleepily down to officially open the celebration. "Merry Christmas!" The resulting clamor was a mix of excited greeting and wondering questions.

"Where's Pop?"

"How come he wasn't up first?"

"Is Dad sick?"

"No, your dad's not sick. He's out helping with one of the boats. He said to tell you he's really sorry not to be here, and he wants you to go ahead and open your presents because he doesn't know when he'll be back."

"What happened, Mom? Is someone in trouble?" Chance turned concerned eyes to me.

"The *Molly E* is on the rocks a little way down the coast, but some of the men think it can be saved."

"Bummer. I hope they can do it. Leo's a good guy." The others nodded in distracted agreement, more interested in gifts than distant disaster.

If I expected to find resentment from the family on this, the first Christmas absence of their father, instead there was a quietly matter-of-fact acceptance. I heard only, "Who hands out the packages now? Dad always does that."

The distraction of problems belonging to others was quickly forgotten in a flurry of ribbon and paper. I placed my unopened gifts next to Ty's; at least we could share that much.

It was the quietest Christmas in my memory, and even that settled down as the kids made a closer acquaintance with their new treasures. Sighing at the loss of the boisterous tradition fostered by their dad, I fixed breakfast, and was wiping up spilled hot chocolate when we received the first in a series of reports from Martha.

"Men have gotten together with Leo and come up with a plan," she said. "Everybody from the waterfront is working on it. Several boats are standing by, including the *River Run*."

The next call relayed a message that I could expect to have Ty's empty fuel drums picked up by one of the men.

"What in the world are they going to do with empty fuel drums, Martha?"

"For floatation, I was told. Some of the abalone divers are working on it from underwater."

"There's no sense in risking lives the way they do," I worried. "What are the chances of their succeeding, anyway?"

"I don't think any of them think in terms of risk, dear. I'm sure all they see is a problem that needs resolution, nothing more. Right now, everyone is quite optimistic. Do cheer up, Bailey. It is Christmas, after all. Good things happen at Christmas."

As early morning wore toward a restless midday, I coerced Martha into joining me in a brief excursion to the site of the ship-wreck. We bumped over the primitive, rutted road topping steep bluffs until we spotted a few silently intent onlookers gathered on a rocky cliff overlooking a cluster of workmen in skiffs, dories and ab boats surrounding the forlorn hulk of the *Molly E*. In the midst of this feverish activity, we could see Leo working lines and relay-ing orders from boat to boat despite obvious signs of exhaustion.

"I can't imagine they'll be able to float her, Martha," I whis-pered. "There are already bits of wreckage washed up on the beach."

"It's lucky there's so little surf," she mused. "Call me supersti-tious, but to have seas this calm in December is a very good omen. There are quite a few inventive men with a lot of experience out there. I'm betting on them."

As we watched, we could see large metal barrels sink slowly out of sight beneath the boat, guided by men in diving helmets and suits.

"What in the world are they doing?" I wondered.

"The barrels seem to be filling with water as the divers guide them," Martha answered without moving her eyes from the action, "and my guess is that they're attaching them to the boat below the waterline."

For a bit longer we continued to watch the slow transfer of equipment from fishing boats to smaller, more maneuverable skiffs and finally to the stricken vessel. With a start, I glanced at my watch.

"I have a turkey in the oven, Martha, and I've got to get back to it. I doubt anyone else is going to make Christmas dinner!"

Back home, the day moved forward in an atmosphere of anxious ennui. Even the usual Christmas exuberance of active children was lacking, so when Chance begged to drive out to the scene of the accident, I reluctantly agreed, certain that only sadness and loss were there to greet us. What a thrill to find the *Molly E* intact and surrounded by abalone boats with submerged air hoses running to it from every direction!

The noise of engines and compressors sounded above the rumble of surf as we watched, wondering at workers silently and intently staring into the roiling water that now surrounded the *Molly E.*

"Just look at that! Every one of those guys looks ready to jump out of his skin."

Suddenly, the *Molly E* shifted and began slowly to rise. Instantly, blasting horns, waving hats, whistles, and exuberant cheers drowned out the surf's roar.

Chance did a little jig, let out a yell, and then breathlessly explained, "I think the water in the drums was blown out by the divers' compressors and are filling with air. It looks like those drums really are going to float the boat."

I stood mesmerized until Chance gleefully remarked, "What a neat Christmas present." Then, cupping his hands to his mouth, he yelled, "Merry Christmas, Leo!"

The damaged boat was soon high enough out of the water for the waiting tow barge to take over. In the deepening shadows of Christmas night, the shattered hull of the *Molly E* began the final leg of an eventful journey.

Ty was soon at home, exhausted and thoroughly jubilant. "This is just about the best Christmas yet! Say, did you leave some turkey for me?"

The *Molly E* was restored to original condition in time for the first albacore run.

16

PULLERS FROM A TO Z

Finding good pullers was an ongoing problem for almost everyone in the fleet. It wasn't due to a lack of volunteers. There was always a waiting line of young men filled with dreams of adventure and a fast buck. The trick was to find one who would stick.

"I wish I could get a seasoned man with a decent disposition. Starting these beginners is going to bankrupt me. They lose gear, sometimes more than once, and at a few hundred bucks a pop, that's an expense I have to eat just to get them useful. Worst of it is, nine times out of ten, they decide the job is not as much fun as they thought it would be, and they jump ship at the first port, swearing they've been dealing with Captain Bligh." Ty's frustration had reached a new zenith.

"Oh, come on, you've had a couple of men that were really good, and you liked them a lot. You might find another one like Bob Newton, or Ford Seles."

Ty smiled grimly. "Bob was with me for only two seasons before deciding he would rather stay married than with the boat. And Ford learned so fast that he bought a boat for himself. Would you have me contribute to the fleet's rocketing divorce rate? Should I try to keep a guy from bettering himself?"

"No, I suppose not." Then, with a giggle, I taunted, "Are you sure that's the reason Bob left? Maybe he just wanted a toothbrush to call his own!"

With a sheepish grin, Ty countered, "How was I supposed to know we both had blue toothbrushes? Anyway, I thought mine was the one on the right."

We both laughed at the memory of the time Ty and Bob discovered they'd been using the same toothbrush for an entire trip. The mix-up was brought to light when Ty complained about the soggy condition of his, and Bob responded with a like complaint. Only after they began to look for water leakage in the storage cabinet was the mystery solved.

Bob was philosophical. "Well, neither of us show symptoms of hydrophobia," he'd reasoned. "So there can't be much to worry about."

Despite the momentary laugh, Ty's current problem remained. It was near the end of the season, and another puller was gone. This latest loss was a case of a young dreamer confronting reality—in this case, too little money. Newly married and expecting a child, Dan's last share had measured out to less than his need, and though he clearly felt both obligation and loyalty, the dwindling season and lowered prices dictated an immediate search for a well-paying winter job.

It was an old problem that I shrugged off with casual words. "I guess you'd better start looking for a replacement. You can't go out alone," I said.

"Why not? A lot of the guys do."

Swallowing hard, I struggled to think of a reasonable argument, finally venturing, "They aren't highliners, either, are they? The boats with a crew do better." I held my breath and remained watchful.

He nodded. "In general. But in slow fishing, the economics of it don't hold. Fifteen to twenty percent of the catch is what a good man wants and deserves, and that's a profitable margin for us both if fishing is hot and prices are good, but as our friend Dan discovered, that's not always the way it goes."

Hoping my thudding heart couldn't be heard, I suggested, "Safety is worth something, surely? So many things can happen out there."

Clucking dismissively, Ty answered, "Things happen no matter where you are, but a careful man with common sense and decent equipment is as safe on his boat as he is anywhere. It makes no sense to take on help when the bite is down to little or nothing, with the price going the same direction. The man's pay comes off the top, maybe leaving the boat with a pretty shaky profit margin."

"You would lose the same amount if you didn't have the help you need in a hot bite, wouldn't you?"

"Not likely to happen at this time of year. Even if I did hit a hot spot, the difference probably wouldn't cover outfitting for the extra man. No matter how you look at it, there are no guarantees in this business. Even so, at this time of year, a man ought to look at facts like these and then do some heavy considering. Could be it's time to hang it up and stay home."

"That sounds good to me!" My opinion was given far too enthusiastically. Ty's frown darkened.

"I'm in this business to make money!" he shot back angrily. This outburst was enough to crack the fragile core of acceptance I still daily struggled to maintain.

"You cannot do this, Ty!" I found myself hissing through set teeth. "All I do is worry, and here you go, talking about making it worse. Why do you insist on putting yourself in constant jeopardy? Your whole family suffers from the awful risks you take!"

Ty stared as my tears began to roll. When he finally spoke, it was with unexpected gentleness though the message was tough.

"You are out of line, Bailey, and I'm sure you know it," he said. "Every job has its hazards, at sea or ashore. I am careful. I don't take unnecessary risks. When it comes to family suffering, that's rot! If it is there, it comes from your attitude. The kids, even Jenny, are comfortable with what I do."

Disarmed by Ty's softened tone, I was suddenly and truly contrite. Ashamed, I nodded and stifled my sniffles. "You're right. It's just me. Martha and Bess, and all the others, stay so calm and accepting of everything their men do. Why can't I?"

I remained at uneasy attention during the long pause before he answered.

"Most of them grew up with fathers in the fishing business, and they married the same breed of men," Ty mused. "For them, it isn't a new game. Haven't you noticed that in the recent flurry of divorces, it seems to be the outsider woman who made the decision? Almost always they had never seen a fisherman before they met the man they married. The usual complaints are about the separations or the uncertain incomes, but sometimes it's as trivial as the smell of his boat clothes or because his fishermen friends aren't like those of her dear old dad. It could be any one of a thousand things that don't fit conventional expectation, but maybe it's just because the same commitments aren't kept that other generations honored."

After this surprisingly serious and thoughtful little speech, Ty put an arm around me. "I know this kind of life isn't easy for you, but for as far back as men, boats, and fish have been around, women have been living it." He gazed at nothing for several moments before adding, "Anyway, I am proud you've stuck it out, Bailey."

I think in that moment I fell in love with my husband all over again, and this time with a bit more understanding.

Thankfully, reports of relatively good catch numbers still being made caused Ty to look for a replacement puller for the last of this season. The matter was briefly settled.

"I'll take Rudy aboard," he declared. "He seems to be a good kid, eighteen, no plan to go on to school. He is kind of colorless, though." Ty shifted uneasily. "His mother came down to give him a plug. She's a single mom, and sometimes it's tough for them to let a kid go, but at least she wasn't with him when he asked for the job."

Rudy lasted for one short trip. He was sick, mute, and a habitual equipment loser. Ty understood.

"The kid was a willing worker, but he just couldn't seem to get the hang of it," Ty explained with a sigh. "He lost three sets of gear. And he said hardly a word, so I was never sure if anything I said got through to him. Of course, I might not have much to say, either, if I had to hang over the rail as often as he did. Worse thing is, he seemed embarrassed at not making it, and that's not likely to do his ego any good, poor kid."

Rudy was replaced by Clarence, who was aboard for the rest of that albacore season. He was probably fifty years old or more, experienced at the job, and was a pleasant, quiet man who read a lot. He wore a colostomy bag.

"No one would guess he wears the thing. He's conscientious and courteous about changing it. The only problem is with his stamina. He doesn't seem to hold up and tires too quickly."

Again, Ty was kind. "He's a good, steady worker as long as the bite isn't too hot. At this time of year, we get isolated hot spots, and that can be a problem, but so far, I've been able to get out in the cockpit to pick up the slack."

Clarence lasted out the season but chose not to return to fishing. The last we heard of him, he was a night clerk in a small mountain inn somewhere in Oregon.

Of all the lightweights Ty dealt with over the years, Billy was a favorite. He was a typical just-out-of-high-school kid dreaming of fast riches and the romance of adventure. Enthusiastic and willing to work, he listened carefully to the opening spiel on basic safety. Among these instructions were rules covering what needed to be done should a man go overboard, and Ty's eyes sparkled as he described Billy's response to the lesson.

"I told him—the first thing to remember is to throw anything that floats in the water," Ty began. "If it doesn't give flotation to the victim, it'll at least mark the spot. That's rule number one. Then you get the boat stopped. You don't want to try to turn around. You want the person to swim to the boat if possible. It would take only a half circle to lose sight of him in calm water, and in a wind chop, it would be next to impossible to keep him spotted.

"The next thing you need to do is provide a way to get him aboard. If there's no ladder, you need to drop a rope with something like a buoy or bumper tire attached, something to hang on to. An exhausted person's dead weight is going to be hard to handle, and anyone pulled out of these cold Pacific waters is probably going to be suffering from hypothermia and shock as well as exhaustion."

Hardly able to hold a laugh in check, Ty stopped his narration to reach over and give my shoulder a slap. "I asked him if he understood how important all this was, and he let me know in no uncertain terms that he did! He repeated every word I said, then spent time chewing over all the maybes and what-ifs of the problem, dwelling on it for quite a while.

"Finally he asked, 'Hey, Cap'n—what if *you* go overboard and I can't find you? Where do I sell the fish?'"

Ty was delighted.

"That Billy just might make something of himself," he chuckled. "He sure has his priorities straight!"

Billy was with the boat only briefly. His parents' insistence on college held sway, but for Ty at least, Billy remains forever famous.

Then there was the good-looking thirtysomething fellow recommended by a friend of a friend. He came to the house one evening looking every inch the prosperous sailor, oozing confidence. Ty and I exchanged dubious glances when he began to sing Ty's praises presented as quotes from our friend. The language didn't ring true. However, the resume he quoted, which included running a small boat out of Northern California, carried weight with Ty, who was beginning to feel the pressure of time off the fishing grounds. Chuck was hired to work the last months of that albacore season. He was with Ty for less than two weeks.

"I should have known he was no sailor when he came aboard with seaboots cut off at the ankle. The guy was okay as long as the weather was flat calm, and he was as entertaining as the devil, though I was surprised at how little he actually knew about the business. After all, he was supposed to have skippered a boat."

We were in San Pedro, where Ty was delivering a skimpy load of albacore from a trip cut short. Troubled and angry, he had made an urgent call asking me to come help watch the scales and weight tallies while he monitored the fish buckets being winched in and out of the boat's hold.

"I'm really sorry, Ty, but don't take it so hard. How could you know? He certainly seemed to be what he claimed."

"Yeah, the jackass was a real con man. He blindsided more people than me."

"Maybe his was an honest mistake. Didn't you try to find out what he expected? What did he say when he jumped ship?"

"Not much I'd like to repeat. But you could be right about it being an honest mistake. He had a big enough ego. I'm certain he thought that whatever experience he had made him a pro, but my bet is that he'd never been beyond sight of land. Looking back, I think the guy was scared green every minute after we hit a good chop. When I didn't run for shore at the first whitecap, he clammed up, got surly and sullen, and then took to his bunk. I thought it was seasickness."

"Are you sure it wasn't? You know how it is with Cord and Chase—pretty miserable."

"Yeah, I know. That's why I went easy on him for a couple of days. When I finally suggested he might be better off doing some of the work, like the cooking, he went berserk, telling me I was a crazy man staying out in that storm, and I could cook for myself. Then he demanded that I head in. Talk about crazy!"

"And I'll bet you went right on fishing. Were you staying out when you shouldn't? I know you sometimes do push too hard, Ty."

"There was no storm. The weather was sloppy, and the wind was up, but it was a long way from driving the fleet from the grounds. He sold himself as a professional, and that's what I expected. What really ticks me off is that the fish were showing up in the best numbers we'd seen in days, and that guy went nuts at the first slop that went over the top of his comfy cutoff seaboots. He should never have been on the boat, and I should have caught on sooner."

Chuck disappeared from our life and the waterfront. His defection came at the right time and place. Word of Ty's need for a new puller quickly spread, and as luck would have it, one of the better boats had been sidelined by a major engine breakdown, and its crewman was looking for a new berth. Before the last bucket emptied, Chaco was working side by side with Ty.

To the world, Chaco probably represented the worst of the waterfront. He must have been in his midtwenties when he first worked with Ty, a simple soul who left his parents' chicken farm as a young teen and had been a deckhand ever since. Swarthy, solid, and perpetually grubby, he was a hard worker generally garbed in black canvas "Frisco" jeans and dark flannel shirts, none of which could be called pristine even after vigorous washing. He swore like the sailor he was and had made himself unwelcome at several bars dotting the West Coast.

"What are you thinking, Ty? You can't take that thug aboard. I've never in my life heard such language!"

Ty grinned. "Maybe so, but he got more work done in half an hour than ten ordinary men would, and he made it look effortless. He knows his business. After that last fiasco, that's what I'm looking for."

"Are you sure? One of the guys at the scales said he's a terror in a fight, and he recently beat up somebody in one of these San Pedro bars."

Ty threw his head back and roared a laugh. "No kidding? There's another point in his favor! This is a tough town with bars full of tough men looking for a good fight. It's nice to know Chaco measures up. We'll get along fine." And they did.

Adventures with his new man were frequent. The first came when Ty called ship-to-shore from somewhere only hours away. "I have to break the trip, Bailey. We've got to get Chaco to a dentist. His jaw's swollen up like a balloon. It's a bad wisdom tooth, and I'm afraid it might go septic. Lucky we're close to home port—maybe you can get our dentist to see him right away."

When the boat pulled up to the dock, Ty was piloting from the flying bridge while Chaco worked the deck. As quickly as always, bumpers were thrown and lines made secure, making me wonder if the emergency was as serious as Ty seemed to believe. It took only a glance for conviction. When he looked up in greeting, Chaco's usual darkly stoic half smile was grotesquely distorted in a puffed and pain-mottled face.

With a gulp, I cried out, "That must hurt horribly, Chaco! Ty, why didn't you bring him in sooner?"

Ty sent a grimace and a shrug in my direction while Chaco let loose a string of angry invectives, the gist of which was that Ty shouldn't have broken the trip for a toothache that could have waited until the trip ended.

The dentist thought otherwise.

A couple of hours' worth of oral surgery left the patient with a mouthful of stitches and a handful of pain pills that he refused to take, claiming, "It'll be okay after a couple shots of whisky. No infection with alcohol."

His preferred treatment must have done the job, because when the boat left two days later, there was only a slight swelling in his jaw. Still, the dentist was adamant about setting an appointment for removing the stitches and an evaluation of the healing process.

A couple of weeks later, Ty again called from sea. "Cancel that dental appointment. We already pulled out the stitches. Fishing's too hot to waste time coming in, and I think Chaco might throw me overboard if I tried."

Much later, I learned that Ty was dutifully preparing to leave the fish in order to make the appointed dental visit when he caught Chaco with a pair of needle-nose pliers, ready to go in after the stitches on his own.

"He was plenty determined and too tough for me to argue with, so I decided I might as well help with the job. I boiled tweezers and cuticle scissors, used some Listerine for antiseptic, and the deed was done. No after-effects, either. I did worry about that a little." With a wink, he leaned back in his chair. "Just call me Doc!"

At Ty's insistence, Chaco most unwillingly went back for a checkup. The dentist spent some time poking and prodding, then reluctantly admitted that his patient was "as good as new" and that, as a doctor, he "couldn't have done the job better." Embedded in Chaco's colorful language, thanks were indistinguishable from indignation at being forced into the follow-up.

I never did get used to the colorful language and was very unhappy when Jenny, still a child, was on hand the day a seagull jettisoned an unsavory load that landed squarely on Chaco's head. Her expression might have been funny had I not been her mother. She stood gaping for several seconds before bursting into giggles. I grabbed her hand and dragged her away, but Chaco's voiced outrage at the seagull followed us up the ramp, turning Jenny's giggle into a hearty laugh.

"That language is terrible, Jenny. I never want to hear you repeat a word of it!"

She looked at me with a twinkle. "That's just Chaco, Mom. He doesn't mean anything. Anyway, girls don't talk like that."

Thinking of her brothers, my retort was heartfelt. "Well, boys shouldn't either."

Despite all evidence to the contrary, Chaco proved to be a worthy friend to the kids, especially Jenny, and in time, even I came to appreciate his fractious character. Certainly Ty did.

"You know, Bailey, it was quite an eye-opener when Chaco and I joined a few others looking for dinner and a drink after we unloaded the boat last night."

Ty was making his report from a telephone booth somewhere in San Pedro, a port town located beside the major harbor associated with Los Angeles, a town so rough that its well-armed police officers routinely patrolled the bars in teams of four.

"It's the only time I've ever gone into one of those waterfront bars without feeling I had to watch my back," he enthused. "Chaco gets real respect in those places—he's as big and mean looking as any of the birds in there. Lucky he's taken a liking to me and is as loyal as they come! Believe me, Chaco is at least as good a backup as Theo's gun."

I exactly understood Ty's reference. Theo was a mild-mannered middle-aged fisherman, a strong churchgoer and family man whose wife worked with him on their small but thoroughly seaworthy boat. Never one to make waves, he was quietly friendly and very well liked. Only those who knew him best knew that he carried a gun, discreetly hidden, as a matter of course.

When a law was passed requiring registration of concealed firearms, Theo went immediately to the authorities to comply. When questioning his reasons for having the weapon, officials appeared to be at the point of denying his request. Theo looked the presiding agent in the eye and quietly said, "You might as well give me the permit. I've carried a gun since I was eighteen, and I'll keep on carrying one with or without that piece of paper."

He received the permit, and I expect he always had the gun with him, though I never saw it. Few people did; one who did was a would-be assailant who threatened Theo late at night on an unlit street in San Pedro. An instantly produced weapon and Theo's steely-eyed pronouncement, "Don't doubt for a minute that I know how to use this," was all that was needed to set the malefactor scurrying into the dark.

Certainly San Pedro, a boiler of hard men and harder women hailing from every country in the world, was legendary for its tough nightlife. Every type of boat imaginable turned up there, from freighters to frigates, all spewing men looking for relief from the boredom of months at sea. Worse, the mix was topped off with local cannery workers, longshoremen, and an unsavory network of "support" professionals.

"Okay, so Chaco is as good as a gun," I agreed. "But why would you want to go in those dives? Everyone says San Pedro is the worst!"

"They're right," Ty admitted, laughing. "It's the only town I've ever seen where cops send two men inside while two others stand watch at the door. Yep, Chaco's a good man to have at your side in San Pedro."

"And still you go in those places!" I hoped my disgust was fully apparent.

"Would you have me miss all the fun?"

Chaco stayed with the boat for a number of seasons, but eventually he, too, left. Oddly, it was to return to his parents' chicken farm when their failing health served to summon him.

With Chaco's departure, we were back to the old question: Who would Ty take on as puller? Once again, it was toward the end of the season, and fish numbers had dwindled.

"This is it, Bailey. I'll fish out the season alone, unless you want to take the job."

"You know I can't do that. I'm needed at home. Jenny's at an age where she shouldn't be left for that length of time. Not now. Maybe later." I was breathless in protest.

"Okay, solo it is. Don't worry, I'll take it easy. I won't take chances, and I'll be with a partner boat the whole time."

This time I understood that protest would be unavailing. The next day I stood on the breakwater struggling to keep a smile as I waved Ty out to sea, alone with his "old girl." Less than three weeks later, he called from Port Angeles, Washington. I knew there was a late season bite up that way and that Ty had wasted no time in getting to it, but delivery there made no sense.

"What are you doing in Port Angeles? I thought you'd unload closer to home."

His voice held an odd note of excitement. "Change in plans. I had to come in for replacement of the pilothouse windows."

Fighting to keep a screech from my voice, I demanded, "What happened? You were in a wreck, weren't you?"

"Not exactly. I hit a rough patch of weather on my way down the coast and got hammered by a rogue wave that keeled me so far over that the inclinator went over the top and stuck there. It took the windows out and soaked all the electronics." At my yelp, he hurried to add, "Don't go batty on me. I'm okay, and the boat's okay. Besides, Wally was close enough if I needed help, but I managed just fine."

Struggling for composure I demanded, "What do you mean by that? You couldn't have gotten hold of Wally or anybody else without radios. I know that much. Did you break any bones? How bad were you hurt?"

"Take it easy! I'm fine! But I had a heck of a mess to clean out of the cabin, and it was plenty nasty and cold getting to shore without windows."

He gave a few more details, annoying me by trying to downplay negatives, but once assured of his safety, other thoughts took hold. "Oh no! We'll have to mortgage our eyeteeth to replace all the electronics, won't we?"

"Relax, will you! I remembered a few things Casper told me. I freshwater washed every piece of electronics in the cabin and hung them on wires in the engine room to dry. When I put it all back together, everything worked like new. No sweat. Now I can finish the season without a worry."

"You come home right now! Do you hear?" I screeched.

"Yes, dear," he simpered in honeyed tones. "But may I please wait until the windows are in?"

17

MARTHA POSES A PUZZLE

"Did you ever sail with Wally?" Martha and I were enjoying a cup of tea in the warmth of her neat kitchen.

"Indeed I did, dear. I fished with him in the beginning." A film of sadness crept into her pale-blue eyes, and her voice wavered hesitantly. "But it was good to have a reason to stay home after our boy came along."

My acquaintance with this attractive, middle-aged, gently graying lady in her pink flowered housedress made it unthinkable that she could have been a serious part of the rough work of commercial fishing.

"What on earth did you do?" The idea of Martha among the rough-and-tumble ranks of fish pullers startled me into blatant discourtesy.

Martha's smile returned with an amused twinkle. "Believe me, dear, I really did fish right along with Wally. Of course, I was young then, healthy, and in good condition."

Disbelieving, I looked at her manicured fingernails and coiffed hair. "But, how on earth did you do it? I mean, you're so...so polished!"

"Now, perhaps," she replied. "It was different then. Fishing with Wally was fun, and I can say that even though in those days, most folks thought it wrong for a woman to work aboard a boat. Fishing was men's work! Tradition, you know, and superstition. But our boat life was good. The sea is a beautiful place and interesting, especially when the weather is fine."

"Then why were you happy to stay home? Why didn't you go back after..." I stopped in confusion, remembering too late that her only child, barely out of his teens, had died years before when the boat carrying him ran afoul of a mill log carried by river floods into the cold sea off the coast of Washington. There were heavy rains that year, with runoff carrying tons of logging debris, as well as timber from flooded holding ponds, far out to sea. Sadly, the boat carrying this cherished child collided with a massive log. The boat went down too fast. None of the three-man crew survived in the icy waters of the northwest Pacific.

"It's all right, dear. I did think about it after our boy was lost, but by then I knew it was best for Wally if I didn't." She sat pensive for several moments before adding abruptly and cryptically, "He's a man. He was better without me."

We went on to other things, but before I left, I mentioned that Ty had suggested that I make a trip with him.

"What do you think? Should I go?"

She smiled her sweet smile. "I think you should. Neither of you will be content until you know."

I didn't ask what it was we were to know.

18

FAMILY

"Hey, Bailey, do you think we can have dinner a little earlier than usual? We've got new problems, and a bunch of us decided to meet tonight."

"Ty! Jenny's all excited about that dance party! I still have to get her outfit stitched up, and you know I've been asked to help chaperone." I sighed. "Oh well, sure, I guess I can manage it."

We were in the off-season, around the holidays. Jenny was spreading her wings, Cole was now in his second year of high school, the twins were worrying me with plans to join the navy after their graduation, Chance was expecting to hear from the army soon, and Ty was so involved with the business that he seemed never to be at home. Adding to it all, my sister was in trouble and unloading on me.

"We absolutely must sit down and discuss something besides the fishing business, Ty! This nonsense about Cord and Chase joining the navy next year is crazy. You know they both get horribly seasick. And why don't they go right on to college, anyway? They'll barely be out of high school."

"There's nothing to discuss! They'll probably change their minds by then, anyway. And what's wrong with thinking ahead? Maybe they'd rather do that than get drafted, like Chance. They'll go to college afterward, no doubt better off for taking time to explore options."

Ty was clearly impatient to get on with his business, but frustration and disappointment kept me at him. "Why must you always agree with the boys? Anyway, you could at least help me with Kayla. She's so unhappy. I don't know what to say to her."

"Tell her she's a control freak and driving you crazy!" With that he slammed out the door but stuck his head back in to remind, "Early dinner, remember. This is an important meeting."

Subdued, I made my way to the sewing machine, where Jenny's unfinished dress waited.

My sister's predicament weighed heavily. She had phoned every day for weeks now. The first call came at eleven o'clock one night, when, without preamble, she wailed, "Oh Bailey, my husband left me!"

"Are you telling me that Wes moved out?" The news was not surprising.

"Yes," she sobbed. "He told me I've destroyed his life and that my boys are miserable because of me. Imagine that ingrate saying such a thing! I've given my whole life to them. He has no appreciation of all the sacrifices I've made. He's the one who makes everybody miserable. I told him over and over what would happen if he let our boys walk all over him. He always takes their side against me and simply refuses to listen to anything I say."

After that first irrational call, I listened to a series of increasingly vituperative ramblings, helplessly unable to give comfort. I came to see that my perfect sister might as well have been named Pandora. She had loosed all the world's ills on herself and those she loved best.

It began the summer before, when her oldest boy, Jeff, paid us a surprise visit. He wanted to go fishing on the *River Run* and made a heartfelt pitch to Ty. I was uneasy and asked, "Do your parents know you're here, Jeff?"

Looking down at his feet, this tall, squeaky clean young man nervously admitted, "Not my mom. I told my dad, though."

"Why didn't you tell your mom?"

"You know my mom. She'd have a Grade A fit and forbid it. She doesn't understand. I'm twenty years old and tired of being treated like a baby. I'm not going to fight with her anymore. I'm just going to do what I want."

"What does your dad think?" Ty asked.

"He said I should go for it, that it would be good for me to be on my own for a while. I don't think he told my mom that, though. Better that way. All they do is fight." The poor kid looked at us pleadingly. "I always wanted to work outside. Something that might be fun. Give me a chance, Uncle Ty. I'll work hard!"

"Well, Jeff, I already promised the puller's job to somebody else. But I'll sure see what we can do about finding another boat for you."

The two shook hands on the pledge, and the gratitude in the face of that boy wanting so much to become a man brought tears to my eyes.

Strangely, Kayla did not hold either Ty or me responsible for Jeff's defection. Instead, she scathingly belittled his father for failing to stop him, all the while assuring me, "I told the old fool that his son is worthless. Exactly like his father." She apparently did not recognize the irony in her words. Despite the obviously genuine pain she was feeling, I wondered how she could call her son worthless, much less put such a label on Wes. In my eyes, he was always a kind, generous man despite his workaholic habits, providing a beautiful home and solid income while trying to satisfy his wife's every unreasonable whim.

I had long since come to agree with Ty, who for years had discouraged me from criticizing Wes for being a workaholic. "Probably staying late at his business is the only way he can keep out of trouble at home," Ty maintained.

Then, as if the problem with Jeff was not enough, Jake fled home to join the "flower children" in San Francisco. Kayla was livid.

"What is the country coming to? Jake was filthy dirty, wearing the most outrageous rags! And his hair is halfway down his back! It's his father's fault. No matter what I wanted Jake to do, Wes took his side. Always 'Let the kid alone, Kayla.' And now he refuses to go over to San Francisco and make him come home."

This last we knew to be patently untrue. Jeff had already told us that his father had gone quietly to San Francisco, found Jake, and done his best to convince him to return to school. Exhausted, I wondered how much longer I would have to listen to my sister's rage.

Fortunately, my sour musings were interrupted when Jenny came romping into the room, trailed by her friend Corinne. "Is it finished, Mom? Can I try it on?"

"Only a couple minutes more, honey. I haven't quite finished the hem."

The happy chatter of the girls was a refreshing change from my doleful thoughts, and I settled back, listening as I finished my handiwork.

Corrine chirped, "Danny really likes you, Jenny. Are you going to dance with him tonight?"

"Nope. He's cute and all that, but he wants to be a fisherman. I'm never going to have a fisherman for a boyfriend." It was a weighted declaration made with a frown.

"Why not? I thought you liked fishermen."

"I do! I'm just never going to let myself fall in love with one, that's all. They're gone too long, and you're always worrying about 'em getting drowned or sunk or something, just like that cute guy Joey last year, or Billy's dad; remember he was lost at sea when we were in second grade? Uh-uh, no fisherman boyfriends for me. It's too hard."

With a lump of sadness in my throat, I sat quietly wondering how my little girl would feel in a few more years.

19

BOAT BRODIES AND STRANGLED JEEPS

My home-front heroes, Chase and Cord, rarely received the accolades they deserved. Chance and Cole were the boys that received a majority of attention through their adventures at sea, but the twins were my special heroes. Because neither of them was able to get past serious seasickness, they were stuck on the beach, and so became the ones I could rely on for help with mundane chores such as looking after Jenny and mowing the lawn. These were duties shared universally in the off-season, but as soon as the boats and their brothers left harbor, it was all up to the twins. There was plenty of complaining about this, which I ignored, more interested in knowing that they were safe on dry land. Still, they were their father's children, and I soon had to accept the restless need of each to break the proverbial apron strings.

It was back when they were in the earliest days of high school that the excited pair burst through the kitchen door. "Mom, Mom! Mr. Andrews says we can come work for him!"

A jumble of noisy information followed, one voice overriding the other.

"We applied…"

"…a real job bussing dishes…"

"His son said we should…"

"…all summer…"

"It's really great, Mom!"

So began the adventures of Chase and Cord on a path to manhood far different from that of their brothers'. They were but two in a long progression of teenaged kids mentored by Mr. Andrews, "Hal" to his many friends and customers. He was owner and popular host of one of the most successful restaurants that now crowded the waterfront embarcadero, and Ty's fish were often in featured menu items. Our families were friends and our children classmates. All exciting new adventures were dutifully and regularly relayed to the kids' dad at sea, and it was not long before curiosity triumphed; he made a home delivery.

As soon as I spotted the *River Run* sailing through the harbor jaws, I hurried down to follow shoreside with the truck as he took the boat up the channel. We were halfway to the buying station, with the boat playing peekaboo between buildings, when I noticed a group of tourists laughing as they pointed toward the bay. Through the open parking lot where they stood, I saw Ty steering from the flying bridge, jauntily waving his white fisherman's cap, exactly in front of the banked windows of Hal's restaurant while the boat circled in the narrow confines of the channel.

"It was so neat, Mom! Dad was spinning boat brodies where everyone could see!" Cord happily reported.

"Yeah, Mr. Andrews told everybody that it was our father!" Chase gleefully added. "And he told people they were eating Dad's fish. So cool!"

The "wheelies" continued to entertain for years, and Hal never failed to express pleasure in the antic and to present a new tale of his customers' pleased reaction each time we dined in his restaurant. Best of all, Chase and Cord enjoyed recognition that didn't involve their brothers, as well as the opportunity to each day tell stories of their own, and they were many.

"Rob slipped and dropped a whole tray of dishes! Every one of them broke, poor guy. He felt really bad. Sure glad it wasn't me!" Cord noted one evening.

"One old guy with a bunch of other people choked and turned kind of blue. Mr. Andrews helped him when everybody else was scared. They were nice, saying thanks to everybody, and they left a heck of a big tip for all the help to share." This from Chase on another day.

I was also privy to daily discussion about the eating habits of the other busboys.

"Did you see Rob eat that whole fish? He snatched it right off the plate before I could scrape it into the garbage."

"I saw that—the lady didn't eat any of it, and those guys don't care anyway, 'cause it's just too good to throw away. I wonder if Mr. Andrews knows they do that."

Apparently that particular young man's growth hormones were rampaging, because if half what I heard of was actually eaten, the kid should have ballooned, but as far as I could see, he remained the lanky teen I'd known from the beginning.

Working for Hal was a boon in many ways to Chase and Cord. Most of the time, they worked separate shifts, learned different life lessons, and consequently made differing choices. It was all good, especially for me, comfortable with the conventional path they seemed to be on, and very happy to have them safe at home.

It was an uncomfortable surprise when, after a year in the job, Chase came home with the announcement, "I quit working for Mr. Andrews. I'm going to work for Scotty, down at the gas station."

With a groan, I asked, "Did you tell Mr. Andrews? You know that is part of having a job; you need to quit in the right way."

With a look of disdain, Chase answered, "Of course I told Mr. Andrews! I was real polite, and thanked him for letting me work in his restaurant, but I really wanted to find out more about engines and stuff. He said congratulations; it was just fine."

Over the few remaining high school years, Cord stayed with the restaurant until he, too, changed direction and found work as a golf course groundsman wearing a hard hat in the shape of a cowboy's Stetson. His golf stories were legion, including those of the serious value in his protective headgear. Apparently not all golfers had perfect control over their drives! Chase progressed from pumping gas for Scotty, to apprenticing in a local auto repair shop, and finally graduating to what had been his goal from the beginning, working on marine diesel engines in Mac's shop.

Mac was a valued member of the fleet's support businesses, well versed in the intricacies of diesel engines. Known as an excellent mechanics troubleshooter, he was honest, cared about his clients, was always amusing and a bit of a prankster. Chase had been with him for less than a month when he came home one evening wreathed in smiles.

"Hey, Mom, did you ever hear of a 'hung Jeep'?"

"Don't you mean 'hung jury'?"

"Nope. Mac hanged ole Colby's Jeep."

Colby was an elderly local-market fisherman, rather more retired than not. He had scattered family that he visited often, and Mac's fenced storage lot was a convenient place to leave his open and battered WWII relic in safety. At the time, Mac and Colby were in a friendly one-upmanship battle that for months had provided much amusement along the waterfront, and Chase lost no time in filling me in on the latest.

"It was crazy, Mom! Mac had a forty-foot crane brought in to move a couple of big engines around the storage lot. Somehow he got the idea it would be pretty funny for Colby to find the Jeep 'on the gallows' when he gets home tomorrow."

Apparently Colby was not nearly as amused as the rest of the waterfront when he found his Jeep swinging an uncomfortable distance from the ground. I'm told that his blue remarks drowned out the laughter of those in on the mischief! The incident marked the end of the battle for top showman, though the two men remained friends, and Colby's Jeep continued to be often seen resting comfortably aground in Mac's storage lot.

20

HUMOR AND OTTERS

R ich with ups and downs, the seasons accumulated, often including alternative fisheries such as bottom fishing, crabbing,
and Ty's favorite, abalone diving.

"You won't believe what happened to Bertie Marshall today,
Bailey!" Divers were still in the hard hat years on the day Ty breezed
in bursting with the latest waterfront tale, laughter deepening the
lines around his eyes. "He showed up this morning with a whale
of a hangover. Lex warned him about going down in his condition, but the kid wouldn't have it any other way. Dumb move, just
dumb!"

According to Ty, young Bertie went down all right, but it wasn't
two minutes before he was yanking on his signal line. They brought
him up fast, but not fast enough: his helmet and suit were filled
with distressing rejections from last night's party.

"Bertie upchucked for the next half hour!" Ty roared with
laughter.

"But, that's terrible!" I objected, shocked. "The poor kid might
have choked inside that suit. He could have died!"

"He was so miserable he wouldn't care."

"That's not funny, Ty!"

"Oh, come on, Bailey." Ty chuckled. "He learned a lesson, one he won't need to relearn."

That particular kind of danger lessened when hard hats were abandoned in favor of face masks, an innovation that was an outgrowth of the Aqua-Lung's arrival. Safer and far less cumbersome than hard hats, they allowed greater freedom of movement, as did wet suits and fins, and the divers were quick to adapt to these changes, especially the younger ones, like Stan.

Stan was well seasoned, a hard worker, a joking teaser, and a great "yarner," all traits that made him popular on the waterfront. Naturally, I was all ears when he showed up dockside with a tale about the "cutest little critter, like a seal with paws," apparently unafraid, and that would playfully sneak up to him from behind, brush his shoulder, and somersault away.

"It was almost like a dog wanting you to throw a stick," Stan said. "He watched every move I made, nosing around while I flipped abs off the rocks. I'm pretty sure it was a sea otter, the first one I've ever seen. I saw him pull up an urchin and head for the surface a couple of times. But he always came back down. He sure was cute."

We all laughed, untroubled by the story.

A few months later, Lex observed, "I don't like these, what you call otters. The urchins are disappearing. Every time I see a couple more of Stan's playmates around, they always pull an urchin and head for the top; then in a minute they come back. They eat many, too many."

Within two years, the urchins had virtually disappeared. Worse, the ab divers were noticing that there were fewer abalone and many more otters.

Then one day word came that Stan had been attacked by a great white shark. It hit hard, removed a chunk of Stan, then characteristically backed off and began to circle, presumably waiting for its prey to weaken before coming in to finish the job. Fortunately, Stan's crew was able to haul him aboard before that happened. Doctors patched him up, but he spent weeks in bed, followed by months of rehabilitation.

Among the diving community, the attack was generally regarded as an isolated accident of wrong time, wrong place. Reports of great whites now seen in places along the coast where they were previously unknown were received with philosophical shrugs by waterfront denizens who noted that the sharks were no doubt responding to the appearance of a new food source, otters.

I thought of Arno and his confidence that sharks kept to open water. He hadn't counted on the abalone's food source, kelp, also becoming home to prime shark prey. He would now need to watch for those "lions and tigers" he once assured me were not a threat in his beautiful underwater forest.

Stan was back in the water as soon as he healed, declaring, "It'll take more than a shark to keep me off the ab beds." Sadly, the cold ocean environment tortured his wounds and stiffened damaged joints, forcing him to spend less time underwater, thus assuring smaller deliveries. My heart ached for him, and I was distressed by other divers who teased him with unfeeling jokes. I found their lack of sympathy unconscionable.

"What's wrong? Are you leaving half your ab catch to the rest of us today?" Bertie began.

"Nah! He's leaving his twenty dozen to feed the otters," someone else chortled, inspiring another to shout, "Hey, Stan, what's wrong, your buckets don't work no more?"

Arno noticed my rising indignation at such merciless cruelty.

"Quit fussing, Bailey," he said, taking me aside. "It's okay. Everybody likes Stan. When we kid around, it makes him feel better. He even makes his own jokes. He tells us that his deliveries are down because when he's underwater, he's so busy looking over his shoulder there's just no time to pick abs." Stan's action was mimed hilariously, and I laughed, forgiving what I couldn't understand.

Recognizing the validity of the advice, I did "cool it" as Arno prescribed. The jibes continued freely amid general glee, and Stan was right there laughing with the rest. In time I became convinced that this compassionate humor is as effective as it is perplexing, and definitely peculiar to men.

21

PETS GO TO SEA

While tromping the docks of various ports visited with Ty, I discovered that pets, mostly dogs, were crew on many boats, worthy companions during weeks and months of lonely sailing. However, the first thing these canine sailors did when they hit the dock was to leave a calling card, usually in the middle of the ramp, or worse, topping a coil of line.

"Toss that line over, Bailey! Hurry up before the tide catches me." Ty was maneuvering the boat into a tight berth, and the outgoing current was running fast. "Quick—before I drift onto the *Ruthie D,*" he yelled.

Of course, a fresh, smelly pile lay in exactly that position to best foil anyone reaching for the rope.

"I can't, Ty! You'll have to back off!" I shouted shrilly over the noise of many engines and was answered with Ty's black glower as the boat roared into reverse, missing the *Ruthie D* by inches.

It took a little time to disabuse the coiled rope of its burden and get myself into a position to toss it, but the boat was at last secured in its appointed niche. I hopped aboard braced for Ty's lecture. His tone had far less fire than I feared.

"If I'd hit the *Ruthie D*, you might have wished you'd thrown the line first and washed your hands later," he said grimly.

I shuddered in disgust. "It depends on the damage. That was a brand-new gift from a *very* big dog."

The retort brought a smile and a pointed discussion of priorities in a boatman's life.

We later pondered pets we had known, such as Angel, the cat that had saved Joe and Elmer from being stranded on San Miguel Island, and Howard's white cat, a fitting mascot for his boat, the *Dove*. Ty began to talk cats.

"Did you know that white cats are often deaf?" Clearly it was a rhetorical question; Ty hardly paused before going on. "Howard was tied up in Coos Bay, and was out on the back deck with the tide running out fast, when he spotted something alive in the current. He grabbed his dip net, reached out, and snagged what was to become his infamous troublemaking boat mate.

"He hauled her in, dried her off, and never looked back. That cat shredded blankets, stole food, and was a general terror. Nothing Howard did seemed to improve her bad manners, but he loved her just the same. It was only when he banged some pots together hoping to scare some of the mischief out of her that he realized she was deaf. She hadn't even looked up."

"Yeah, I know, Ty. I've heard all about that cat. She was locked in the cabin most of the time because in port, and even at sea, she would sit staring into the water until fish schooled up around the boat. Then she'd go after them, practically dangling from one claw in the process. Worse, when the boat was in port, she took every opportunity to jump ship. She always came back, but in her own time."

Ty nodded. "You got it. That's not a good thing for a man in a rush to get out to a bite. Howard spent half his shore time looking for a cat that couldn't hear, and that hid when it suited her mood. I can't count how many times he swore he was going to go off and leave her."

"A wonder he didn't. Anybody else would have," I said.

"Well, sure, and his worrying about that cat in port was one thing; it was something else aboard ship. Howard knew it was only a matter of time before she fell in the drink permanently. He had to do something."

Ty was quiet with his thoughts until I finally asked, "Well? What did he do?"

"He married Ginny."

Of course! I laughed, thinking of Howard's perky little stay-at-home wife, Ginny—known for her love of cats.

Not long after this, Arno, abalone-diver-turned-fisherman, was one in a fleet of perhaps twenty boats following a hot bite fifty or sixty miles off California's Central Coast. In good weather—meaning not too sloppy—he was trolling out of sight of other boats when he spotted a big dog of Labrador-spaniel mix swimming purposefully toward nothing.

"All I could think was, why in hell is a dog swimming out here in the middle of the Pacific?" Arno said. "Man, when that poor mutt spotted me, his eyes nearly bugged out of his head, he was so happy."

Once Arno got the dog aboard, he recognized him as belonging to Bill, on the *Widow H.* Arno judged that the dog had been in the water for so long that even fifteen minutes more might have finished him. Once in his rescuer's care, the dog made a halfhearted try at shaking himself, drank a little fresh water, staggered into the cabin, curled up, and "slept like he was dead," Arno recalled.

"I got on the radio and gave Bill a call asking him where his dog was. 'Right here with me,' he says. 'You sure?' I say, and when the dog didn't come to his whistle, he was pretty upset. So I told him I picked him out of the drink, he was fine, and we'd make delivery when we got back on land." By all accounts, dog and master shared a "lickin'-good" reunion a week later.

The incident remained under heavy discussion for many weeks, having inspired countless wind and tide projections, studied charts, and a dozen wagers. None bore fruit; no one was ever able to authoritatively say how much time the dog spent in the water or how far its swim had been.

Ty also found himself with an uninvited pet on one occasion. Both Chance and Cole, very young at the time, were with him when an exhausted land bird sought haven on the *River Run*. It was a little garden-variety finch, probably carried offshore in a strong wind and without strength to fly back to land. It thrived for over a week, quite unafraid to steal crumbs from plates and chocolate from mugs. It became a pet to the boys, perching on their shoulders or snuggled against their necks for warmth. It was a sad morning when their tiny friend failed to join them at the breakfast table, sadder still when its cold, flattened body was found in the kids' bedding.

During a few of these years, popularizing exotic pets was the rage, and the fishing fleet was not exempt. Ben was one of the most respected fishermen in the fleet, and he had seemingly remained stable through a difficult divorce, so it was a shock to learn that his long-standing boat puller had weighed anchor, leaving his job without warning.

Shortly after this news made the rounds, replete with intriguing hints that an interesting replacement had been found, I joined Ty in San Francisco. The day after my arrival, I spotted Ben laughing with a beautiful dark-eyed girl as they walked arm in arm down the embarcadero.

"Did you know Ben was here in San Francisco, Ty? I saw him walking down the street with a stunning girl today."

Grinning, Ty looked up from the study of his charts. "You've seen his new boat puller, have you? I hear she's quite a looker."

"You can't mean that girl is his puller! No, Ty, this gal looked classy. No way the type." I was confident. "You should have seen the outfit she was wearing—it cost a bundle, I can tell you, obviously tailored to fit. Boy, I wish I had a figure like that."

"Fishing for a compliment, are you? Well, she's the gal. Gossip is that she's pretty clear about who runs the boat, and it isn't Ben. No, Ben can have her. I think I'll stick with what little I've got." Grinning wickedly, he went back to his charts.

I gave him a playful poke. "No, really, Ty, did he take that woman on as his puller?" At his nod, I persisted. "Where did he find someone like her, anyway? Who is she?"

"I hear she came on to him in the bar at the Mark Hopkins. Beyond that, nobody knows, or cares. Sounds like a nice problem to have." He turned that wicked grin on me again. This time I didn't continue the inquiries.

The next day, Ty and I were heading for a special lunch at a posh waterfront restaurant when we spotted Ben and his girl on the other side of the street. They were creating quite a stir. Padding along beside them was a tawny, sleekly muscular leopard on a golden leash.

"Is that Ben?" I whispered, not able to pull my eyes away from the astonishing sight. At Ty's silence, I turned to see his jaw gone slack: my unflappable husband was at an utter loss for words.

Ben's foray into the heady world of exotica didn't last. Not long after, I heard that his regular puller was back on the job. Word was that his beautiful puller had thrown down the gauntlet: the leopard would sail with them, or she would not. Witnesses said it was a contentious breakup, but the next time I saw Ben, his eyes twinkled in the old way, and he wore a small, sly grin I hadn't seen before.

This little escapade continued to amuse me until a situation of greater import filled my thoughts. Once again, Ty found himself without a puller, and it was late in the season.

"Come on, Bailey," he urged. "You might as well quit stalling. There isn't a better time than right now to get your hands dirty. At least make a stab at it—see what the job is, feel what it's like. You can say no, never, and that's okay, but if it's no, I'll take her out alone for whatever good fishing is left."

As he looked steadily into my eyes, I thought of Ben walking down the street with a beautiful girl on his arm and a leopard at his side. Why that memory arose or why I sensed that another gauntlet was thrown, I can't say, but in that instant and without hesitation, I made the commitment. "Okay, let's go," I said.

Perhaps I thought of the danger in his fishing alone; maybe I thought of another kind of danger.

22

BAILEY TESTS THE WATERS

What a time to make my first trip as the *River Run* puller! The storm was taking its toll, and Ty was driving me nuts with his grumbling and pacing. Always nervous and impatient when sitting in port for bad weather, this time brought him to near frenzy. Sausalito was fast losing its early appeal as a good place to wait. With nearly a week of the remaining season gone and no break foreseen in the weather forecast, he was getting downright surly.

"What lousy luck!" He snatched the white cap from his head and slammed it down on the galley table. "Just when the fish were showing up in decent numbers, we get beaten off the bite."

At my alarmed jump, he smiled weakly, took up the mistreated cap, slapped it over his rumpled curls, grabbed my hand, and pulled me out the door. "Let's take a walk before I go stir-crazy."

"Good idea." Hurrying to keep up with his long-legged stride, I said lightly, "I guess I must be proving how right that old superstition is about women on boats causing bad luck."

Ty grinned for the first time in hours, saying, "Could be, but I'm willing to test the devil on that one." With me in tow, he made his way rapidly down the docks toward Howard's boat, the *Dove,* where it was secured and temporarily untenanted, its owner opting to wait out the weather with his wife in their near-by home.

"After I check Howard's boat, we'll try a new restaurant. Maybe we can find a few laughs."

"Doesn't Howard worry about leaving the boat?" I found it interesting that a man would go off, as they all seemed to do, for extended periods while leaving this valuable and seemingly vulnerable asset untended.

"We do the same all winter at home, you know. Tied up snug in a proper place where there's no danger of damage, why not? There's always someone on the lookout. I'm probably not the only one keeping an eye on the *Dove.*"

Done with Howard's boat, found safe and secure, we continued our quest for dinner and diversion. As we walked, Ty anxiously went through the gamut of a puller's duties for the twentieth time, and although I'd felt confident when my decision to fish with him was first made, his repeated warnings about hard work and long hours were taking a toll.

"It's your job to run the lines, get the fish out of the water and on deck. I'll see to getting them down on the cooling racks. But after they're frozen, you might have to help stack them in the hold."

"Yes, I know. I know! You sound like you don't think I can do it."

"Of course you can. But that's not all. You have to remember that it's also your job to keep the decks clean and do the cooking. Think you can do that?"

"Sure. And what are you going to do all this time," I teased, trying to hide my nervousness, "lounge around demanding fresh coffee?"

I knew he would do as much of the hands-on fishing as I. However, only he could find the fish, navigate, and keep the boat running. I also knew that a novice aboard would double his workload, a fact probably adding to his current stress. These were sobering thoughts.

When we first talked about my sailing with him, he made it seem so simple that I was convinced it would be no more than a happy adventure. Now here I was, stuck in this prolonged state of limbo with doubt clouding pleasure. Instead of adventure and a hypothetical nose-thumb at tradition, I paced the waterfront in delayed anticipation, almost as anxious as Ty.

Luckily, it was not all waste. While the idle hours brought tight nerves to the trapped fishermen and led my captain to restless frustration, I found each day a boon of information. With me at his side, Ty regularly prowled the docks. He was at home in this hive of activity, and before long I noticed that we were continually drawn into groups made up of highliners—that is, men known to make the most successful catches. I hadn't realized until then that Ty was one of them, though Wally often dropped hints of his protégé's growing reputation. It was also during this prolonged wait that I was introduced to Ty's seafaring nickname.

The two of us were walking back to the boat after a downtown excursion and had taken our first steps on the docks when a white-capped fisherman disengaged from a cluster of others knotted around a pile of seine nets. With a wave, he yelled, "Hey, Zorro! Over here. You ought to hear this."

Ty joined the group while I continued to the boat, full of questions. He stayed away far too long for my curiosity, and I was out on deck as soon as I heard his first step on our ramp. "What was that 'Zorro' business?"

I was amazed to see him color with embarrassment.

"Nothing. It's my radio handle, that's all. We all have call names." He began to busy himself with a dangling line but soon shamefacedly looked up to say, "You know that my mom named me Tyrone after one of her supposedly heroic ancestors?"

I nodded, remembering the prideful reference by my mother-in-law to a family ancestor, a British naval privateer who had made inroads against his country's enemy of the moment.

"Well, I made the mistake of telling Howard that story. It was while I was still with Wally, and somehow my full name slipped out." He went back to teasing the loose line.

"What does Zorro have to do with your name? Or with Howard?"

"Oh, you know his imagination." At that time I didn't, but I let it go as Ty went on, "He ragged on the subject until he finally hit on Zorro. You know? The movie character Tyrone Power played?"

"That's just plain nuts!"

"Yeah, but that's Howard for you." My usually confident, purposeful mate writhed with embarrassed indignation at this perceived loss of dignity caused by a man he admired—such a battle in a man usually the first to laugh at an inanity! I looked away as his misery continued. "He told half the fleet that I must be something special with a name from a long line of heroes. But it was no stopping there! He put out over the air that I'm a ready-made hero, good-looking enough to be Zorro." Ty gave the frazzled line a final slam before ending, "What a bunch of hooey that is—that guy has black hair!"

I'd managed to contain myself through the whole ridiculous outpouring until this final absurdity, but now there was no stifling the giggle that quickly became a full-blown laugh. Red-faced, my darling looked daggers at me and then, in high indignation, brushed past on his way to the boat cabin.

With a teasing simper, I followed. "Oh, Zorro, my handsome hero! Take me, I'm yours."

We had just reached the galley door when he gave a sudden hoot and turned with smiling eyes to make a lighthearted grab, wrestling me into the privacy of the cabin.

WAITING OUT THE STORM

23

THE FLEET

We were among the first to leave the harbor in that exodus of working boats that always follows a storm. The pent-up anxiety that seemed to hover in a dark mist over the waterfront during the long wait disappeared with the shoreline. The banter that began on the docks with the first reports of dying winds followed us as we sailed under the Golden Gate Bridge, through the choppy "potato patch," and out onto the high seas. All three of our radios buzzed with chatter. Everyone was keyed up and feeling good, happy to be on the way after spending too many days off the grounds.

Our partner boat on this trip was, of course, the *Dove*. Despite, or maybe because of, the Zorro nickname, Ty and Howard had already shared many adventures. Though meeting personally only once or twice before, I now felt I knew Howard well, not only from the day or two spent together while waiting in Sausalito, but from Ty's wild tales. There was soon proof of their authenticity.

We were only moments past the bridge when the boat's short-range CB radio crackled to life with Howard's easily recognizable drawl. "Zorro, you there? Say, any fireworks between you and Bailey yet? Are you still speaking, or has she already marked off her side of the boat?"

"Nah," Ty picked up the radio's microphone and casually answered. "No danger. She prefers her fireworks closer to the bunk."

"Ty!" I choked. "Don't say things like that over the radio! Everyone out there can hear you!" My cheeks burned as Ty chuckled, looking pleased. I knew he was showing off for his friends, but I was too green in this new society to appreciate the form of its compliments.

Smarting at his casual treatment of what I regarded as my reputation, I demanded, "What did he mean, my side of the boat?"

"It's only an old fisherman's fable. Once at sea, if you discover you can't stand your boat mate, there's no escape. They say it's either murder or staking out one side of the ship." Mock seriously he added, "I've heard it said that one pair painted a line down the center of the boat, bow to stern, and didn't speak for a whole season."

With a snicker, I retorted, "Make a few more radio calls like that last one, buster, and you might find yourself banned to the life raft!"

Otherwise, my first hour at sea went smoothly despite the queasiness brought on by unfamiliar smells and the boat's incessant and unpredictable rocking. Happily, it took only minutes on deck, feeling the wind and smelling the salt, to set me straight. I waited there for Ty to show me how to take care of the outrigger poles, my first seagoing duty as puller.

The poles are usually let down while the boat is running in the calm waters of the bay, but in deference to my inexperience, Ty opted to do the job himself after we were under way. Once in open water, he could set the iron mike—automatic pilot to the uninitiated—and without hurry show me how best to approach the task.

The *River Run*'s poles, like those on most West Coast trollers, were forty or more feet in length. When folded up against the mast while in port, they towered out of the way. At sea, they dropped to a forty-five-degree working angle that also helped to reduce roll. It was always a treat to watch those big white workboats transform into something almost dainty as the poles, with tag lines attached, let down. To me, five or six trollers working an area on a blue day looked like seagoing butterflies in a breeze, with their fishing lines, like wing tails, dragging behind.

On that first day of lessons, I watched uneasily as Ty scrambled over the spray-dampened deck, working to push a pole free of its holder while the boat bounced in the wind-chop, token of the passing storm. This was very different from what I experienced while playing sailor in calm waters, and as I saw my husband slide around the deck, my hands grew clammy in sudden recognition of a serious oversight: I knew not even the rudiments of how to operate a boat. The horrifying truth was that there was absolutely nothing I could do for Ty if the unthinkable happened and he went overboard.

With heart pounding, I clutched frantically at a dangling boom rope while screaming, "Hang on! Ty! Be careful!"

Ty stopped wrestling the stubborn pole and turned to stare at me in surprise as he swayed with the jolts of restless water. With a questioning eye and shake of his head, he went back to work. Seconds later he triumphantly held up a short, frayed line. "Found the culprit. It looks like somebody tied the poles to the mast."

Appalled, I demanded, "Who would pull such a dangerous stunt as that?"

"Well, I suspect Howard. This does look like his handiwork." Chuckling, he went back to the poles.

"Why do you laugh? That is not funny! You could have fallen overboard!"

He paused to give me an incredulous look before finishing with the poles. In passing me on the way back to his electronics, he gave my shoulder a gentle pat while hiding a smile.

By the time we were again together in the cabin, I was calmly rational, almost laughing at myself, and said lightly, "You might want to teach me how to stop the boat, unless, of course, you think you can swim faster than it goes. Fair warning: if you fall over-board, you're on your own."

It was some hours later, after we were well settled into routine, when Ty began his lengthy and conscientious spiel featuring safety. Included were man-overboard instructions, and though he smiled and spoke lightly, his eyes were serious. I listened well, remembering that shudder of total helplessness.

I also remembered Billy.

"Hmm," I ventured as he ended his recital on the man-overboard issue. "Now, let's see, where do I sell the catch if I can't find you?"

Ty laughed. "You're a fast learner, and you sure do have your priorities straight!" He chuckled all the way through the next lesson—how to use the radios.

At the time I sailed with the *River Run*, radios were the pulse and beat of the fishing business. Every boat had at least three. They were the all-important communication between boats hidden in the distance and unpredictable seas. They were also navigational tools, fish-finding aids, and ship-to-shore telephones. I soon discovered that they were entertainment, as well.

Once again the CB radio, affectionately known as the "Mickey Mouse," crackled to life with the inquiry, "You there, Zorro?"

With a wink, Ty reached for the radio. "What's on your mind, Rag Mop?"

"It looked like Bailey had a little trouble getting your wings out. Too bad that old tug of yours is giving her trouble so soon," Howard cooed sweetly.

Ty pointed to the *Dove*, sailing ahead, then with a grin responded, "Yeah, she had a little trouble, but took care of it, no sweat. Hey, don't worry about my pretty *River Run*. You'd better think about that leaky bucket you call a boat."

"Best bucket in the fleet," Howard teased back. "By the way, be sure to tell Bailey that if her captain goes on making her work with bad equipment, I'm always looking for a good deckhand."

Soon other calls streamed in with some light reference to my presence. One regular wore the handle "Cyrano," and he drew from a cornucopia of "learned" witticisms. I looked forward to catching his calls, enjoying a voice with a peculiar squeak that enhanced the nonsense. Most often he jousted words with another regular labeled "the Professor." Whenever those two took over the airways to bandy wits, everyone listened. I always visualized them as a pair of wizened old men chuckling into their whiskers.

The dread that swam through my first hours at sea drifted away in the fun. I began to enjoy myself. Even my initial queasiness disappeared. It seemed Sal's prediction might be right. We would have a "helluva good time."

Our good time followed us through the long trip from harbor to fishing grounds, Ty alternating four-hour sleep watches with me. We didn't reach our target position until the next evening, when I was surprised to see boat lights dotting the sea as far as I could see. "Just look at all the lights, Ty. Is that really the fishing fleet?"

"Sure is. It's the spot, and it looks like half the fleet is already here and bedded down for the night. I have to find a good place for us to shut down, too."

"Why can't you just turn off the engine? Water is water, isn't it?"

"The boat should be no less than a couple of miles away from any other boat," Ty explained. "We definitely don't want to be below one with a sail." He went back to peering through binoculars in lengthy study of every light. "Each boat has a different drift pattern. Size and structure, both above and below the water, are main factors, but a boat with a sail picks up the lightest breeze and has to be watched especially close."

"Why do they have sails? I thought all the fishing boats were motor powered."

"Some of the guys use a sail as a stabilizer and swear by it. It's a different approach than the 'flopper-stopper' stabilizers that we hang from the poles on each side of the boat. Most of us use this method and think it is more efficient. Their official moniker is 'chain-rigged paravane stabilizers.'"

He went back to his study while moving slowly through the area, watching the radar, measuring distance between lights, and testing the wind. Eventually, he threw a satisfied glance in my direction. "This spot looks good. We should be fine here, but I'll be checking all through the night. The radios are on, and if anybody spots a freighter coming through, we will soon know."

With that he shut down the main engine, and the boat went quiet.

Adrift for the night with radios still for the first time all day, we could relax in review of the day's events. We hashed over Howard's trickery, along with memorable radio calls, and were beginning to wind down when Ty asked, "You weren't actually scared back there when we started, were you, Bailey?"

"I guess not, really," I answered, believing it as I melted into his arms for the first of the many nights of warmth we would share, finding pleasure in the rhythms of the sea.

24

WHISKY LINES, JIGS, AND
SETTLING FOR LESS

As promised, Ty taught me how to start and stop the main engine, what gauges to watch, and how to use the radios. He also schooled me in the intricacies of dealing with the bait jigs that trailed from the poles angling out from the boat's deck.

"Watch it, Bailey! Geez, look at that tangle!"

It was several days into the trip, and we were standing together in the cockpit at the stern of the boat, he on one side, I on the other, pulling in gleaming silver albacore as fast as we could. We were on a hot bite, and for a while it was fun, working side by side. I thought I had it wired, with everything going just right. Then I grabbed a wrong line, a fish ran out across another line, and I didn't know what to do about the resulting mess.

With a searing oath, Ty let go his lines and stepped over to my side, where he pulled in the snarl while I sniffled, fighting an all-out crying jag. While he ranted on in peppered language, I cowered in a corner of the cockpit. He had forgotten me, absorbed as he was with the situation, but when his glance slid my way, he was all unsympathetic attention.

"Okay, okay! Forget it," he ordered firmly. "We've got to get this mess cleaned up." Still sniffling, I got to work.

Once we had the tangled lines on deck, I fought knots and replaced jigs while Ty, back at the helm, went hunting for the lost school of fish. Fortunately, he was able to find it, or one like it.

He soon rejoined me in the cockpit, where I was again pulling fish. Trying to forestall a lecture, I apologized. "I'm really sorry, Ty."

I should have stopped there but couldn't restrain a bid for sympathy. "It's hard, working with all these jigs. How many are there, anyway? I can't keep track of them, and they're stickery." In proof of the complaint, a hook grabbed at my gloves, then bounced out of reach as I heaved a fighting fish aboard.

"For crying out loud, catch that line!" Ty yelled with none of the sympathy I had tried to drum up, instead launching into the lecture I didn't want to hear. "It is not that hard! There are only four hooks on each pole. That's eight. Add the two stern lines, and you have ten—eleven with the whisky line! The whisky line is the one running out from the top of the mast. You've got to get it right. Unless the albacore think they're following real bait, they'll disappear, and so will our profit!" With a shake of his head, he added, "You do know that the jigs are supposed to look like baitfish following us, don't you?"

Once again fighting tears, I nodded. "Yeah, I guess."

Trying to control his irritation, he went on, "No guess to it. There is a system to all this. Every jig goes on a line different in length and position from the one next to it." He made several steps back and forth in his inches of space, took a deep breath, and then, struggling for patience, went on, "The idea is to be able to pull any separate line, at any time, without a disaster."

He stepped aside in thought for several minutes, then came back to continue more gently, "I guess we need to get the whole thing mapped out for you. You need to remember that the line nearest the end of the pole is called the intermediate line, and it is about ten fathoms long. Next one down is the long line, about twelve fathoms, and then the short line, seven fathoms, and the chain line, five fathoms. The two lines dropping off the stern are called stern lines, and they're only two fathoms long. With the fifteen-fathom whisky line, our eleven jigs are arranged to mimic a natural bait school while letting us pull in one line without affecting another." He sighed and retreated to his side of the cockpit.

We were hard at work again, but eventually the bite slackened, giving us a breather. Shamefaced, Ty came over to put an arm around my shoulder. "Sorry about being so hard on you. I should have explained this end of the business before now. I went a little crazy because fish don't always bite, and when they do, we have to land all we can. It's our living. We can't waste time untangling lines."

"I know, and I'll try harder. It's only that I didn't know what to do."

"Forget it. It was my fault. I should have brought in the whisky line. That's the one you got hold of, and it shouldn't have been out in this kind of fishing. We can't fool with it when the fish are hitting. Not only is there too much time lost in pulling fifteen fathoms of line up to the boat, but the hooked fish on it could pull free and sound, hide in deep water, with the rest likely to follow. Mistakes like that can lose the whole school, as you saw."

"I thought the fish on that line was coming in just fine."

Ty nodded. "I know, but between the current and the wind, there was just enough drift on our setup to get us in trouble. You saw the mess. We're lucky we didn't lose more gear than we did." His tone lightened as his ire settled. "Forget the whisky line for now. We want to keep it for slow days, for the odd straggler that we wouldn't ordinarily catch."

"But I heard Wally telling a story about how, one day, the whisky line catch was the best of his whole trip."

"But that's not the entire story." Ty was grinning. "Wally tells a good tale, and it is true. Sometimes that line is worth its weight in gold by bringing a whole boatload of albacore up close enough to spot the rest of the jigs. It happens once in a while, but we don't need to think about that in a hot bite. Let's keep it where it belongs, picking up just enough stray fish to buy whisky!"

We sailed on over the endless, restless waters, seeing other boats only now and again, or occasionally crowded on a small school of fish. Boredom was buried in hard work, and loneliness in radio chatter. To my mind, the journey was without plan or direction. Sometimes we sailed in never-ending circles over the fish schools. Sometimes we went hunting, sailing first into the sun, then away from it, north then south, wandering aimlessly, it seemed. But sometimes it was full speed on a straight course.

The bite had disappeared, and we were bucking north at a good clip in response to a reliable report of fish showing up off Oregon. I tossed aside the book I read and carried a fresh cup of coffee to Ty, on watch in the wheelhouse.

As I handed it over, I asked, "Where are we, Ty? How far are we from land, and where are we going?"

With a look of surprise, he took the offered cup. "Right now, we are about a hundred or more miles off the Oregon coast. Up in this part of the country, we find fish from about ninety to one hundred and twenty miles offshore, almost never less than sixty miles. Down lower, off Southern California, the fish are usually found from three to four hundred miles out, but every once in a while, the right current will bring them in much closer."

He sipped his coffee as he explained, "Albacore are a migratory fish that follow certain warm ocean currents, about sixty-two degrees, as they swirl through the Pacific. Because we know when and where these currents are likely to show up, we know the right places to explore."

"Albacore are always on the move, aren't they?" As I had spotted the schools from my position on the flying bridge over the past weeks, they reminded me of a flock of birds, hundreds moving as one, flowing like a silver stream below the ocean's surface.

"They're territorial, too," Ty answered. "We tend to think of land animals as the only ones that stake out territory, but if you climb up to the top of the mast when we're on a good bite, you can watch the action. I was amazed the first time I saw it—the main man darted out from the school that followed our jigs in an effort to fight off fish from a new school trying to move in. It reminded me of an old rooster guarding his hens."

I smiled but was thinking of other things. "Are we really over a hundred miles from land? That's scary, Ty."

With a laugh, he said, "What difference does it make how far out we are? After the two or three miles from shore that anyone might be able to swim, it doesn't matter if it's six, sixty, or six hundred miles. Your chances are the same."

With a grimace, I retorted, "Comforting thought."

Again he laughed, then went on, "Like all living things, fish need food, and, same as the rest, they're apt to congregate around the best sources for it. That is usually where there is an upwelling of currents full of the nutrients necessary to countless varieties of sea life, each of which will probably end up as dinner for something else. Seafarers have names for these special spots. The Davidson Sea Mount is one, and Rodriguez Dome, 1908 spot, and the Escarpment are others. That last one is only sixty to seventy miles off the Santa Barbara continental shelf. In between any of them, the sea bottom is mostly desert, offering little to support food fish." He grinned and eyed me. "We'll be going to one or the other of these upwelling locations before this trip's done. Stick with me, and you'll see them all."

"Well, if what I've seen so far means anything, there won't be much to see! Anyway, how do you decide where to start in the first place? I know you don't just go sit and wait at one of those places."

"The first reports usually come from long-distance tugboats as they cross the Pacific. Most of them put out a fish line and then send a radio report on what they pull in. You have to remember that the biggest part of the ocean is a sand desert where only migratory fish following the currents are found. Once in a while, a sailboat or a yacht will give a heads-up. By comparing this kind of information, we can make a pretty good guess about the currents and where fish might turn up. Other than that, we go exploring on our own. Fuel's cheap at eleven to fifteen cents a gallon."

"Thanks loads. I sure feel better now that I know exactly where we've been, exactly where we are, and exactly where we're going!"

I struggled on, learning a little more each day about keeping the lines in the water, the jigs in order, and how best to boat the fish. Meanwhile, I loved watching Ty, admiring the ease with which he worked the cockpit and at the same time managed everything else. He was constantly back and forth between the wheel and the radios, or battling the temperamental radar or glitchy old WWII loran that was almost impossible to read. Sometimes the engine or the refrigeration demanded attention belowdecks. Meanwhile, he kept us clear of other boats and on course while we ran at exactly the speed needed for our school of imitation fish to swim at the right depth. He had to be a navigator, an engineer, a mechanic, an electrician, and something of a creative wizard, with frequently makeshift tools. I found it a wonder.

It was also intimidating. Finally, on one of my particularly discouraging days, I asked, "How did you ever learn to do all that?"

With a grunt and a raised eyebrow, he replied, "How does anyone learn to do anything? You just do it until you get it right."

So I kept on doing.

Then one day Ty stood watching as I heaved a lively fish up out of a choppy sea. "You might make a boat puller yet, Bailey. You're turning into a real sailor!"

Somehow, the compliment took the sting from the blisters, hook punctures, and wire cuts I had accumulated despite the heavy protective tire-tube "nippers" covering my hands. After Ty's stamp of approval, it was easier to forget all these little hardships, even the pervasive fish gurry that seemed to stick to everything it touched.

Ty was right to warn me about the hard work. Those first days were brutal, with the fish turning up in quantity everywhere. Luckily, the weather remained good, a blessing I didn't recognize until later, while I learned the mechanics of the job and the trick of using boat action to flip the big white-meat tuna aboard. My arms muscled, and my hands toughened with callous. The day came when I didn't have to call Ty to help pull lines or stack frozen fish, and watching him slide precariously in sea wash was no longer a fearful thing.

Still, all was not perfection. The boats fishing around us reported making larger catches than we had. "This isn't working out too well, is it, Ty? You did better with your hired pullers."

"It doesn't matter, Bailey. We'll catch up."

"Sure. I just need a little more experience. And I am getting faster, aren't I?"

"You're doing fine. Anyway, it's nice working together. We can settle for a little less."

As pleased as I was to hear that Ty didn't regret having me aboard, I noticed his frown with the suggestion that we could "settle for less."

RUNNING THE BOAT

25

MURDER ON HER MIND

The *River Run* was a wooden boat, deep keeled and vee bottomed, with a generous cargo hold. A fine, seaworthy vessel designed initially for salmon fishing, her sizeable hold also worked well for albacore fishing; however, when carrying weight that varied daily, adaptable ballast was necessary. Without it, the boat would bounce or roll dangerously in the mildest seas, and in response to this situation, a system had been devised wherein fifty-pound lead ingots were moved from the refrigerated hold to the bow of the boat as the weight of frozen fish forced the stern deeper and the bow higher. As the hold filled, it was necessary to balance the remaining ballast there also.

Handling the ballast was a puller's job, but Ty had been taking care of it, no doubt in deference to my novice status. This boon did not last; the inevitable day came when I was called upon to assume my rightful duty, and I found myself in close relationship with those ugly chunks of lead.

"You mean I have to carry every one of those things forward? They're heavy!"

I was excited and happy to get out on deck despite the inky darkness in that hour or two before the sun showed its first dim rays on the horizon, eager for this early start. I hoped to match yesterday's catch, the biggest day yet. We had caught so many fish that there wasn't room for all of them below on the refrigerated cooling racks. The last of the catch bled and cooled overnight on deck, waiting for morning to be transferred below. But before this could happen, frozen fish had first to be removed from the cooling racks and stacked in holding bins.

"You'll have to help with it, Bailey, if we're going to get in a full day. I've got to move leads out of the hold before I can stack what's frozen and get these deck fish down to the cooling racks before the sun is up. The ballast has to be adjusted before we get under way." Busily, he lifted bars up through the hatchway. "You shouldn't have any trouble getting forward and aft. We're not moving, and the weather is down. You lugged Jenny around long after she was heavier than one of these."

Sighing, I picked up the first of those fifty-pound leads and headed for the bow of the boat, slipping in the fish blood that covered the deck. Disgusted, I paused to grumble, "It's going to take hours to clean up this mess," then continued on to the narrow passage between the cabin and the low side rail of the boat, concentrating on keeping my footing sure and my burden safe.

By the time the sun crept close enough to the horizon to light the morning, all the necessary ingots were transferred from the stern to the bow, each bar cradled in my arms as I sidled slowly along with my back hard against the cabin wall. This narrow deck space was several feet long, and passage usually required clinging to a shoulder-high grab rail installed on the side of the cabin. After carefully arranging the last lead with the others, I paused to flex my back and admire the first glints of sun on sea.

One glance, and I nearly strangled on a choked scream. Below, a parade of dark shadows slowly circled the boat. Accenting the horror, an occasional sharp black fin broke the tranquil surface of the water surrounding us.

Frozen, heart pounding, I tried to think. It would not do to scream for Ty. He might slip and go over the side or miss his footing while trying to reach me along the narrow passage. Going back that way was unthinkable, yet it was the only way to reach the stern, where Ty worked. After a moment of frantic consideration, I braced myself for a new ordeal. Back I went, this time nearly wrenching the grab rail from the side of the cabin in the journey.

"Bailey!" Ty dropped the fish he held and hurried to my side. "What's the matter? You're white as a sheet."

Without answering, I pointed to the evil patrol. Ty stared for a moment, then threw his head back and laughed himself to tears.

Dumbstruck, I stood wondering. Had he not recognized the threat? Had the sight deranged him?

When I finally found my voice, I croaked in horror, "Those are sharks, Ty. Dozens of *huge* sharks!"

After he'd gotten control of his chuckles, my lover observed, "You don't see them jumping aboard, do you?" At my look of disgust, he lightly added, "They only smell fish blood draining off the deck. Once we get under way and you get everything scrubbed clean, they'll go away."

If ever murder crossed my mind, it was at that moment.

FISHING ALBACORE

26

GALLEY COOKS AND PORPOISE

IN QUICKSILVER

The days stacked up, as did the fish in the hold. One morning while inspecting the catch, Ty poked his head up through the freezer hatch and announced, "Another day of this kind of fishing, and we can head for the cannery. We're close to a full load."

"It doesn't seem we've been out that long." The job kept me too busy to think of time. "Your trips are usually longer, aren't they?"

"It's going on three weeks. Lucky the catch has been good because we'd have to head for shore anyway. The way you're feeding us, we're running short of supplies." Ty rubbed his belly. "Nice to have you along if only for the grub."

I laughed. "Next time, I'll choose the groceries. Guys don't know beans about cooking."

That last was unfair. Ty's boat help was always well fed, and it was he who lectured me on the importance of regular, hot, and nourishing meals when at sea. He also insisted that while our kind of hard physical labor and incredibly long hours must be sustained by a sound and adequate diet, regular naps were equally necessary. We took advantage of any lull in the fishing cycle for necessary sleep, in compensation for days that began at dawn and lasted until dark, no matter the time zone. I now understood both points, especially the one about sleep after fishing the northernmost grounds, where darkness might last as little as four hours.

Although I spoke as though my job as Ty's puller was more than a onetime adventure, it was not my intent to desert home and family for life at sea. Who would, when the "head," toilet to a landlubber, was housed in a cubbyhole accessible only from the outside deck, fresh water was limited to a seventy-gallon tank, and the kitchen was a three-foot suggestion, rightfully called the galley.

The *River Run*'s galley was equipped with a big ever-burning oil stove that served for both heating and cooking. Its tiny linoleum-covered counter was partnered with an even tinier sink. Cupboards were tucked willy-nilly between beams and studs, and, to keep them from becoming projectiles in rough weather, canned goods were thrown haphazardly into storage benches where boat action quickly settled them into a lock of immovable tin. These bench lockers flanked a small table with a raised edge designed to keep items from sliding to the deck. Refrigerated food was stowed in heavy cardboard boxes and kept on shelves just inside the freezer hatch, where regular refrigerator temperature reigned.

Even so, inconvenience and lack of space were not the worst of cooking aboard a seagoing vessel. On my first effort as galley cook, I found myself slipping and sliding from one end to the other of the miniscule area surrounding the hot stove as I screamed for Ty.

"Quick! Come help me! There's water everywhere."

"What the hell happened?" Looking scared, he dropped his radio microphone and came running.

The teakettle rolled around underfoot, bumping and rattling to add zest to my squawks. "I put some water on the stove, and as soon as I turned my back, the whole thing went flying."

Looking relieved, Ty lectured, "You can't be yelling like that, Bailey. I thought something serious had happened."

"You mean this isn't serious?" Furious, I was not open to a lecture. "How do you expect me to cook with pots and pans flying all over the place?"

Fortunately, Ty's sense of humor saved us both from living on a divided vessel. Characteristically, he began to laugh.

Indignant, I responded, "Why do you always think everything is funny? This is not funny! How am I supposed to work in this mess?"

"See this?" He pointed to a neatly stacked maze of brass rods and wing nuts bolted to one side of the flat stovetop. "What did you think this was for? You've got to tie things down to keep Neptune from playing tricks." On inspection, the rods proved to be the framework of an adjustable grid designed to keep a variety of pots and pans in place on the stove's surface.

I never again forgot to secure the utensil of the moment, even in ordinary seas, and beans, spaghetti sauces, stews, pot roasts, and thick soups were soon primary to my menus. Not only healthy and sustaining, they were good choices because they could be left to cook unattended in tight-lidded containers for hours at a time. The gentle heat of the ever-burning oil stove coupled with the incessant stirring motion of the boat created an ideal environment for those old-fashioned favorites. The always preheated oven was good for baking potatoes, cookies, and dense breads, too, as long as the weather was reasonably calm and there was enough time to prepare them.

That was the beginning. Now I was an accomplished galley cook, and Ty was right about the supplies. They were getting slim. In my zeal, I was overgenerous with almost everything.

"What say we barbecue the last steak tonight, Bailey? The weather is perfect for it." Ty always carried charcoal and oak bark along with a small waterproof metal box that opened to become a portable grill.

"Okay! Baked potatoes, too, and canned peaches for dessert." I knew that would be the last of both but was ready to sacrifice them for a celebration. Sadly, nothing fresh remained on ice.

Evening found us in our night drift nursing a last cup of coffee as we lingered beside the dying embers of the little grill, the sun long gone in a pink-and-gold burst.

"I think I will get at the dishes before I fall asleep on my feet." Reluctantly, I boosted myself up and into the cabin.

The clean dishes were safely stowed, and I was beginning to eye my bunk, when Ty called, his voice lilting with excitement. "Come look, Bailey! Hurry!"

Rushing outside, I found Ty staring into a night brilliantly clear, the air's usual sea nip tamed to velvet, and stars so close that you could almost feel their cold heat. The sea was satin smooth, and though it was hours past the sun's last wink, you could see into endless depths now aquiver with phosphorous, and electric with life. That great ocean expanse had drawn its nymphs together in a light show that far outshone any Broadway production.

Trailing long, graceful streaks of liquid radiance, dolphins raced, chased, and cavorted around us. Wrapped in iridescence, they danced on a dazzling otherworldly stage—"Like porpoise in quicksilver," Ty whispered, as if fearing he'd disturb them—coming up out of the depths in great, twisting, arcing leaps that left showers of sparkle indistinguishable from the starry horizon. Heaven and Earth were one in a kaleidoscope of shimmer.

Over and over again, the troupe leaped and whirled in a show that held us locked in unearthly time until the sea emptied and the night became ordinary again.

The next morning, the radios were quiet later than usual. When the chatter did begin, it was subdued, though we learned that the phenomenon had been widespread. Oddly, no one seemed eager to discuss it. Howard's only comment was, "Sure nice Bailey was with you on such a pretty night, Ty."

Fishing was good that day. By nightfall, Ty announced that we had a full load. By the next morning's wee hours, we were well on our way to shore, a long and uneventful trip with plenty of time for introspection.

Relaxing on the bunk, I daydreamed of sailing into our home port. Although never very poetically stated, I'd often heard seagoing friends speak their heartfelt fondness for our PG&E tower lights visible at night for many miles at sea. In my half-dream state, it was easy to imagine how it would feel to watch their winking welcome grow brighter with every lonely hour, a beacon that spoke of comfort and safety. I suddenly yearned for home.

"Well, what about it?" Ty startled me out of my reverie. "Are you sorry you came along?"

More slowly than I'd have responded only hours before, I answered, "No. I really liked being out here with you." A little doubtfully, I added, "It was good, but awfully hard work."

"You wouldn't go again?" He sounded surprised.

As suddenly as it had come, my doubt was gone. "I'll go anytime you want. But we have to think about the kids. It's no good their having part-time parents."

"No. But one or two trips a year wouldn't be a bad thing. Besides, they'll be out of the house before we know it." After reflecting for a moment, Ty added, "Chance is experienced enough to go out with Wally next summer, and he's looking forward to it. The twins seem pretty happy in their dry-land summer jobs, with Chase learning how to work on engines, and Cord learning the waiter business. It looks like time to put Cole to some serious work with me. He wants to go, he wants to learn more, and he's been driving me crazy about it."

I jerked erect. "And I'll bet you encouraged him. He's a child, Ty! It's too dangerous! The work is too much! No! No more of the children."

Ty stared. "What's the matter with you? He's been with me for at least a week every summer for years, and it's been good for him. It's what the kid is begging to do."

"No. It's bad enough worrying about you and Chance. Now you're telling me I'll have to think of my baby boy out there, too? No."

"Listen to yourself!" Glaring, he went on, "None of them are babies. You sound exactly like your silly sister. Only a few minutes ago, you were telling me you liked being out here, working hard. Well, so does Chance. Why not Cole? Your 'baby' or not, he needs to figure out who he is, just like the twins and Jenny, too, for that matter." He ended the lecture by spitting out, "Always scared! Don't you know *life* is dangerous, Bailey? It comes with birth!"

I flung myself out of the cabin to sit on the hatch, brooding until Ty, wearing a conciliatory smile, came to sit beside me. By then some degree of common sense, or perhaps resignation, had returned.

"Sorry. That was foolish of me. I can't stop Cole or Chance any more than I could stop you. I'll have Cord and Chase safe at home, anyway." I sighed, "I'll worry, but I'll try not to let it show too much."

I leaned into Ty's comforting arm for several thoughtful moments. In the end I looked ruefully into his eyes and said, "Anyway, what kind of mother would deny her kid a chance to see porpoise dancing in quicksilver?"

27

OF WHISKY FAIRIES

Our last fish were caught somewhere off Northern California, calling for delivery in Eureka. My only previous visit there was a brief one with all the kids in tow, and I looked forward to this chance to better explore the historic town. I couldn't know that events marking the end of my debut as a boat puller would be memorable for much more than exploring a new harbor.

"We'll deliver at Tarantino's. He runs a good restaurant next door, too." Ty was happily preparing for landfall. "You've never spent much time in Eureka, have you? It's kind of rough, but interesting. I think you'll like it."

"If I can get a good shower there, I'll love it."

"Don't worry. The buyers keep a nice bathhouse for us with enough hot water for a fleet." He rubbed his hands together in anticipation. "Last one in is all wet!"

It was early evening when we reached our destination, too late to do business. Howard had beat us in by a few hours, so we tied up next to the *Dove,* rafted outside Wally's *Mariner.* Waiting side by side to catch our tie lines as we pulled in, Wally and

Howard radiated good cheer, a bit of beer, and the refreshing effects of long hot baths. Seeing them standing there together made me smile at their differences. A slightly graying Wally, all wire and energy, contrasted amusingly with Howard, a stocky, stoic-appearing young man whose solid muscle masqueraded as corpulence.

"Ahoy there, Captain!" Wally doffed his clean white cap in greeting to Ty, then turned to me with an exaggerated bow. "And a special welcome to your first mate."

Howard tied the last line to a cleat with ease born of experience, then smiled slyly. "I don't suppose you'll show the whip marks left by that slave driver you've been working for, will you?" He scrambled smoothly over the railing to surprise me with a bear hug, and a handshake for Ty. "Or did Zorro get himself assigned to one side of the boat?"

Before I could think of a pert retort, Wally hopped aboard carrying four glasses and a bottle of Scotch. "Celebration is the order of the evening," he advised, pouring out his offering. "You brought luck, Bailey. We haven't had fishing so good in a while. There is no other explanation." He lifted his glass in salute.

Grinning as happily as Wally, Ty and Howard raised their glasses to me. Dazed, I lifted my own glass and immediately burst into tears. "But I'm dirty and I smell like fish!" I wailed. "We can't celebrate this way."

With drinks still held high, three startled faces froze in baffled wonder for a space of seconds. The sight forced a teary giggle.

"Three handsome men offering a toast to a lady deserve more than fish gurry and a truly disgusting sweatshirt." I struggled for a playful tone. "But, if you're game, so am I." In innocence, I tossed the toast down my throat and immediately felt the hefty gulp's flame that left me gasping. Even as I choked, I saw those three wondering, wildly funny expressions dissolve in laughter. For me, that toast was a farewell to more than one cherished notion of propriety. In that moment, years of foolish social conditioning floated gently away.

For many hours I had anticipated with relish the promised hot bath and a meal that didn't require constant vigilance to keep out of my lap. Booze and partying held no place in those plans, but there was no resisting the warmth of such an outlandish welcome. I relaxed, enjoying the novelty of this strange method of socializing.

Drinks dispatched, I was directed to the ladies' bathhouse, where soap, shampoo, and unlimited hot water taught me what luxury truly is, perhaps as only weeks of saltwater bathing can teach. I lingered long in the misty warmth but at last could dawdle no longer. After so many weeks at sea, the ground seemed to roll under my uncertain seaman's legs, but I made it without mishap back to the dock. Fresh-shaven and smelling of soap, Ty waited in the boat's cabin, his clean shirt almost wrinkle-free. How handsome he was, free of his smelly, oil-stained boat clothes!

The restaurant was bustling with a mixture of tourists and fishermen. As we walked toward the table where Howard and Wally waved, I heard Sal's unmistakable roar. "Hey! There's Bailey and Ty!" Scrambling through close-packed chairs, her booming voice and tumbled words turned every head in the house. "I heard you was sailing with Ty. When did you get in?" Loudest of all was her joyful shout: "Ain't it a great life?"

Ignoring the tight smiles of other restaurant patrons, she bumped up to give me a hug and smacking kiss I knew must leave a smear of vermilion on my cheek. Still, I was delighted. "I didn't know you and Jim had gotten this far north," I babbled, returning the hug.

"We got here all right. Just in time for the engine to conk out. Jim's been working on it all week." She bugled her laugh. "We'll probably get out again about the time the fish leave. Hey, join us up on Two Street when you're done here. We're going barhopping up to the Bird Cage. It'll be fun!"

I joined my gentlemen and was busy studying the dinner menu when I was startled to hear the unmistakable squeak of Cyrano's voice coming from a table next to us. Recognizing a favorite performer who had eased boredom with his radio nonsense during long sailing hours, I quickly turned with a smile for my envisioned whiskered ancient.

Instead, I looked into deep-green eyes set in a smoothly youthful face. The only vestige of my imagined ancient mariner came as he stood in greeting, his long, lithe body unfolding to reveal the hint of a potbelly.

"You must be Bailey. I see you're with the right folks."

I stuttered a few words in acknowledgment, even managing to speak something of appreciation for his radio offerings, but it was strangely disarming to find the comfortable old friend of my mind in such a different skin! I returned to my menu with the sudden comprehension that most of my radio friends would forever be shadows in a different reality.

It might be that circumstances made this particular meal seem extraordinary, but I will always remember it as one of the best I've had: fresh swordfish expertly seasoned and grilled, pilaf with a touch of lemon, and vegetables al dente. It could have been the perfect end to a happy evening, but there was more.

"Hurry up. We don't want the others looking for us." Ty waited outside the powder room door while Wally and Howard went ahead.

"Hurry up? Don't we have to unload early tomorrow morning?"

"We can have a drink up at the Bird Cage. There'll be plenty of time to sleep in before we have our turn at the hoist. There are a lot of boats ahead of us." He grabbed my arm and pulled me out to the street. "There's a piano in the bar that hardly ever gets played. It is a little out of tune, but nobody there knows the difference."

Ty is one of those nonprofessionals who love to make music. We've always had a piano that he will play by the hour, even now. His forte is ragtime and honky-tonk, and he plays well enough to please his listeners, though I always worry.

"The owners might not like to have strangers fooling with their piano," I warned.

Grinning like a kid at Christmas, he answered, "Nobody's going to mind."

He had drawn me to the doorway of a big, dingy, poorly lit cavern. Drifts of cigarette smoke rising from the noisy crowd obscured the atmosphere. A yellowed tin ceiling towered above an unlikely assortment of partiers lolling about the once grandly ornate bar and well-abused tables left from another generation. Pushed against one wall was a forlorn spinet piano with a highly powdered woman in a skimpy dress leaning at one end in deep flirtation with a man in a once white fisherman's cap.

Gasping, I sputtered, "We're going in there?"

Before Ty could answer, Sal's big voice boomed, "Hey, Bailey, over here! Come on in and have a drink."

Never before had I been thrown together with so many strangers in a place as bizarre as the Bird Cage, though I suppose they were not really strangers. They certainly were no strangers to Ty. In seconds, I found myself holding a drink and hearing someone yell, "Ty's here! Open the piano!"

Ty quickly launched into his brand of honky-tonk while Wally guided me to where Howard, Sal, and Jim waited. It wasn't long before our table was jammed, and we all watched the crowd go from noisy to rowdy. Glasses multiplied across the top of the piano. Chairs were pushed back to make more dance space, and I was swept up in a lively two-step with a complete stranger who, incidentally, was a great dancer. The place was jumping, and Ty was playing better on that raunchy old piano than I ever heard him play before.

Empty glasses were quickly refilled, and it seemed that anyone who walked past the door couldn't resist coming in. Although the crowd was largely made up of fishermen and visiting wives, it also included local workingmen and their girls, some intrepid tourists, and two or three tired-eyed ladies whose business was a mystery to me. Social barriers evaporated in the noise and smoke.

Over the evening I tried to keep track of Wally and Howard and found it impossible. I did see Wally several times make his way to the piano, where he hung around for a moment or two, joking with Ty, then disappear again in the crowd. I also noticed Howard hopping from table to table, sometimes leaning over to speak in a confidential way to someone who would then make his way over to the bar. Occasionally, he joined me to make some silly remark about one or another of the dancers out on the floor where Jim and Sal were showing off. Always he wore an odd grin that I attributed to too much whisky, though there was no other sign of it.

The Bird Cage didn't empty until the bartender reluctantly announced the closing hour. "Sorry, folks. I'll lose my license if I don't kick you out. Come back tomorrow."

"Probably the best day he's had in a year," Sal whispered loudly.

A troop of us headed off toward the docks that lay several deserted and seedy streets away. We had gone only a few yards when Wally stopped the procession at a weed patch. Pushing aside a few blades of dead grass, he pulled out a cache of overflowing glasses.

"Why, look at this, will you? The whisky fairies have left their nectar!"

A roar of laughter went up. The conspiracy between Wally and Howard was clear. Howard had kept the drinks coming for the pianist, while Wally spirited them from the piano and into the wilderness of the Eureka waterfront.

Sal grabbed me by the waist in a joyful twirl, shouting, "Men! You just gotta love 'em!"

It was a riotous trek home, with numerous discoveries of the whisky fairies' largesse along the way. Most of us tumbled aboard our boats in the early hours too weary to notice that several more vessels had come in.

28

BREAKFAST AT THE WHISKY DEL MAR

The clang and clatter of machinery brought me slowly awake. Ty was nowhere in sight, though a pot of coffee steamed at the back of the stove. It took two cups of that life-giving brew before I was ready to face the world.

Too soon, my wandering man bounced aboard looking as fresh as a summer morning while demanding, "Hurry up, Bailey. We're having breakfast at the Whisky del Mar."

"Whisky," I groaned. "Don't mention that word to me." I couldn't believe my husband was suggesting such a breakfast. "I want some eggs and toast."

"Oh, come on! It's a café! The Vista del Mar."

Dubiously, I agreed. "Okay, but no saloons, and it better be good."

"I guarantee a regular truck driver breakfast. Hurry, though. Wally is up to unload in a couple of hours, once Howard's done, and he wants to introduce you to his brother."

"What brother?"

"Virgil! Wally's brother. He got in during the middle of last night and tied up in front of Wally." Ty's grin widened. "Wally spotted the boat while preparing the 'fairy nectar' surprise."

I knew that Wally had a brother in San Diego, but I thought fishing was simply a pastime with him. Most references I heard were either of his scholarly or political exploits or of some ridiculous entanglement the two brothers shared in the past.

"What are you talking about? The only boat I see in front of Wally is that great big thing. Anyway, what would Virgil be doing here?"

"That great big thing is the *Titan*, Virgil's boat, and he is here for the same reason we are. He has a full load."

"But I thought he was a teacher or something. The way Wally talks, he's a really smart guy."

Ty looked at me with a frown as he hesitantly said, "His wife still teaches at Cal State University—" Annoyance and dawning replaced the frown. "Haven't you figured out yet that there are damn few dim-witted fisherman around? And just so you know, Virgil gave up university life when he got frankly tired of the personal politics involved."

Noting the tone of annoyance, I silently allowed him to hurry me up the gangplank, but as soon as we hit solid ground, I persisted. "Well, why didn't I hear him on the radio? We heard everybody else."

Impatiently, Ty answered, "You did hear him! You heard the Professor every day we were out."

"Professor? You mean that guy with a quote for everything, the one who jousts words with Cyrano? He calls you Typhoon? That's Wally's brother?"

How could it be that one-half of my favorite shipboard entertainment was Wally's brother without my knowing it? Wondering, I soon realized that I knew even less about most of those whose voices I heard daily. Nicknames and boat names were their identity at sea. Ashore, I heard conventional names and home ports that had nothing whatever to do with radio tags or boat names. The identities seemed not to mix, but it didn't matter because I would recognize them anywhere. I knew exactly what they looked like by the timber and tone of their voices! Silly me.

One vividly hilarious exchange between the Professor and Cyrano took place over several days, all relating to booze and its effect on imbibers. It kept the whole fleet eagerly awaiting each day's session of verbal upmanship. Only one of the exchanges stays with me, and it was one of the less "lofty" offerings—probably why I remember it. The banter usually dealt with Shakespeare, Thomas Hardy, or Balzac.

Cyrano, with his squeak, on this day came up with a comic distinction between alcoholic and drunken sailors: "When ashore an alcoholic seaman goes to meetings; a drunk goes to first-class bars."

The Professor was quick to reply, "'Tis a sad commentary with little hope that you offer. It is a well-known fact that a sailor never wishes to embarrass a friend and will not be insulted when offered a too-small glass of whisky—he will merely swallow the insult."

As I remember it, after several days of amusing and vaguely insulting repartee, the Professor ended that particular session with a suggestion for a sailor's obituary: "This man liked his whisky so well, he is gone to where he can light his cigar with his finger."

"The Professor is Virgil? Really, Ty?" I still couldn't believe what I heard.

"One and the same! That's Wally's big brother, and he isn't called Professor for nothing. You should see the library he has crammed into that boat. He's read everything from Nietzsche to Louie L'Amour, I think!"

"But why does he call you Typhoon? Every time he does, everybody within a thousand miles comes back with some joke that embarrasses you. What's that about?"

He cut me off with a curt, "Nothing," then quickly diverted my attention to a discussion of Virgil's and Wally's family history. By the time we reached the restaurant, I was so busy digesting new information that I'd forgotten all about Typhoon.

My first impression of the affectionately known "Whisky del Mar" was less than stellar. This dusty stucco rectangle sat in the middle of a graveled waterfront lot dotted with battered trucks, dented sedans, and an occasional Cadillac under an early layer of salt and seagull droppings. The words "Vista del Mar" staggered above the doorway in faded red lettering, while salt-crusted windows sported neon signs announcing a variety of beers and the fact that the place was OPEN. In my many later visits to the Vista del Mar, I discovered that this sign was never dark. The bar was closed only during those hours decreed by law, but other than that, no matter the hour of day or night, the place was open, a haven for hardworking men whose lives were lived outside the governing tick of a clock.

In vivid contrast to the establishment's externals, the pleasant odors of fresh coffee, frying bacon, and hot cinnamon rolls enveloped us as we stepped through the door and into a straightforward dining room of clean linoleum counters, chrome stools, and well-worn Formica tables with matching chairs. A series of boat photographs and Coca-Cola advertisements adorned all the walls but one—that wall boasted a mirror and well-stocked bar backing a short length of counter jammed with white-capped men.

"I thought you said it wasn't a saloon," I whispered to Ty as I eyed the bar patrons with beer bottles in hand.

"It isn't, if you want breakfast. Look, there's Wally over there with Virgil and Karl."

"Who's Karl?"

"Virgil's boat puller. Been with him longer than anyone remembers." Ty pushed me toward the trio.

With his customary flourish, Wally introduced me to Karl, instantly throwing me into confusion. This man perfectly fit my preconceived notion of Wally's brother, greatly resembling Wally himself in stature and wiry energy. Virgil was a tall, well-built man of middle age, almost regal in appearance and manner. I looked doubtfully from one stranger to the other, wondering what sort of prank was under way, but when Virgil shook my hand, he appraised me through eyes the identical brown of Wally's, bright with the same intelligence and humor, though perhaps more keen. As he bent in acknowledgment of our meeting, his focus was so direct it might have shut the world away. This was no compliment peculiar to me. I observed that he took the same intense interest in everyone he met.

Formalities complete, we settled in our chairs to wait for breakfast. I used the moment to study the newcomers and was startled to notice coolness between Virgil and his longtime shipmate, Karl. Several times I caught looks between the two far more frosty than friendly. Wally and Ty noticed, too, and I wondered at the amusement I caught in their exchanged glance.

Hoping to ease possible tension, I began a conversation with Karl while Virgil, Wally, and Ty discussed industry problems. "Karl, have you any idea why Virgil calls my husband Typhoon? When I ask Ty about it, he either ignores me or makes a joke."

"You don't know?" Karl looked at me in amazement. "That very first season he fished the *River Run* on his own, a doozy of a storm came up faster than anyone expected and caught us all outside. Him being a new captain on a first-time boat, we figured he'd turn tail and run, but he did the smart thing and hung tight. He said, 'Wally stuck it out with the *River Run* through the Columbus Day blow a few years back, and I'll stick now. She'll make it fine.' And, by golly, he took her through with flying colors. He took to heart the fact we'd lost a good part of the fleet in that storm, mostly boats trying to fight their way back to shore."

He paused for a moment, then with a sheepish grin, went on, "From the way he handled that storm, we all just started calling him Typhoon: it kind of fit with Ty. You know, as a sort of compliment?"

I didn't wonder that Ty hadn't told me. He wanted to avoid the hysterical tantrum he knew I would throw, complete with accusations of unnecessary risk and failure to consider his family. I saw it all clearly and blushed.

Hesitantly, Karl changed the subject. "The fellows have been joshing you, I know, but you need to keep in mind that fishermen like to tease. It isn't meant to be mean, so don't you go to worrying about their foolery."

This nice little speech caught me by surprise. "Oh heavens no, I don't take offense. I like entertainment as well as the next guy! Especially Virgil's radio nonsense."

Karl smiled. "As so we all do. You're all right, missy!"

He had endeared himself to me in that moment, and on impulse, I blurted, "It's too bad you didn't reach port early enough to join the party last night, Karl. It was fun."

Karl shot a malignant look in the direction of Virgil and raised his voice. "Seems like I missed more than one party last night."

Virgil answered stiffly, "Yes. It is a shame when a shipmate won't let his partner in on a heady evening."

For several minutes more, during any opening in the conversation, increasingly heated jibes were exchanged between the two men eyeing one another in clear hostility. I held my breath, wondering if it might not be wise to run, or at least hide under the table. Apprehensively I glanced at Wally and Ty, hoping for intervention before things got out of hand, and found the sight nearly as upsetting as the brewing warfare. Wally was all but rolling out of his chair with suppressed laughter, and Ty's grin reached for his ears.

This odd reaction finally caught Virgil's attention. He paused, then slowly and melodramatically turned a questioning finger at Karl while growling, "You didn't..."

"Not me! Are you saying you didn't...?" Karl straightened with an air of indignation and continued to stare with malevolent suspicion into Virgil's eyes until both men registered sudden enlightenment and turned as one to glare darkly at Wally.

Hardly daring to breathe, I gazed, spellbound, as Virgil demanded, "All right. Out with it, Wallace!"

Karl cryptically added, "A certain rat jumped on the wrong ship."

We all sat frozen in the electric atmosphere until Wally burst into a vibrating belly laugh, startling me into spilling a glass of water. At this, Virgil and Karl rose in tandem, mayhem in their glances.

Weak with laughter, Wally stood to face the pair with protesting hands lifted. "Wait, wait! I had to do it! I couldn't pass it up!"

Virgil and Karl stared grimly for a full second. Then accused and accusers fell all over each other in peals of laughter.

I sat in silent wonder at the sight of grown men abandoned in gleeful insults and promises of retribution while the waitress, who'd been gallantly trying to serve breakfast, mopped water from the table.

It turned out that when Wally found the *Titan* tied off next to him after the late night with the whisky fairies, he gathered several of the pilfered glasses, a discarded rum bottle, and various raunchy party detritus found in an alley, then sneaked aboard the *Titan* to carefully arrange a scene of debauchery. The professed idea was that on awakening, Virgil and Karl would each think the other had committed the cardinal sin of having a night on the town while slighting the other.

Puzzled and indignant, I waited until the turmoil settled down to the rattle of silverware before asking, "How could either of you imagine something that supposedly wild could take place without being heard?"

"One might believe that noise from a dozen boats' refrigeration units running all night would drown out anything for a man tired from a long run into harbor," Virgil slyly suggested, then added with a twinkle, "but I should have known better. Karl doesn't drink rum."

I laughed with the rest, though wondered at the whole preposterous scene. Back on the boat, I badgered Ty for an explanation. "Virgil and Karl really scared me. It looked like they were truly fighting." Ty gave no answers, only smiled knowingly.

The battle didn't stop there. In retaliation, and over Wally's protests that he planned to do it himself, Virgil and Karl rounded up all the glasses and returned them to the Bird Cage's grateful bartender. Included with the service were suggestions on how to handle a certain thief next time he visited.

When later I shared this odd adventure with Sal, she laughed, slapped her knee, and happily yelled her usual, "Men! Ain't they great?"

Despite the fun and newly felt sense of purpose in my adventures at sea, watching the twinkle of lights topping our hometown PG&E stacks draw closer through the night made my heart sing. When we reached harbor shortly after dawn, their billowing steam made the welcome complete.

Home! I could hardly wait to get through the door in anticipation of a joyful reunion with my children. Instead, I returned from my first working voyage to Jenny's accusatory silence and the boys' indifference.

29

THE GOLD OF MEMORIES

In our first few years in the fishing business, while the kids were at their youngest, family vacations were nonexistent. Time was always at a premium and the workload so intense during Ty's stays in various ports that the children were rarely included. During the off-season Ty was far too absorbed in maintaining, repairing, and upgrading the boat to take time away. This was good for the boys, who enjoyed working, or at least pretending to, with their dad, but Jenny and I had little share in it. Ty was the first to notice this disjoint in family activities.

It was near a season's end late in October, and we were settling down after a difficult delivery in San Pedro when Ty said, almost angrily, "We need a family vacation!" At my surprised start he added, "I mean we should do something together that's fun for everybody. I've been thinking about it ever since John on the *Isla B* told me that when his youngest boy started college and the whole family got together for a send-off, he felt like a stranger in his own house. He says he doesn't know his kids at all, especially his girls.

"It made me think of my mother wishing she had known how quickly the four of us would be gone. She thought it couldn't happen soon enough when she was up to her ears in lunch boxes and teen drama, but then one day she looked up and we were gone. After that, she said all she could think of was time wasted on clean floors instead of picnics in the park." He looked intently into my eyes. "Is that going to be us, Bailey?" There was only one answer, of course, and so began our domestic maneuvers in reaching a decision about where to go, what to do, and when to do it.

When Ty first came up with the idea of exploring the Santa Barbara Channel Islands from the boat, it didn't in the least match my wishes. I dreamed of sophisticated entertainment, trains, cities, and museums. He spoke of learning opportunities in a kids' perfect rough-and-tumble vacation setting. I saw little educational benefit and no vacation at all.

"I should think you'd be sick of the boat by the end of the season," I complained. "It's nothing but work. Why can't we do something civilized?"

The debate wove through several weeks, with noisy input from each of the kids to match Ty's insistent teasing. Even Jenny surprised me with her vote for the islands despite a new interest in ribbons and pretty dresses; fascination with her brothers' activities tipped the scale. Eager to test new water "toys" and convinced that they would find a Spanish gold cache hidden on an island, it was a no-brainer for the boys. In the end, tired of arguing, and tired of the accompanying noisy turmoil, I reluctantly agreed. So it was that during the coast's best weather season, we began our annual autumn pilgrimages to California's Channel Islands, trips that, over time, became adventures filled with the truest treasure—the gold of memories.

Our first departure found the boat piled high with vacation gear and a mountain of food. The trip was uneventful, despite worry over a couple of mildly green faces, but once in the quiet waters surrounding the islands, all was bliss. The anchor was hardly set in the chosen cove before the kids were clamoring to begin their play, with Cord giving orders.

"Come on, guys, let's get the skiff down!"

"No! Get the surfboards. They're best for looking around," Chance countermanded.

The argument abruptly ended when Ty stepped in. "Can it, men! First things first: Skiff in the water and tied off to the boat, surfboards stacked at the side of the cabin, and fishing poles stowed aft in the cockpit with the snorkel gear! Got that?"

I watched the resulting flurry while laying out sandwiches in the galley, thinking how nice it would be if the boys took out the garbage and mowed the lawn as quickly at *my* order!

Hefty sandwiches had dwindled to crumbs when Ty stood up to command, "Okay, pay attention, all of you! I'm laying out the rules, and you can bet you'd better follow them." The order was met with good-natured grumbles, but lazing bodies straightened as he continued, "Rule number one: You will never be in or on the water unless there are at least two of you together. Got that?" Voice stern and eyes steely, Ty clearly intended to make an impression.

"Yeah, Dad, we know. You tell us all the time." That was Chance, chafing at the oft-heard warning.

Ty's glance hardened, and his voice rose. "Well, I am telling you again. Out here it's even more important. You will have at least one buddy with you at all times!"

After a few seconds of hard-eyed silence, he went on still more firmly.

"Rule number two: You are never to leave Jenny alone! That is an absolute rule. If it's broken, we go home. Jenny, you have the same responsibility. You must make sure you are with one of your brothers every minute. Furthermore, each one of you is to keep everyone else out of trouble, too. Do you hear me?"

Even Chance, from his lofty position as oldest child, joined the chorus of nodding heads. Ty stared hard at each in turn. When he spoke again, it was in the same stern vein, though softened in tone.

"For today, stay in sight of the boat. You are not in home waters, so be a little cautious, okay? Tomorrow all of us can explore farther outside this bay."

They were gone then, splashing and yelling in a clutch of surfboards. Ty watched them off with a wryly wistful smile. "Well, there they go, Mom. You won't have to listen to their racket for a few hours."

"Do you really think they'll be all right? After all, they are just kids."

He gave me a strangely inquiring look. "Do you really believe that? No, Bailey, they're not just kids. The boys are probably a lot nearer to leaving the nest than you imagine, and Jenny won't be far behind." It was a jolting thought. "Stop fussing about them. They'll be fine. If I didn't believe that, I wouldn't let them loose." I fought the idea, but I knew he was right.

The kids spent hours either on or in the water, returning only to grab sandwiches or exchange surfboards for skiff or snorkels, and I soon lost any unreasonable fear for my babies. Watching them told me once again that they were all capable and confident in the water, perhaps safer there than on the streets of home. I should not have doubted because I watched Ty teaching them from infancy. With his history of lifeguarding and competitive water sports, he had all his offspring swimming—or at least confidently floating or dog-paddling—before they could walk.

None of our children remember their father's lessons, but I do. They were sessions of hand-wringing watchfulness for this young mother whose water skills ended with a weak sidestroke. I remember one panic-stricken grab for toddler Jenny, preventing her from making an exuberantly fearless jump into a pool and then dealing with her screaming protests and Ty's chiding. It was no surprise to find her always one in our flotilla of surfboards.

These annual island outings continued through our children's tender years and onward, until they are now a jumble of happy memories, pockets of sun and sparkle, years no longer bracketed in chronological order.

The then-open and mostly uninhabited islands were a wonderland of trails punctuated by evidence of past pioneering, all irresistible to an adventurous spirit, and though the latest water sport was the kids' usual activity of choice, they were often drawn ashore in search of treasure, preferably a hidden pirate's cache. This last despite Cole's confidential aside, "I bet any old pirate would have come back and dug up his own gold a long time ago, but I guess we should look for it anyway."

The sea was always the great attraction, and each vacation saw activities change with the latest technological advance. Year by year, Ty and I listened with satisfaction to the kids' increased knowledge, understanding, and respect in wondering descriptions of their underwater world as it became ever more accessible.

Snorkeling was the first intrigue, and with it, they all fell in love with that same watery world described by Arno as a beautiful jungle populated with fish rather than birds darting through its trees of kelp. That lovely image, no doubt, saved me from much worry over the kids' earliest adventures, and I gradually came to believe past apprehension regarding life in partnership with the sea was gone. But then, maybe not—lapses were frequent.

"You be careful! There are all kinds of dangerous things hidden in the rocks and kelp." As I watched Jenny off to explore, I tried to keep my voice light, but Ty was quick to catch its quiver.

With a smiling glance, he whispered, "Yeah, you know all about the giant octopuses and man-eating sharks that lurk everywhere, don't you?" I giggled sheepishly at this reminder of the most recent lapse.

Ty and I sometimes found ourselves abandoned by our adventuring kids, and we used those hours to explore the ocean-fashioned nooks, crannies, and caves along the varying shorelines. This was a pleasant pastime, and skiff or raft were comfortable despite my distrust of the meager protection offered by a stretch of rubberized plastic or thin layer of plywood between the creature-filled depths and me. I was especially chary of the turbulence churned at those points where land meets sea, and Ty was quick to take teasing advantage of it.

"We aren't going inside there, are we?"

We were at the entrance to a large, often-photographed cave carved over the millennia by the beating of wind and tide into the sheer face of Santa Cruz Island. I was already clutching at the skiff's railings.

"What if we get caught in there? Aren't the waves hitting the back walls awfully hard?"

Grinning, Ty brought weight to the oars, shooting us straight into that dim cavern of echoing splash while I screeched and clung. Inside, with boy-like triumph he announced, "See? Calm as a lake in here." I hurled a few uncomplimentary words at him while violently bouncing from one side of the rocking dinghy to the other. "Sit still!" he snarled angrily without the triumphant grin, and the rightness of the command quickly brought me to my senses.

In truth, there was very little sea action inside the grotto. I settled down, following Ty's instructions, allowing the action of lapping tide against the sculptured stone walls to calm and open my senses to this unknown. The changing colors surrounding us were spellbinding, and we explored, admired, and exclaimed for some time, lost in the beauty and wonder of nature's work.

Eventually Ty teasingly remarked, "Look how clear the water is. You can see all the sharks and octopuses hidden in the rocks."

Startled, I looked down, and there they certainly were, huge creatures, threatening as they tumbled in and out of shifting shadows. Instantly, I dropped to the bottom of the skiff, hoarsely demanding, "Get us out of here!"

I was so filled with horror at the thought of what was beneath our flimsy little craft, that it was several seconds before Ty's laughter registered.

"No, no! It is not funny, Ty! Hurry!" I sputtered. "We have to get out!"

Choking back a laugh, Ty said, "Hey, get a grip! I'm sorry, Bailey, I was kidding. Take a look; nothing's down there! What you see is light and shadow surging around the bottom as swells roll in and out over rock fallen from the walls."

Gathering courage, I peeked down into roiling reflected light and felt my cheeks grow hot. Despite embarrassment capped by annoyance at my husband's lack of sympathy, I couldn't withhold a forgiving grin at his smirk, but nevertheless ordered, "You get this boat out of here!"

Of course, the entire entourage was entertained that evening with Ty's narrative featuring Mom's sharks and octopuses.

After the "sharks and octopuses" episode, Ty was vehement in his insistence that I learn to snorkel. "You've got to get over this, Bailey. It's good that we can make a joke of it, but I don't like Jenny hearing your fear-talk. She's impressionable. You might put some of this nonsense in her head. More than that, you could have capsized the skiff jumping around the way you did. I worry that if you ever actually ended up in the water, you'd panic to the point you couldn't be helped. You need to have a look at what's really down there."

So began my introduction to a world unimagined by dry-land dwellers. It was slow going at first, but Ty's patience brought me at last to a day when I could float, breathe through the snorkel, and finally keep my face below the surface of the water in fascinated wonder.

"Why didn't anyone tell me how great snorkeling is? How incredibly beautiful it is down there!"

My enthusiasm held strong until the day when, poking around in wonder at the diversity of life on the face of an underwater cliff, I came face-to-face with a moray eel. He was lurking in a seaweed-decorated chamber, awaiting delivery of dinner, said meal being anything edible that he could snap up with his wickedly sharp teeth as it drifted past.

"Your mom could win a swim race against any of you," Ty chortled. "She beat all records in getting away from that fellow. Churned up quite a wake, she did!"

His story was not quite true, though it was more than a week before I could be cajoled back into the water. Still, Ty was right about snorkeling. Most of my more irrational fear disappeared.

Our annual "yachting" vacation continued in much the same pattern until introduction of Jacques Cousteau's Aqua-Lung, as it was first known. Scuba diving was born, and discovery of the freedom it brought with its individual compressed air tanks immediately captured the imagination of our children. That sport became the focus of island life. With scarcely a thought, my family joined the fish community, though it was without me. I still didn't completely trust that beautifully foreign water world.

Ty nearly always dove with the kids. He claimed it was a security measure, but I noticed that his eyes sparkled in anticipation before every dive. These excursions left me to my own pleasures, and I savored the solitude. I was perfectly content to loll on deck with a book while enjoying the fresh salt air and uninterrupted quiet, or better, going off with my fishing pole. Those crystal-clear channel waters made it fascinatingly possible to watch a fish approach the bait, tease it, circle about ignoring it, and then make the ultimate rush to the hook and destiny as dinner. I became expert at locating and boating our meals.

"Did you know your mom thinks like a fish?" Ty turned a big sheepshead fish on the grill. "It takes someone who thinks like a fish to catch a fish, you know."

"Then how come she can't swim like a fish?" chortled one of the boys, dodging my mock cuff on the ear.

"Careful, kids. You might get hungry tomorrow, and your mom still does the cooking." Ty brandished his barbecue spatula as he glanced at the big fish sizzling on the fire pit. "When she can't get me to do it for her, that is." Our evening dinners were always generously seasoned with laughter.

Many of our dinners were made up of the day's seafood catch, and they might have put a gourmet chef to shame. I may have been the expert at bringing in rockfish, but as the kids grew older, my catch was easily outshone by their underwater harvest of scallops, abalone, and lobster. Anyone who has ever tried it knows that seafood caught and cooked on the spot is heaven's own food, especially when it includes the big clawless western spiny lobster. They give their Maine cousins a lively contest for flavor.

Most of the memories are of sunshine and laughter, but even paradise has its clouds. There was the time when we sat on deck enjoying the last of an afternoon sun. The kids were worn-out from the day's activities, talking quietly together, while Ty and I enjoyed an evening toddy. The boat swayed gently at anchor in the middle of a wide cove encircled by the precipitous cliffs dotted with the brush, grasses, and stunted trees of Santa Cruz Island. We idly watched a small band of sheep from the many that roamed the island, and had remarked at their apparent agility as they worked lower across the face of the cliff.

"Look at that one, Ty! It must think it's a goat." I watched the animal as it stumbled uncertainly over a narrow outthrust of rock. "I wonder if all that bulked-up wool keeps it too far from the face of the cliff."

I had no more than uttered the words than the rocky ledge gave way and the poor creature, bleating horrifically, plummeted with a shower of rock into the sea many feet below. We all rushed to the boat railing in helpless horror, knowing we were too far away to do anything to save the animal. It bobbed quietly on the surface. There was no struggle, and we were comforted by the thought that death had come quickly, probably from injuries received in falling rock.

In the greater scheme of things, this incident was a natural and minor tragedy and accepted as such by the boys. For Jenny, it was not. She was haunted by the cry of the falling animal, and it was several days and another island before she again became her spirited self. Ty and I could do little beyond hope that this harsh introduction to the reality of death was eased by all that surrounded it.

Almost from the beginning, various friends joined these annual excursions. On one particularly memorable year, there was a gaggle of boats and friends making the trip with us. When our little fleet dropped anchor in one of the large and quiet island bays, we were surprised to see a beautifully sleek sailboat, well rigged for world cruising, already settled there with a man and woman standing topside to watch our arrival.

Gritting his teeth, Ty whispered to me, "Uh-oh! They're probably not going to be happy about sharing their space with the hoi polloi."

With some trepidation, we went about the business of making our boats secure. Happily, the snubbing of commercial boats sometimes practiced by such yachters did not materialize. Rather, we were hailed aboard for the cocktail hour. The kids preferred to enjoy what was left of the day with liquid pleasures of a different sort, but the rest of us clambered en masse onto the boat's varnished deck, where a smiling not-yet-middle-aged couple greeted us with drinks and an odd accent.

We spent several days in island-hopping friendship with Berna and Zele, New Zealanders as eager to learn about us and our country as we were to learn of theirs. During those lovely sun-and-fun-filled days, more than an exchange of histories was gained. Notions about the yachting community built upon the fears and prejudices of others were put to rest, and lively conversation introduced a world larger than the one my family knew. I was ready to think that Ty's need to escape the bonds of convention and boredom was a gift. We were sharing a journey of discovery not to be found in the old life left behind.

THE ISLAND VACATIONS

30

TIES THAT BIND

I t was a long time before I made another working trip, a time of changes and surprises. One of the first occurred on the day Cole breezed in with a new friend in tow. Introductions were casual.

"Mom, this is Carlos, from Chile. I've invited him for dinner."

As we shook hands, the uneasily questioning eyes of a smoothly attractive young man with an air of quiet culture met mine. Of course, he had no way of knowing that unexpected guests were a given in our household. I quickly reassured him with my own invitation and welcome.

In our home, the kids' friends were always welcome and were frequent guests at our dinner table. Carlos, however, was different than Cole's usual school chums, a little older, and displaying considerably more social sophistication. Eyeing these two attractive young men standing together in easy chat, I was amused by the thought that Carlos's white smile against his bronzed Latin features, in contrast to Cole's summer tan and bright beach-boy curls, was no doubt a sight destined to create havoc among the ranks of local maidens!

Cole had been sailing with Tiny Moore, a local fisherman. With a trip that ended within easy reach, it was decided to outfit for the next trip from the comfort of home, but when they pulled in before dawn, it was to find Tiny's usual boat berth occupied. Forced to tie up amid the transient vessels at one of the public docks, they found themselves next to the fishing schooner *Santa Fe*. The two boys met while throwing and catching mooring lines.

During dinner Carlos told us in careful, accented English of his cruise to Hawaii on a Chilean friend's sailboat, a pleasure craft that ended its carefree travel there. Carlos's aim, however, was to reach the United States, where he would continue his education. The *Santa Fe*, having fished its way to Hawaii, happened to tie up near the sailboat. Acquaintance between Dane, the *Santa Fe*'s skipper, and Carlos led to an agreement that Spanish lessons for the two onboard children would pay for Carlos's passage to the continental United States.

During the several days Cole was in port, the two were inseparable. When it was time for the boats to sail again, Carlos stayed ashore, moved in with us, and began his studies. He was soon a cherished member of the family, though our already-filled household was now bursting at the seams. Still, he was probably no less comfortable than he had been on the *Santa Fe*.

The *Santa Fe* was one of several schooners operating within the West Coast fishing fleet. This particular boat design is notable for sailing comfort. With a schooner's cabin situated at the stern, the most stable location on any boat, the crew is assured a smoother ride. As fishing boats, they often carry husband-and-wife teams, though rarely live-aboard families with young children, a rarity on any fishing vessel.

I once hinted to Ty that a schooner was a boat I would be happy to sail on. His answer was a terse, "It would be without me."

His perception of this particular boat style when used as a troller was clearly unfavorable. In his eyes, cabin placement on the stern severely limits the helmsman's view, and while in general only a nuisance, could constitute real danger when maneuvering. Then, with the hold located forward, moving fish from the stern cockpit to the bow hatch wastes time and energy. Notwithstanding, those who own and fish schooners usually swear by them, claiming they would have nothing else, but Ty remained unconvinced.

Of them all, the *Santa Fe* was of particular interest to me, especially after Carlos became a part of our family. A good-sized vessel with an unusual amount of living space, it was the year-round home to a family of four, including two children, a boy and a girl close in age to our kids. The family sometimes wintered in our port, mainly to take advantage of its marine support professionals, and we often socialized.

I was fascinated by this family's lifestyle. Dane and Charlotte were intelligent, educated, and could be called Bohemian, while their children were bright and well homeschooled. Theirs was a family with intriguingly unconventional ideas and habits. One of the most surprising was learning of their previous experiments with communal living, and the fact that Charlotte, in particular, had found it comfortable. It was hard to comprehend folks in a business notable for the fierce independence of its adherents enjoying such a life.

I liked Charlotte, and we visited anytime they happened to land in our port, or in a strange harbor where our husbands were delivering the latest catch or making repairs. When in our port, her children were frequent visitors to our home, nice kids who seemed to enjoy being there, though the big attraction was no doubt the TV. I often stumbled over one or the other of them lying belly down, mesmerized by a device still many years out of reach to a working boat.

One winter, the *Santa Fe* was holed up for repairs in our port for several weeks. As usual, Charlotte was my frequent visitor, full of hopeful plans for discovering the perfect spot where there would be a permanent house to return to between fishing trips. Dane did not share, and never had, her enthusiasm for the idea, so I was surprised at the plans she delightedly shared on the day they were to ship out, all boat work complete.

"Dane decided it's time to move down to our little ranch in Mexico. He put a well in first thing after we bought it. The water has been a godsend to the villagers. Now he wants to concentrate on building a house."

"I didn't know you had property in Mexico, Charlotte. I thought you had to be a citizen to own land down there."

"Our boy was born in Mexico City. We made sure our baby would be a Mexican citizen so we could buy land in his name.

We've owned the place for ages. Dane decided that now is the time to go down and stay for at least a couple of years."

"So, do you think your kids will be happy there? How big is the town?"

"The village is small and primitive, but the country around is beautiful. The kids aren't really interested in the place, but once they settle in, they'll get a kick out of helping the villagers, I'm certain."

I couldn't help but wonder how her children felt about this new venture and how the locals there might feel about well-meant but unsolicited aid from children of a different culture. It would certainly be an adventure for all concerned, I decided, and no doubt a broadening one.

I watched the *Santa Fe* sail off, grateful for the delivery of Carlos into our life and sending best wishes for a bright, adventuresome future for Dane, Charlotte, and their children.

31

FISHING GOES POLITICAL

With the *Santa Fe* gone, I was left to chew on the many problems facing the seafaring industries we depended upon. The abalone divers were fighting a desperate war against an adversary warmly appealing to the public, and their foes were winning the battle on all fronts. The sea otters had arrived in enough numbers to decimate the abalone beds with their voracious appetites, leaving as evidence empty, freshly broken shells littering the ocean floor. The otters were not limited, as were the divers, to picking only adult abs of a specific measurement—they killed indiscriminately, including, in effect, mothers, fathers, and babies. It would likely be many generations after the otters picked the pantry bare and moved on, for the ab beds to recover. The truth was clear, yet authorities continued to deny the problem.

This desperate situation hit close to home one morning, when I was visiting the docks and came upon Stan and Bertie Marshall, lolling in unhappy contemplation of their bleak future.

"There's nothing left for me here where I've lived all my life. It's pretty damn maddening that a guy trying to make a living good enough to support a family is put in second place to a seagoing weasel." Bertie sighed, kicking at a stack of rope.

"Yeah," Stan agreed. "Every time I remember that first one that came down to play with me, I wish I had taken my ab iron to him. Too bad they're so cute. Folks go all gaga watching them float on their backs, gorging on what might have been my kids' college education."

Bertie nodded. "Too bad we're dealing with such unfair competition. There just ain't nothing cute about an ab, is there?"

I thought about Foy's abalone ballerina and the show it put on. Definitely cute, but unfortunately a show not available to the public.

"Maybe something could be done if it wasn't for so much money being poured into stirring up sympathy for the otters," Stan ventured.

"Not a chance for us peons while politicians use their clout to back the pet projects of their big-money donors," Bertie answered grimly. "I think we're shafted but good, pal."

I headed for home, reflecting that even if the public could see Foy's pet abalone perform, they probably would demand a law criminalizing human consumption of the mollusks. I briefly contemplated life without tender, succulent abalone, appropriate for breakfast, lunch, or dinner, and one of my favorite seafoods, but soon shook off these depressing thoughts. The ab business no longer affected me. Ty had long since recognized the futility of this particular battle and now focused all his energies on the albacore and salmon fisheries. There were problems enough there.

Worn-out with unpleasant ruminations, I turned to more pleasant thoughts of Cole currently sailing on the *Lil*, the good-sized boat owned and operated by Tiny Moore, an enormously corpulent, loveable bear of a man not many years older than Cole, and a well-seasoned member of a long-established local seagoing family. The two were steadfast friends, probably because skinny Cole's voracious teen appetite was carefully tended and appreciated by his sympathetic boat captain.

"How great is that, Mom! Tiny cooks a whole chicken for each of us. He keeps huge tubs of ice cream in the freezer, pounds and pounds of meat, and lots of stuff ready to eat anytime you want."

I smiled, remembering the time Howard hosted his neighbors to a pancake breakfast aboard the *Dove*. Everyone had finished and was sitting with coffee when Cole jumped aboard for a quick visit.

"You want a couple of pancakes, Cole?" Howard casually offered.

More out of politeness than hunger, Cole answered, "Sure! I already had a pretty good breakfast, but I guess I could eat a couple of flapjacks."

Howard beat up a bowlful of batter, baked it into a half dozen good-sized cakes, and set the steaming pile in front of his guest, who devoured the stack with gusto as everyone else chatted and traded news.

"I can fix you a few more—I've got plenty," Howard offered as Cole scraped syrup from the plate.

"Well, I'm not too much for pancakes, but a couple more might be all right."

Poker-faced, Howard repeated the exercise with the same results and, after Cole had cleaned his plate for the third time, made a fourth offer.

"Thanks anyway, but I'm really not too much for pancakes," Cole answered, pushing his plate away with an air of finality. "I did have a pretty good breakfast earlier. I think I'll pass."

After Cole left, Howard laughed until he had to sit down. "I just wanted to see how much that skinny little guy could pack in," he explained. "Sure don't know where he puts it!"

No one would ever say the same regarding Tiny. Despite his weight, however, Tiny was an excellent fisherman and boatman with a delightful personality hidden in a quiet, shy manner. He was diligent about his work, and there was nothing lackadaisical about his approach to it. Despite his girth, he displayed surprising athleticism and energy.

One day, Cole let me in on the only recognized work avoidance by Tiny.

"You know why Tiny named his boat *Lil?* Because it only takes three letters, all straight lines. He hates painting fancy names. He says the curves are hard to do, and he's never going to own a boat that doesn't have a name with straight lines, the fewer, the better."

I'd been down at the boat with lunch and had felt widespread unrest as I greeted friends on the docks. Cole's interest in such mundane things as Tiny's peccadilloes had eased me away from thoughts of the difficulty and disappointment swirling across the waterfront that day, and it kept me smiling until I reached the house. The phone was ringing as I came through the door. Fish prices had plummeted once again.

Soon after, Ty blew in from a meeting with Virgil, Wally, and a few others. He was venting with a vengeance.

"Those SOB buyers down south are doing a real job on us this time," he snarled. "We can't go on this way, and Virgil wants me to help get our local fishermen banded together. The way things are is killing us. Without warning, the buyers dropped the price again."

"I know. Martha called. She said Wally is as much up in arms as you are. It isn't right that the buyers can jerk you guys around like that. We all know they need the fish. We all know the market is there for it. We all know where the profit from your hard work ends up."

I remembered the first time there was an unannounced price drop on albacore. The *River Run* was under the hoist in San Pedro, making a delivery. Ty was furious when he was told that he would receive full price only on what had been unloaded before the call came, and the new, lower price on the remainder. We had taken a real financial hit, as did everyone else, and most of these hard-working men harbored smoldering resentment.

With a sarcastic turn of lip, Ty said, "The buyers claim there's a glut of fish. Horse pucky! Do they think we don't understand that they're taking advantage of the fact that the bulk of the year's catch happened to show up late and concentrated within a couple of weeks? We sell frozen fish that go straight to cannery process-ing, and nine times out of ten, they don't even warehouse it. Those greedy so-and-sos are afraid that, for once, they will have to pay for refrigerated storage at their own expense."

It was, Ty contended, no accident that the big buyers waited until the fish began showing up hot and heavy, with boats lined up three deep to unload, before announcing a drop in price.

"Think how hard it is for all of us with a year's worth of bills stacked high to sit it out with our catch in the hold, losing prime fishing time while watching money go up the flue in refrigera-tion fuel. Those guys bank on the pressure getting to us. They know we have to sell at whatever they want to give. What else can we do?"

Muttering and pacing, Ty ranted on.

"The buyers have us behind the eight ball. The law says we've got to have a market order before delivery, and market orders have always been set by the buyers—you know, a gentlemen's agree-ment, nothing on paper. The bigger buyers have every advantage, and they generally take it. Virgil is right. It'll take the whole fleet working together before we can make any headway. Now, what

I want to know is how these fishermen, independent cusses that they are, will ever come to see that."

The answer came a few days later when word reached us that several of the Oregon fleet had drawn a line in the sand when the price dropped from an already low $250 per ton to $200. Fed up, they decided to sit tight and refuse to sell, risking everything with a threat they clearly intended keeping, to dump their fish rather than sell at prices too low to cover operating costs. It was a strike, of sorts, and there were enough good and honest, or maybe just needy, buyers to recognize the legitimacy of the stand.

A few days later, Ty gloated, "Be damned if that didn't get some attention! The dealers brought the price back up, and it made a few more of our independent yahoos see what a little organization, negotiation, and hanging together can do!"

That was the beginning. Within months, the Professional Fisherman's Association came into being, established first by a group of San Diego fishermen, including Virgil. A board of directors and board president were selected, and most of the fishermen from the major ports banded together to form a series of chapters covering the West Coast. Ty was the first director from our branch of the organization and, soon after, president of the board.

The first necessary steps had been taken. The next was to convince the buyers that this new association was to be taken seriously. When prices again started fluctuating unreasonably, the fishermen began "channeling" the fish, meaning all deliveries were made to a single chosen buyer until the rest fell in line. Soon, agreements were reached and channeling abandoned as long as negotiated contracts were honored. The business was stabilizing, but the buyers were not yet ready to give up their long-held hammerlock on the process.

"Can you believe it, Bailey? Now those so-and-sos are trying to get around the contract by claiming they need to grade the fish," Ty groused. "If they find a missing fin or a broken tail, they throw it in a separate bin and call it a second—and worth less money. It's all such a bunch of bull! Every fish goes straight to the canners frozen solid, and those graded second-rate are in exactly the same condition as those they grade A-one. You can bet that no matter what the grade, they all get processed in the same batch."

That particular crisis didn't last long. It took just one courageous—or incensed—fisherman to bring the buyers around. It happened in Coos Bay, Oregon, when Hal, on the *Judy K*, watched the grading of his delivery.

Hal had a reputation for being particularly conscientious about the handling of his catch. On this day, he quietly watched as the grader put aside a pile of "second-rate" fish. When the man finished his chore, Hal walked calmly over to the pile and began pitching the snubbed fish, one by one, into the bay.

The shocked buyer began a frenzied dance, shouting, "What the hell are you doing?"

"This boat doesn't sell second-rate fish at any price," Hal explained. "If it isn't first-rate, I don't sell it." He reached for another "second" in the pile.

Frantically, the buyer begged, "Wait! Wait! We'll see what we can do about this. Maybe those fish aren't that bad."

"You're damned right they're not bad, and if all you horse's asses think they are, over the side they go!"

The thoroughly rattled buyer tripped all over himself rescuing the rest of the "seconds." Grading was abandoned, soon to become an industry insiders' joke.

The hard work and early sacrifices of these men stabilized the industry at a critical time. Contracts and established market orders that were put in place did remove much uncertainty in a business already uncertain by its nature, and helped it to expand and flourish.

While many major buyers had a bad name within the fleet, most small operators were held in high regard. They could almost always be depended upon for honesty at the scales and often provided much-appreciated perks such as errand vehicles, hot showers, and a friendly welcome.

One such buyer came to my attention when I was called upon to drive up the coast to Oregon where Ty was delivering his latest catch. It was a long and tiring drive, but in some ways a mission of mercy, for I brought not only needed boat parts to Ty, but a variety of essentials for other members of the fleet.

All during this long drive, my overriding thoughts were bound up in the hope that Ty was able to get a room in Brookings, the miniscule port village adjacent to the docks where he waited. The loading docks would be jammed with noisy refrigerated vessels and trailers. Sleeping on the boat would be no fun—aside from the fact that we'd be submerged in noise, we'd also have the puller as our roommate!

All season, fishing had been especially good up on that part of the coast, making it logical to deliver fish to the nearest small port buyer, saving hours of sailing time getting back to the hot spot. Many factors entered into deciding where to deliver at the end of any trip, but in hot fishing, one factor outweighed all others: balance between speed and end payout. The higher payout at large canneries often wasn't enough to cover catch time lost in travel to and from the grounds. This was one of those times.

"I got a room for tonight, Bailey, but it may be tougher for tomorrow. A lot of boats are in right now."

"If we have a place for tonight, what more do we want? I'll be on my way as soon as you are," I promised.

"Whatever else, this is a great place to unload, well worth losing the freight cost. We'll make it up by getting back on the fish in half the time. The fellow running the place is a great guy, and his wife is just as nice. You'll like them."

"Will I meet them? Do they hobnob with lowly fishermen?"

"You judge. They've invited us up for drinks before dinner, and then we'll all go on to a place they know somewhere up the road."

The evening was as wonderful as advertised. Marilyn and Dick were friendly and world-wise. Their home was lovely, perched as it was on the highest point of the peninsula embracing the harbor, and we were welcomed into it with the casual warmth usually reserved for the oldest of friends. We drank, dined, found answers to problems of the world, and laughed our way into early morning.

"There's a buyer you can trust to do right," Ty declared as we waved our good-byes and headed toward our hotel room. "He's sure different from the 'Forty Thieves' down in San Pedro! I wouldn't walk two feet away from the scales when those guys weigh us in. With Dick, no matter where I stand, I know I'll get the same reading I'd get from myself."

Sadly, in the way of time and distance, Dick and Marilyn were lost to us. They went farther north, established a small, specialized cannery catering to sportsmen, then, like the restless sea that served us all, moved on to other shores. Brief as our time together was, I never think of those two without remembering dear friends and feel certain that they also remember dear friends when they think of us.

32

MR. WHITE, THE LANDLORD

Chance was out of the army and had taken a job as line tender, working abalone with his best friend, Knute Callahan, diving San Miguel Island.

Knute was successful, one of the most hard-core divers on the coast. By hard-core, I mean he ran six hundred feet of hose, as opposed to the more common three hundred feet used by most hookah-gear divers. Those extra three hundred feet mean a lot more work for both diver and line tender. The pair had left for San Miguel on a fresh trip the day before, with beautiful, flat weather ahead. So I was startled, next morning, when Chance unexpectedly popped into the kitchen just as I took an apple pie out of the oven.

"Whoa! You scared the heck out of me; I almost dropped the pie! What's the matter? Boat problems?"

"No, no, nothing like that, Mom."

His tone seemed a bit dejected, and I thought that he and Knute must have had a little falling-out. "What happened? You guys fighting?"

"No, nothing like that."

"So tell me what's going on. The weather is beautiful," I said.

"That apple pie sure smells good. Can I have a piece?"

"It's *may* I have a piece? And no, you cannot! It has to cool first, and anyway, it's definitely no, until you tell me what's going on!"

He shrugged and looked to the ceiling. "Well, the plain truth is, as hard-core as Knute is, he kind of wimped out on me."

"Wimped out?" My voice rose in an unbelieving screech. "Knute Callahan?"

Chance smiled that disarming little-boy smile that he uses so judiciously, and said, "Well, I guess I can't blame him. After all, he *is* the worm on the hook, so to speak, and I'm nice and dry up on the boat."

"Worm on the hook" sounded pretty ominous to me. "Tell it!" I commanded.

"Apparently Callahan met the Landlord. You know, Mr. White?"

Of course I knew that the Landlord and Mr. White were none but Mr. Great White Shark! Chills thrilled through my body. "Just tell me he's all right, Chance," I pleaded. "He wasn't bitten, was he?"

"No," he said, "just got the crap scared out of him. Needs to take a little time off. Say, can I have some pie now?"

"It's *may* I have some pie now!" I couldn't help it; I'm his mother.

While I sat at the kitchen table with my third cup of coffee, Chance dug into his second piece of pie and told the story.

"We got to San Miguel after dark last night and dropped the hook, ready for a good night's sleep. Beautiful weather all the way down. Heck, it's still beautiful weather!

"Anyway, we got up early and ran around to the west side of the island and what we call 'the shark park.' You know, where J. W. got bit.

"We found a nice little patch of kelp about a quarter mile off-shore, maybe forty, fifty feet deep. It's a gorgeous morning, and we were both in really good spirits.

"Callahan was suited up, I fired the compressor, and he took off on the first dive. I always throw plenty of hose overside even though he isn't going far until after breakfast. This lets me get started with the bacon and eggs, and then I signal when everything is ready with a good yank on the hose.

"In the galley, I had the radio going and was whistling along to some old tune before stepping out to the back deck to pour out the bacon grease. I was leaning over the rail when I heard splashing, followed by a huge thump. I turned around and nearly dropped the frying pan overside!

"There Callahan stood on the back deck, full-rigged, fins on, weight belt, regulator, and mask, as well as a puny little bag with three abalone in it. I was shocked! Aghast!

"Knute always swims up to the outdrive on the stern, hands up any abs, then his weight belt and regulator, mask and fins before climbing up the outdrive, which he uses as a ladder. But here he was, standing like an apparition frozen to the back deck! When he finally moved, he tore off his mask, spit out the regulator, and shut down the compressor.

"'Why, you son of a gun, Callahan! I didn't think you were that hungry. I haven't even started the eggs!'"

"He ignored me, saying only, 'We are going home. I just met the Landlord, and we are going home!' Period. I could tell he meant it. 'We'll eat on the way in,' he said.

"Just like that, the trip was over. I let him calm down a little before asking the usual stupid questions.

"'How big was it?'

"''Bout the size of a Cadillac, a *big* Cadillac!'

"'How close?'

"'Too damn close! Maybe five feet away,'" Chance quoted, then paused for my reaction.

"Wow!" I breathed.

"Yeah," Chance continued, "then Knute told me, 'It cruised by and looked right at me with an eyeball the size of a big black pie plate, and when it swam off into the murk to circle around, I *knew* I was about to get eaten. Then I looked up and saw the boat. I don't think I ever swam that fast, even when I was on the swim team in high school.'

"I'd say not," Chance commented, "because he must have hit the surface going ninety miles an hour. It's not easy climbing the outdrive with fins on, not to mention the weight belt and a bag of abs. He must have looked like one of those missiles that submarines shoot off, and it sure looked like he had landed straight up on the back deck!"

Chance was eyeballing the rest of the apple pie.

"So where is the boat?" I asked.

"It's down in Santa Barbara. Charlie Pierce gave us a ride home."

"How long do you think Knute needs?"

"Well, he's pretty tough, Mom. I imagine about the time the weather gets bad, he'll want to go."

"He's a football fan, isn't he? Maybe he just made up this stuff so he could watch the play-offs."

Chance pondered briefly. "No, he was really shook up, I could tell. I don't think you can fake a run-in with Mr. White."

I should send some pie over to poor Knute, I thought.

"Mom? *May* I have another piece of pie?" Chance wheedled with a grin.

"You may," I sighed. Fat chance of it reaching Knute Callahan's place, anyway.

33

A DECISION MADE

By the time spring arrived, I was thoroughly worn-down by a nonstop schedule centered on the needs of Ty and business, kids making worrisome choices, the unabated woes of Kayla, and now the failing health of both my parents.

"I think I'll just run away, Ty. I'm sick of everything."

"Okay, run away with me. Make a salmon trip while Jenny helps out at the old girls' camp. She'll be too busy to think about us." Ty's smile told me that the invitation was real.

"What about the boys? The navy won't take them until September."

"Don't start acting like your silly sister. Those boys have jobs, and they don't need a keeper."

Hesitantly, I pointed out, "Cole is still at home, and I can't send him to my folks. They already have too much to handle."

"Cole doesn't need a jailer, either. Good grief, he'll be a senior in the fall, and he has a lot better sense than you imagine. He could stay home with his brothers, but he might like to make a trip on the *Mariner*. Wally's been talking about it, and you know how much good he's done for Jeff. I think it's a good idea. He'd learn a lot and be a better puller for me next summer."

Unprepared, I gasped and groaned, "It's too soon for him to be working with a stranger." At Ty's look, I bit my tongue, finally saying, "Okay, so Wally isn't exactly a stranger."

A little pacified, I began to warm to the thought of time away from the current bedlam in my life, when thoughts of my sister crept in. "Oh, Ty, I really don't think I should leave Kayla in the state she's in. She doesn't have anyone else to talk to."

"Damn it, Bailey, who else would put up with her? Tell her to go talk to a shrink before she drives us all crazy."

When I gently suggested just that to Kayla, she was, as I feared, outraged. Realizing there was nothing I could do for her, I decided it was definitely the right time to go fishing.

34

DEVELOPING A BACKBONE

On the first day of my first working salmon trip, I decided that to fish for salmon is but a distant cousin to fishing for albacore. Everything about it seemed different, and I was intimidated by a whole new battery of challenges, the hardest one being an unexpected introduction to mal de mer.

"This is ghastly, Ty. I'm so miserable I could die." We'd been on the grounds little over an hour, and already I'd been at the rail more than once, retching, and not much caring if I went overboard. "I was never sick before. Why now?"

"Sorry, but we don't even have Dramamine aboard to help you. I didn't think about seasickness. Eat a chocolate bar. Sometimes that helps."

"Oh yuck," I groaned.

"Never thought I'd see you turn down candy," Ty laughed. "I can take you back to town. We're not far offshore. But if you can stick it out for a while, chances are you'll get over it."

The chocolate helped, and I did stick it out. Then with the relief provided by chocolate, I found myself sleeping hour after hour. "I didn't come along to sleep, Ty," I whined, secretly enjoying his unusual degree of solicitude.

"It's okay, Bailey. Sleeping seems to be part of it, and anyone can get seasick. Certain conditions get to everyone, one time or another. For you, the slow boat action that comes with salmon trolling does it. Some people can handle the quickness that comes with albacore fishing but can't take the slow roll that comes when we're after salmon. With others, it's vice versa. Anyway, we'll take it easy today. You'll be fine tomorrow." He didn't look happy when he said it, but I was too lazy and comfortable in my warm bunk to ask questions.

He was right. The next day, after a quiet night anchored in "Domingo's Hotel," a small anchorage inside Blount's Reef, so named for its proximity to Domingo's Creek, I was up before dawn, ready to eat everything in sight and eager for work despite the nippy springtime air. Convinced that I would easily pick up the routine, I took my cockpit station and then sat back, staring at a series of lead weights in varying sizes, each adorned with monofilament line and lures. Each metal sphere sat in its own hollow carefully tooled into a length of timber, where it waited to be snapped to wire and rolled out from a set of electric "girdies," three-spool line winders.

"This isn't the way the lines were before. What am I supposed to do with all these things?" I complained.

"Take it easy and I'll show you. You'll want to get it right, because each one of those lines with all its gear costs me a couple hundred dollars. We don't want to lose too many."

"Oh boy," I groaned, "here we go again!"

Once I was introduced to the tools of the job, I realized that my albacore trip actually had prepared me for a little of what I faced when fishing for salmon. At least I knew enough to use the action of the boat to advantage and understood the need for keeping the lines in their proper order. All I had to do was figure out which lead went on which line, and how to work the all-important girdies designed to smoothly lower and raise the heavy weights and any fish that were caught. After watching Ty push levers and snap mono lines to wire for a few minutes, I thought I was ready.

"No, no! The fifty pounders go on the bowlines, closest to the boat. Those little twenty-pound weights go on the dog line, farthest out. The thirties go in the middle. Don't get them mixed up, or they'll snag each other, and we'll lose the whole setup!"

"Okay, okay! And each one of these balls takes the line down with a spread of six of these thingamabobs on it?"

"You've been around this stuff for how long now, Bailey? For crying out loud, you should at least know their names and what they're for." Embarrassed, I shook my head but thought to myself, *Why should I know?* There were a lot more interesting things about the business than all these bits of metal and string.

With a sigh, Ty went on. "Those 'balls' are lead weights to carry the lures down to the right depth. And the 'thingamabobs' are the lures, jigs, spoons, or hoochies. The type and color we use is determined by what the fish are feeding on. See the hooks? And remember the flashers." He held up a thin strip of artfully twisted, very shiny chrome, saying, "One or two of the line spreads on each side of the boat need one of these somewhere in the middle."

"Why? What do those things do?"

With thinning patience, Ty answered, "Those 'things' spin as they're dragged, twisting and catching the light, making the salmon think they see darting bait. But nothing will work unless we are using the right lures. See these hoochies?" He pointed to a colorful array of lures in several shapes and sizes. "We have to use one that mimics either what they're currently feeding on or something they want to feed on."

"And how do we know what that is?"

"The best way is to look at their stomach contents, easy to do when the fish are cleaned. We might find that the lure we're using is close, but maybe one closer to what they're eating would bring a bigger catch. That's something you need to pay attention to."

What confidence I had managed to dredge up was shaken. "Oh geez, I'll never get the hang of this. I wish you hadn't told me how expensive the gear is. Now I'm scared to death to do anything; I might lose it all."

With a returning grin, he answered, "Good. Maybe that thought will keep you straight."

With that, he moved back, and I watched as he threw out the drag boards, one on each side of the boat. These were an arrangement of three chains on a flat triangle of heavily painted wood some three or four feet across. Immediately on hitting the water, the shear created by the chain and wood dragged the boat down to a speed even slower than the original slow half-knot speed we were already traveling. We were now moving at the crawl most likely to attract salmon. It was also with precisely the motion most likely to send me running for the rail.

"I can't do this," I sniveled. "I'll never figure out how to do the lines, and I'm going to be sick again."

Before I could work up a good howl, Ty stood towering above me with his arms akimbo and his feet solidly planted. "Cut that out, Bailey! If you're sick, get up and walk around. Otherwise, settle down and go to work. Feeling sorry for yourself won't help, and I'll be damned if we're going to lose another day of fishing to baby you."

Startled speechless, I watched him turn on his heel and go back into the cabin to watch the radar and the depth finder.

Swallowing sniffles and indignation, I got down to work. Slowly I figured out how to get the heavy gear in the water with the help of the weight-bearing girdies, and the fish back up and in the cockpit without mishap. For whatever reason, seasickness was forgotten.

Nothing more was said about the matter until several hours later. We sat with hot coffee and sandwiches when Ty gently lectured, "You should know, Bailey, that this is not entertainment. Every hour the gear isn't in the water means less income. Lost time is lost fish and lost dollars. What we do is hard work, but it's the way we make our living, and the seasons are short. I like having you on the boat, but my purpose is to earn the best possible income for my family. I think this is a good way to do it, and I hope you're as serious about it as I am."

Ashamed and embarrassed, I could do nothing but nod while inwardly vowing to measure up as best I could.

After a couple of days, I had a pretty good understanding of the intricacies of the gear and began to tackle the next step, cleaning, washing, and icing the fish. This job Ty alone had handled until now.

"My hands are freezing, Ty." After watching me wash, gut, and gill a beautiful big king salmon, Ty taught me how to remove blood streaks from its belly. All this was accomplished within minutes of its landing, an absolute rule of Ty's, sometimes at the expense of other hooked fish dragging for an extra moment. The fish was then placed under wet gunnysacks to cool and finish bleeding, and was now ready for a second wash and belly icing. "I can't ice this guy. My hands are so cold my fingers don't work."

"You can wear gloves for that," was his unsympathetic answer. "Come on, this isn't even cold weather. We're at the end of June, for crying out loud. If you want cold, you should do this during the first weeks of April."

Long past tears and argument, I shrugged and reached for a pair of heavy gloves. "Okay. I'll try."

"Atta girl, toughen up those lily-whites!"

"Just what I need." I smiled. "One thing I know for sure, it's a whole lot easier to handle albacore than it is to deal with salmon. You just freeze the whole albacore and stack it in the cribs. Nice, though, that salmon come slower and are counted in numbers, not tons, like albacore. Less of them in the hold, even iced down, means that I don't have to pack ballast. Another bonus with salmon fishing is incidental catch. I do love having those fresh bottom fish to cook up for dinner. The only incidental catch with albacore is a big fighter boated with its middle gone from a shark bite!"

"Just goes to show there's benefit to everything!" Grinning, Ty lifted my cap and tousled my hair like he would one of the kids. "Albacore go to canning, but salmon is sold fresh, and I sure hope everyone who tastes it wants more. Getting it to market in prime condition is the only way I know to make that happen, so you'd better make sure you do it right." He started back to his radios, pausing only long enough to turn with a grin. "Do a good job with that belly ice, now."

Later that day, as I sat with a warming cup of coffee, Ty explained a bit more about the habits of salmon. "Unlike albacore, salmon want cold water, and that's usually well below the warm surface. Our job is to determine what depth that is and then get our lines down to it, complete with the right lures. We don't need to sail far offshore. By that I only mean that we don't have to travel two or three hundred miles out to sea."

"You didn't like a couple of the fish we caught yesterday, Ty. Why? They looked okay to me."

"Those were humpies, and there's no market for them; we hardly ever catch them south of Washington. What we're really after are Chinooks, the ones people call king salmon. They are the best, and if we want to make money, that's where it is, but coho, also called silvers, are good, too."

Catching the fish was one thing. Getting it to market in the best possible condition was another, and always the primary aim. With this in mind, salmon trips were never more than eight days, the maximum time the fish were considered fresh. Sometimes winds kept the boat on the anchor, and a one-day blow might be ridden out in some little coastal cove without serious consequence. Anything more could mean holding the catch too long. We were already a week out, but because of the initial time lost to my ills, the trip was still within limits. I had time to learn one more lesson.

The winds rose. The seas got choppier all day, but fishing was good, and Ty was anxious to put in that one last good day. By late afternoon we were several hours offshore, and conditions were worsening. In the cockpit I was thoroughly soaked with spray when Ty ordered the gear brought aboard and me into the cabin to dry.

"It's going to be bumpy going in," he said, "but it was worth it to stay out today. How many fish did we pull?"

"Twenty-eight. That's pretty good, isn't it?"

"Good enough for who it's for! Get something hot to drink, and then warm up in the bunk. It's going to be a long, rough ride."

"Worse than this?" Already, I couldn't take a step without clinging to the ceiling grab rails. Even then, I was thrown around enough to bang against the cabin walls. "How can I drink anything hot when the sea is like this?"

"This isn't so bad. There's a pretty fair wind, and we're sailing against the tide, that's all. Get some sleep, and you can spell me on watch in a little while."

"I can't sleep bouncing around like this."

"Sure you can. You've been up since four o'clock, and you missed your midday nap. But first get something hot in your belly. You were pretty chilled."

Despite much of it ending up on the front of my sweatshirt and more on the deck, I did manage to drink a cup of hot chocolate before crawling into my bunk.

"Better wedge yourself in," Ty warned.

"Okay," I muttered as I drifted off, hardly aware he'd spoken.

My awakening was rude and painful. A particularly mean breaker had hit hard, throwing me to the cabin deck in a tangle of blankets.

"You okay?" Ty helped me to my feet.

"I think so. Just my ego bruised a little."

"Doggone it, I told you to wedge yourself in!"

"Sorry. I guess I went to sleep too fast." I glanced up, noticing that Ty was looking tired. "Did I sleep long?"

"Only a couple of hours." He grinned through his weariness. "Anyway, I was listening to Virgil talking to that fellow on the *Jay C.*"

The captain of the *Jay C* was well-known to me by reputation. By all accounts, he was not destined to become one of the most successful, or respected, members of the fleet. He was a "careful" sailor. He left port only after ascertaining that fish were located and that the weather was ideal. Moreover, he was another of those would-be sailors who kept his seaboots cut off at the ankle, and he made for port at the slightest hint that spray might wash over their tops. Despite all this, he was considered an amusing "nice guy." This assessment did not change the mild resentment of seamen hard at work on the grounds who were the target of his inquiries. Virgil was no exception, and he had not only a sense of humor, but strong convictions about parasites. Even nice ones.

Wide-awake now, I giggled and said, "Oh boy, what did he say?"

"Well, the weather's screaming northwest right now, you know."

"I certainly do! I've got the hot chocolate burns and the bruises from getting tossed out of my bunk to prove it. But what happened?"

"The guy wanted to know how the weather looked. Said he heard fishing was pretty good where Virgil is, but there might be a northwest wind." Ty chuckled. "Nice as you please, Virgil told him, 'Yeah, fishing is good, and holding up. Come on out. Not much wind. Only a little light air out of the northwest.'"

"Whoa! Poor guy, is he in for a surprise!"

"Oh, a couple of miles out, and he'll turn tail, but I bet he doesn't call Virgil again."

We had our laugh, and I took the watch while Ty got a few hours of sleep, well wedged into the bunk.

FISHING SALMON

35

HOWARD AND THE COLD WAR

The fish were delivered and I was standing hesitantly at the phone booth, feeling antsy about my boys after trying unsuccessfully to get a call through to our home phone. I started with annoyance when Ty hollered down the dock, "Bailey! Hurry up if you're coming with me."

Swallowing my irritation, I shouted back, "Don't be in such a rush. I still haven't gotten through to the house."

"Call again when we get back. Somebody's going to need this truck pretty soon. Come on, we haven't got all day!"

"Okay, okay, I'm coming." Reluctantly, I left the phone and joined Ty in the battered old dockside truck. "It's too early for them to be at work. Why aren't they answering?"

"Who knows?" Unconcerned, Ty got the truck under way. "Quit fussing. We'd hear soon enough if they were in trouble. No news is good news!"

"I guess. Anyway, I'm glad Cole's with Wally, especially with Jeff aboard. Those two will have fun together. They've always been friends despite the age difference."

"Yeah, it'll be a race to see which one can get into a jam first." Ty grinned. "Jeff isn't wasting any time trying out his new freedom. Roy Millson from the *Jessie M* told me that his man and Jeff celebrated Jeff's twenty-first birthday in San Francisco. Roy says he had to haul them both out of his fish hold next morning. Damn fool kids had fallen in and were so far gone that they couldn't get out, so they just went to sleep! Boy, was Roy ticked!"

"Did Wally know? Oh geez, what will poor Kayla say?"

"What do you mean, poor Kayla? How would she know anything about it?" Then Ty chuckled and waved his hand in good-natured dismissal. "Ah, nobody was hurt, and the kids learned a lesson. At least they should have from the tongue-lashing Roy gave them. He said he was so mad he'd have fired his man, but he couldn't because it was his own son! Wally didn't mention a word of it to me, probably because he was afraid Jeff would get a blast from me, too, and the kid already felt bad enough."

I was indignant. "Why do you men think that kind of stuff is funny, anyway? I just hope Jeff isn't going to get Cole in trouble."

"Believe me, Cole won't need any help. Probably, Cole getting Jeff in trouble is what you should worry about."

"Be serious, Ty. Surely you don't want to see your son, or my nephew, get in trouble? Jeff's always been such a nice boy."

"I am serious!" Ty snorted his impatience. "There's nothing wrong with either of them that working in the real world won't fix. Wally says Jeff's a fast learner, responsible, and a first-rate worker. That shows a pretty good work ethic and tells me that his dad's influence took hold in spite of his mother. Not only that, the last time I talked to him, he told me he plans to go back to school in a year or so. He just wants to make his own decisions for a while. He'll be fine. So will Cole."

"I just don't understand why boys insist on getting themselves in one mess after another. Why can't they simply do what's right?"

"Who's to say what's right? Kayla? Besides, real boys need to test limits and explore boundaries. It's their God-given job, and all your female fussing isn't going to change it."

I didn't have a chance to argue the point. We'd reached the door of the grocery store, where the next hour was spent boxing up a few weeks' worth of food. We made it back to the docks before the truck was needed, and I immediately raced for the phone to learn, as Ty predicted, that everything was fine at home. The boys had only gone surfing before work, and I had to listen to Cole's indignant chides.

"Mom! We're fine! Why do you worry so much?"

Why *did* I worry so much? I wondered. Their lives were already out of my hands. I knew I had to back away from pretending I could protect them. It was time to loosen the strings, if I could.

I brooded quietly over this new thought as we carried our supplies down to the boat, but Ty again began to hurry me as I stowed lettuce and tomatoes. "Come on! Make it snappy, Bailey—Howard is coming up the line, and if we get out right away, we can hook up and partner with him. He says the weather let down a little."

Feeling better at the news, I smiled inwardly while tweaking Ty's funny bone. "Are you sure he didn't steal Virgil's line?"

"Not a chance. He's got his own line." Ty grinned back, cheerful once again. It always went that way. Once the groceries were aboard and stowed, last chore before leaving port, he lost that tense, purposeful persona that I detested. He was right about Howard, though. Howard was always his own man. He was one of those who was a solo fisherman; he fished alone and claimed to cherish the solitude.

I thought about Howard and how he and his wife, Ginny, had become important friends to us. She turned out to be as much a renegade as her new husband and would dare all sorts of adventures. A cat lover, cute as a button, and happily busy with a full-time job, she was a good match for him. Most important, they shared a love of devilish fun. Ginny was the one who sneaked several pairs of Ty's jeans into my sewing room while I was away, and sewed the bottoms of the legs closed. She missed enjoying Ty's frustrated bewilderment that soon gave way to laughter as he tried on pair after pair to discover the same flaw, but she heard plenty about it later!

The memory set me to giggling, remembering other moments with one or the other of those two. One was the time I

met Ty in Moss Landing and been nearly overwhelmed by a singularly unexpected gift: a crystal ball exactly like one you'd see
on a Gypsy fortune-teller's shawl-draped table. I had coveted
that beauty from the first moment I laid eyes on it during a rare
window-shopping excursion Ty and I made in San Francisco. Of
course, I had no expectation of ever actually owning this beautiful and expensive item, let alone that Ty would remember how
it had enchanted me. But my thoughtful man had not only gone
back and purchased this exotic beauty, but had managed to get
it back to the boat and kept safe over heaven knows how many
miles of turbulent seas.

Howard was on hand when Ty presented this supremely meaningful gift to me, and I had spent the rest of the day cooing over my
precious new treasure, polishing it and pretending to see the future hidden in its center. Howard joyfully egged me on, and when
the time came for me to head for home, he sweetly offered to carry
it to the car. Ty and I chatted happily as, loaded with suitcase and
jackets, we walked slowly along behind Howard, in whose arms was
carefully cradled my tissue-swathed prize in its sturdy box.

Imagine my gut-wrenching dismay when Howard stumbled on
loose gravel and the box flew from his arms. In horror I watched as
the box crashed to the ground amid sheets of fluttering tissue. I was
so stunned I couldn't even scream. Ty silently laid an arm over my
shoulder as poor Howard turned to face us, stricken nearly to tears.
I watched, heartsick, as he bent to retrieve the fallen treasure, then
approached us in obvious misery.

In the next minute, I was hysterically pummeling him with
my fists, laughing and crying at the same time. My crystal ball was

perfectly intact—the prankster had it zipped safely inside his jacket through the whole performance. It was a full ten minutes before I could forgive him, and even longer before I could forgive Ty for being a coconspirator.

Certainly our days were filled with many light moments and uproarious laughter, yet new worries were gathering like storm clouds. Chief among them was the new Cold War, a chilling reminder of the flames of World War II. For the fishing fleet, the threat took the form of enormous Soviet ships dragging "roller reefer gear" through what were traditional US waters, then unloading catches to even bigger mother ships, in reality gigantic floating canneries set up to process the fish at sea. These Soviet draggers often worked tandem in overlapping patterns, with their giant dragnets leaving a naked ocean floor in their wake. Their huge nets were fitted with big plastic or rubber rollers through which a lead line was threaded, and they rolled seamlessly over rocks and snags, taking up everything in their path. The damage done was so serious that some areas were virtually decimated.

Ty, like of the majority of his colleagues, believed that the United States' territorial jurisdiction, which extended only twelve miles from the coastline, was not enough.

"We need control of all our traditional grounds, at least out two hundred miles," Ty fumed. "Those Russians are sweeping up everything—it looks like a deliberate bid to wipe us out! Meanwhile the Soviets have closed thousands of miles of the Bering Sea to their own boats. Those are some of the richest fishing grounds in the world! It's hard to believe that there isn't some kind of scheme in that. Instead of sticking to their own resources, they're working the West Coast right up to our twelve-mile line. A top priority with our association must be to urge Congress to enact the proposed two-hundred-mile limit. Let's hope it happens soon."

The situation with the foreign trawlers had caused worried debate for many months, and by the time we headed out to meet Howard, who fished alone, scuttlebutt was rampant.

"I hear it's a good idea to stay clear of those big trawlers," one of the fishermen reported on the radio. "John on the *High Tide* was nearly run over this morning. He had the right-of-way, and they knew he was there. They have no respect for the rules of the sea, and they're too big to argue with."

After that, the radios sizzled with talk of the foreigners, attendant dangers, and lost fish. Ty simply ignored the chatter, somewhat easing my fear.

The boat was on automatic pilot, plowing its way upstream against a wind-chopped sea, and we were eating grilled cheese sandwiches when Howard's drawl came through on the radio.

"Hey, Zorro, take a look off to the northeast, maybe four miles or so. Tell me what you think."

We were running some fifteen miles offshore, the *Dove* only a mile or two away. Ty reached for the binoculars and jumped to the window. Within seconds he was grabbing for the Mickey Mouse radio transmitter.

"Yeah, Rag Mop, I've got it in my sights. That's one big fish. I hope it's friendly."

Standing next to Ty near the window, I could see a dark, mammoth-sized, torpedo-shaped object bristling with wires and antennae resting low in the slop. At first, I couldn't imagine what it was, then recognized a conning tower and the outline of a submarine. With a gasp, I instinctively moved close to Ty, who slid a comforting arm across my shoulder. Suddenly, the periscope seemed to move, and the huge black beast sank slowly beneath the choppy water. We watched the wake of the conning tower until it was lost in sea froth.

"What do you think, Zorro?" Howard's voice was calm. "Theirs or ours?"

"Not a clue, Rag Mop. It didn't stick around long enough to get a good look, but I don't think it's ours. One of ours wouldn't need to hide so fast. Usually a sub in hiding only surfaces to make speed or get fresh air, and does it at night when there is less chance of being spotted. It sure looked like they didn't want to be seen by us, so why were they on the surface in daylight?"

"Beats me," Howard returned.

The sighting was immediately reported to the authorities, and soon we could see planes circling the area. There was nothing to do but continue on our way, wondering what we had witnessed. Whether it was connected with the foreign fishing fleet or something more sinister, we were never to know, but the incident certainly jangled nerves already tense. News of the sighting spread fast—the radio always had plenty of listeners whatever the conversation—and submarines were a hot topic by the time we reached good fishing.

Despite the radio talk and my renewed apprehension, this second salmon trip was much the same as the first, except better because I was more comfortable in the work and no longer seasick. The mysterious sub was talked out by the time we were ready to head for shore. We were packing up for the trip when Howard's leisurely drawl beckoned through the radio.

"Hey, Zorro, I'm going to partner up with you for the run home if you don't mind."

"Okay with me, Rag Mop. Not a good idea to travel solo these days."

A few hours later and closer to port, Ty muttered a startled oath and began to fiddle with the quirky old radar. As always while moving, particularly in the shipping lanes where we now sailed, he was on constant lookout for other boats while keeping a close eye on the radar screen for anything outside his immediate vision.

I dropped my book. "Something wrong?"

Reluctantly, he answered, "No, probably not."

At his tone, I got up to look. Without a word, he pointed to two blips on the screen, one at a distance but very intense, the other close to us and moving away on a course toward the first. "That's Howard." He put his finger on the closest blip.

"Where's he going? That other signal looks like it must be a freighter or something." With a gasp, I realized the significance of my words. "Oh geez, could that be one of those big trawlers?"

"I've been watching it for the past hour, and it's a working boat for sure, a big one." With that, Ty reached for the radio handset and keyed it, still watching the radar. "Hey, Rag Mop," he called, "you going exploring?"

"I might be," Howard drawled. "Go on. I'll catch you later."

"Not a chance," Ty returned. "I think I'll tag along to see what you find."

"No!" I panted. "You guys are both crazy! There's no telling what could happen!"

Ty looked at me with disgust. "What are you talking about? They're fishermen like us. So they're getting orders from some fat landlubber a thousand miles away. They can't be looking for an incident any more than we are. We can hang back a little if that'll make you feel better."

I was about to plead further when Howard's voice came back on the radio. "Okay, Zorro, it's your call. If I lose the battle, you can let the world know I took on the Cold War all by myself."

One look at Ty's grin and I knew further objection was futile. Nervously, I took to the bunk, curling up like a child as we followed Howard. Eventually Ty quietly said, "Look at the size of that thing. And look at the stretch of its net!"

Despite being desperately fearful, I hurried to the window. Shuddering at what I saw, I whispered, "That looks like a good thing to stay away from."

Ignoring me, Ty demanded, "Hand me the glasses. I want a closer look."

I grabbed the binoculars from their holder and passed them over. With my naked eye, I could make out what seemed like dozens of men crowding the rails of the dragger as the comparatively miniscule *Dove* drew near. "It looks like the whole crew is ready to jump Howard. Can you see what's happening?"

Ty was silent, intent on what he watched.

Frantic, I begged again, "Tell me what's going on, Ty!"

"There's nothing to tell. Just a bunch of guys waving their arms and jumping around, almost like they're throwing things. It looks like something's happening, all right, but Howard seems fine."

When the *Dove* at last moved away from the dragger, Ty got on the Mouse to inquire, "You okay, Rag Mop?"

"Hunky-dory. See you when we get in."

It was many travel hours later, but the minute we were safely tied up, Howard jumped aboard the *River Run*. Wreathed in smiles and giddy with triumph, he dumped packages of Russian cigarettes, chewing gum, and a couple of lighters on the table. "I don't think they're any different than we are."

"You going to tell what happened," Ty demanded, "or are you going to pontificate?"

Howard was never an easy man to know, though it was easy to see him as a fun-loving, unusually intelligent man with a quirky sense of humor and a deep sense of curiosity. At first glance he looked commonplace enough. Of medium height, he carried bulk that might be perceived as corpulence. Quietly gentle in speech, his smile radiated boyish innocence. All this was decep tive: that soft-looking bulk was in fact hard muscle, the sweet voice concealed a resolve of steel, and he had been free of any kind of innocence since the age of fourteen. He told his story with a complete display of this quixotic mixture, his masculine language and muscular gestures in odd contrast to his lilting voice.

"When I first pulled up, there was a lot of laughing and jeering," he began. "One guy, he looked like an NCO or something, pointed at my boat and measured it out with his fingers, then pointed at their ship and threw his arms wide, laughing like a hyena while he did it." Howard's smooth features contorted in imitation of the man's expression while he aped his inches-to-feet hand-measurements. "Didn't think much of my little *Dove*, I guess."

"He was making fun of you!" I exclaimed.

Ty just grinned and said, "Your little boat, their big ship. What was your comeback?"

With a mischievous smile to match his twinkling eyes, Howard demonstrated in pantomime, sticking out his chest in a little cock strut, indicating with his hands the smaller comparative size of the *Dove* to the leviathan trawler, then pointing to himself proudly and clearly saying, "It may be small, but it's *mine*."

Continuing the pantomime, he pointed to the imaginary Russian trawler, holding his hands wide to admit its superior size, then pointing at each crew member with a questioning look meant to ask, "Whose boat is it?"

Howard's shrugging gestures were so expansive and his expression so mobile that a whole gallery of bewildered faces flickered before us.

"You could see they didn't make out what I meant, so I repeated that prideful dance pointing to my little *Dove* and then at myself, and then at their big ship and at them with a 'Whose?' kind of confused expression." Howard flailed his arms in wide measurement, shaking his head in wonderment, enacting a sad little mime of fruitless pointing and questioning that ended in a questioning shrug with outstretched arms and uplifted palms.

Then, with chest out and thumbs under his armpits, he repeated his happy dance that clearly said, "My boat may be small, but it's mine. Your ship might be huge, but...whose is it?"

Aghast, I asked, "Didn't that make them angry?"

Howard chuckled. "Nope, it brought down the house! They got the message, all right. They showered me with gifts! I tried to throw some of my junk over to them in return but couldn't get it high enough. Those ships are tall!" He said it ruefully but soon grinned. "To tell you the truth, I was surprised at the reaction to my little act. The whole bunch went crazy. You should have seen them laughing, wrestling and punching each other. The NCO-type guy got a real ragging. I think even he envied my little *Dove.* You could see that personal ownership was not a new idea to any of them. When all is said and done, they're only fishermen, just like us."

The three of us sat in thoughtful silence. Finally, Howard observed, "Doesn't change the fact that they're ripping us up, does it?"

"Nope. Sure doesn't," Ty said as he sat fiddling with a pack of Russian cigarettes. Both men wore a look of regret.

36

Radars and Survival

"I've got to break down and get a new radar, Bailey." Ty had made his last salmon delivery and was now at home, outfitting for the albacore season.

This latest announcement wasn't really a surprise because the vagaries of the old radar had been a regular complaint from the beginning. Still, it was a blow.

"Shoot! It seems like every dime we make goes right back into the boat," I complained.

"You've replaced every radio and added I don't know how many other gadgets. On top of that, you had to do that big refrigeration overhaul last year, and it's all so expensive! We'll never get ahead."

Ty grinned. "I guess it's true when they say, 'A fishing boat is nothing but a hole in the water that you pour money into.' But you know as well as I do that this is necessary."

He was right. The last month had proved it so. Another local boat was gone with no survivors in a circumstance that made it seem possible that radar might have saved the day.

Sighing, I glanced over at Ty. "Yeah. Maybe Lennie would still be here if…"

"Yeah—all those ifs! Still, even the best radar won't save your skin unless someone is watching it. Maybe something was going on that took them away from the pilothouse. It's hard to imagine Lennie being irresponsible. He was one of the most conscientious guys in the fleet, and I know he had good equipment." Ty shrugged philosophically. "No matter. We'll never know what actually happened. Anyway, that's not the whole reason I've got to bite the bullet and go for it."

I knew that, too. My last salmon trip had taught me that. "It's because of Soviet trawlers and strange submarines. I know."

"That's only the beginning. I need it because there are more boats in the business, and more coming. It's getting harder every year to avoid collisions. Even freight traffic is heavier—international trade is booming."

But the most important reason for keeping up with new equipment, Ty explained, was because of growing changes in the business. The latest costly refrigeration overhaul was due to market demand pushing for colder core temperatures in fish that are shipped out. "If we want to be competitive, we have to stay up with the technology," he groused.

Then, in a cheery effort to lift the somber mood created by the loss of Lennie and his crew, he went on in a lighter tone, "If all this technological improvement keeps up, we're going to get so efficient we put ourselves out of business."

I smiled at the idea of being overefficient, but soon went right back to brooding over our latest seafarers' heartbreak.

"The only thing I know about Lennie is what I can pick up from his wife," I mused. "She's pretty vague, and it would be heartless to badger her with questions. Do you have any idea what happened?"

"All any of us know is what Cal, captain of his partner boat, could tell. He says they were traveling north twenty or thirty miles offshore, ten or eleven o'clock at night, about five miles apart somewhere above San Francisco. The weather was clear, no fog and a sloppy sea. Cal said he'd been standing watch and had seen freighters, but there seemed to be no threat, and plenty of distance. Lennie was moving ahead on a steady course when Cal stepped away long enough to grab a bite to eat, gone only a few minutes. When he got back, Lennie's blip was gone, and there was nothing else showing in the area." Ty sank back, quiet.

"That's it? Just like that? Didn't anybody do anything?"

"Of course they did. As soon as it was certain that there was no radio response, all the boats in the area converged on the spot. Nothing was found, not a trace."

I sighed. "Yeah, that's about what I heard."

"Most of the men figure it was one of the freighters. Those things move fast. They think it might have hit him without knowing it, or hit him and kept quiet in order to avoid legal and insurance hassles." He was pensive for a moment or two, then said, "I'm charitable enough to think that if such was the case, they at least made sure there was no hope of survivors before leaving."

"Don't those big ships have radar? Surely they would see a boat nearby."

"Our boats are so small they don't always show up, especially a wooden boat like Lennie's—or the *River Run*. Unless there's a pretty good metal reflector, the bounce may not show up on a radar screen. Or an image will show up as a ghost, too fuzzy to take seriously, especially in bad weather, when rough seas sometimes show shadows all over the place." He hesitated and cleared his throat nervously before continuing, "I've been thinking—even something made of steel might not show up if it was low enough in a sloppy sea." Another pause as he shook his head doubtfully. "A man on night watch could visually check a ghost if he had one on the screen, but if something big enough to sink a boat without a trace was black, half submerged, and running without lights, well…"

Gasping, I caught his thought. Visions of a frothy little wake left by a sleek black submarine sinking into the deeps leaped to mind. "Could it be? The best of men with the best of equipment wouldn't be a match for that!"

"No. But you know what, Bailey? I think we better keep our thoughts at home. Probably a pipe dream, anyway." Sitting quietly slumped in his chair, he looked up with a wry smile. "Anyway, detection technology is getting better all the time, and if I want to stay in business, I'll need that new radar."

With a thumping heart, I said, "And I suppose you aren't going to quit, are you? So I guess tomorrow you'd better order the best radar made." I gave him a commanding stare. "And a bigger steel reflector, too."

37

A Seaman's Support

Alvin Casper, electronics expert extraordinaire, had established his shop in our home port. A native of Arkansas, he found his way to our little fishing town via an indirect route that began with a stint as an electronics technician for the US Navy. He found himself stationed on the California coast, where electronics and coastal life in all guises became his profession and his passion. Once out of the navy and established in business, fishermen with home ports as far away as Port Angeles to the north and San Diego to the south were soon making the ultimate sacrifice of time on the grounds to take advantage of his expertise.

Casper, as he was simply known, had gained fame from his development of a superior "brain box" for the automatic pilot universally found on seagoing vessels. Previous to his knowing touch, automatic pilots were driven by mercury switches that were undependable in rough weather and required careful adjustment. By replacing these with diodes, a newly developed electronics component, he created a substantially more dependable instrument.

Further refinement quickly followed, with remote controls providing greater efficiency and more freedom from the wheelhouse. He had earned the admiration and loyalty of our local fleet, the first beneficiaries of his creation, and in time, that of the entire West Coast fleet as word of the brain box, and his skill, spread.

One of those surprising characters so often seen among men associated with the industry, Casper appeared at first glance to be a typical land-loving midwesterner, tall and lanky, with a blandly innocent face and a leisurely drawl that somehow belied the bright-red Mercedes convertible parked outside his neat waterfront shop. Locals often saw him roaring up or down dockside ramps on various errands. His gray-blue eyes above a slow, lazy smile always welcomed those who entered his shop, but he seldom spent time in talk of anything but business.

For some unremembered reason, I was with Ty on the day he went to Casper for the new radar. Ty got right to the point.

"You'll be glad to hear that you won't have to pin my antique radar together again, Casper. Order up a new one for me, will you?"

Casper rose from his workbench and ambled over, reaching for an order book as he came. "Been wondering when you'd see the light, Ty." With heads together, they looked at a couple of catalogs, briefly spoke their obscure jumble of codes and numbers, then shook hands as Casper concluded, "Likely, it'll be here before the week sees Sunday, but you'll have to wait your turn to get it hooked together. Sorry, Ty, I'm swamped, and I aim to keep you boys in order here. Don't want no shootin' irons deciding who comes first."

The whole transaction took place in less than fifteen minutes, and before we were out the door, Casper was back at his workbench.

"It sure didn't take long to spend our kids' inheritance in there, did it?" I was surprised at the lack of chat between two men I knew to be good friends.

"Didn't you see the work lined up back there? He doesn't have time for chitchat."

"I wonder how he keeps track of all that junk piled up back there. It's amazing that the place still looks neat and clean."

"Better not let some guy hear you call his season's worth of electronics, junk!" Ty laughed. "Casper knows down to a missing screw every item on that bench, and who it belongs to. What I can't figure, though, is how he stays civil when he's drowning in work and some jerk who wants what he wants, right now, badgers him on the hour!"

"All that may be true, but I hope he gets to you before the next season is gone. You can't wait forever for something that important."

"He'll get to me as soon as he can, and he's fast. Anyway, I don't want special treatment. He already puts our local guys ahead of outsiders, and that's good enough for me. I'd rather be confident that no one is hustled in ahead of me."

"How do you know he doesn't do that? You would never know if he did."

"Casper has ethics. More than one guy has tried to bribe him and gotten the heave-ho for his trouble. Not that I blame a man for trying. There's nothing worse than being stuck in port waiting for repairs while a good run is going, and you sit losing money because you can't get your boat out to it. Nope, Casper is a straight shooter. I hope he stays that way."

Casper's wife, Clara, was a quiet little woman who wore her straight hair pulled back in a knot at her neck. Obviously devoted to her husband, she was always very pleasant in a modest, retiring way. They had had no children, and she was clearly homesick for Arkansas.

"I visited Arkansas once, ages ago," I said to her one day over coffee. "I thought it was lovely."

Clara's pale eyes brightened. "Oh yes, it is real pretty. We lived out by the lakes, in the northwest corner of the state. I really don't think there is a nicer place anywhere. We had so many friends—we all got together after church on Sundays for potluck. I wish folks out here did things like that." She sighed wistfully. "But Alvin is happy and doesn't mind the way they do here. We used to get together in the evening, sometimes, too. But even if our friends were here, Alvin's hours are so long that we probably wouldn't do much of that either."

The radar was received and installed, all in turn, and when Ty next sailed, it was with a confidence due largely to Casper's ministrations.

In fact, our centrally located port boasted several top-notch support businesses. One was our refrigeration expert, Dean. If he had a second name, I never heard it. He was a shadow more than a personality. He darted quietly from one end of his well-lighted workshop to the other, whirring one machine, grinding another, always with eyes in a distracted glaze. Like Casper, he was a jewel to the fleet and always busy.

Now, as Ty described the latest glitch in his refrigeration system, Dean stood silent, listening intently with head cocked and eyes thoughtful. When Ty finally wound down, Dean gave one brief nod and said, "The compressor will probably have to be rebuilt. I'll be down to take a look tomorrow morning at seven thirty."

Dean was like that. All business. I left the two men in discussion and went to wait outside in a sun struggling against fog. When Ty joined me a minute or two later, he exuded relief.

"Dean says that if it's what he thinks, and I don't remember a time when he's made a bad guess, he should be able to get at it right away. He'll do it, too. There's no better troubleshooter on the coast when it comes to refrigeration. He'll find the problem and get the fix done right. Nice fellow."

At a glance, I could see that Ty's compliment was sincere. For myself, I wondered how he knew that this quiet, apparently unexceptional man was a nice fellow. But nice or not, his diagnosis was on the money, and the compressor swiftly repaired to a state like new.

Next door to Dean, Rick held forth as a welder, mechanic, and machinist known within the fleet for his excellent work. On the early side of thirty, he had a strikingly attractive face, and his physique was well developed. However, I sometimes wondered if he knew the purpose of soap and water because both he and his gar-ments were invariably coated in oily grime. Even his hair, which might have been light blond, looked as if it had been spiked with axle grease.

The first time I met Rick, I was sent to retrieve a boat part that needed welding. Without thought, I stuck out my hand in introduc-tion and then had to stifle the urge to snatch it back. His responding hand was as black as coal, and I'd bet that his fingernails hadn't seen sunlight since he was ten. He was, however, courteous and atten-tive, though extremely uncomfortable. I thought my poorly hidden dismay at his offered hand was the reason for this, but later learned that he was always miserably ill at ease with strangers.

I was not convinced that Ty had made the best choice when next he hired Rick to put a new steel bow on the boat.

"Do you really have to hire that guy?" I asked querulously.

"Why? What's the matter with Rick?" Ty looked up in surprise.

"He's a grimy mess," I declared in disgust. "It took me half an hour to get the grease off the steering wheel after I picked up that welding job. Who's going to follow around on the boat, cleaning up after him?"

"What do you think I keep you around for?" Ty joked.

"Not for cleaning up after messy workmen, that's for sure. I have enough of that at home!" I grumped with a half smile. The matter wasn't worth an argument, and besides, I wouldn't be living on the boat while the messy job lasted. "Okay, no skin off my nose. I'm just glad to hear you're adding more metal. Are you doing it for better radar bounce?"

"Well, no, but it might be a help in that way. I'm doing it because the wooden bow is deteriorating, and replacing it with steel makes good sense. The job can be done faster, less expensively, and it'll be longer lasting than with wood. Rick's the logical one to do the job. I know it will be done right."

During the month or so that Rick worked on replacing the boat's bow, I came to appreciate him and to admire his work ethic, all the more after learning that he'd had a tough childhood, shuffled from one place to another. Sometime along the way, he married and was proud to introduce his wife, a plump, pleasant young woman who shared his pride in their home. I eventually came to wonder why I didn't immediately see beyond his greasy hands.

38

SUNNY SIDE OF DARK POSSIBILITY

Despite their uncertainties, the next couple of years were as rewarding as they were exciting, too full and too busy to dwell on dark possibilities. We hardly noticed the disappearance of the Soviet trawlers after the two-hundred-mile jurisdictional control over US coastal waters became law. The long, hard fight had been celebrated when it was won, but the victory was tempered by new problems created in a heady period of growth and good times.

As the industry and the fleet grew, newly built boats nudged out of service most of the old whalers and WWII vessels adapted from the needs of an earlier day. War-surplus engines and electronics increasingly gave way to newer, more efficient designs and innovations.

Insurance premiums began to skyrocket, in part a reflection of the growing fleet that often brought with it inexperienced and untested skippers with more macho than sense, forcing the insurance companies to cover big losses by increasing premiums. This financial brunt was resented by veterans like Ty, whose years in the business reflected responsible decisions that led to fewer accidents. It was impossible to walk the docks without hearing of some new grievance.

"Did you hear about that jackass who turned into John's circle? The crash brought down John's boom and smashed up his bow. Lucky both boats weren't lost."

"Not nearly as bad as the clown who came full bore up to the docks and smashed dead center into Telly. He managed to save the boat, but he had to replace both the engine and the refrigeration."

The list of complaints grew until one day Ty came in to report, "Some of us were talking down at the docks today about setting up an insurance pool like that one that was started in Oregon—so far, it looks like it's paying off for those guys."

Always eager to keep a little more of our hard-earned money, I was enthusiastic. "A few of the gals have been talking about it, too. Shirley says her brother is in that pool, and he's happy with it. Can our boats get in with them?"

"No, we have to set it up in California in order to meet all the regulations. It doesn't matter—it's likely to be a good deal if only because a private nonprofit organization can pick and choose members. We won't have to take in hotshots who don't know the difference between bravado and business."

No sooner was an insurance pool a thought than it was a fact. Now aware of what could be accomplished by working together, a group of savvy men banded together to form their own insurance group. Ty was named director from our area, one more responsibility added to many others.

"The insurance pool is working out pretty well, Bailey," Ty announced one day over a lunch of homemade tuna sandwiches from our ever-present store of canned albacore. "I like working with this bunch. We've got a conference coming up in Santa Rosa next month. We decided to invite all the members and their wives. It seems a good time to make a party of it."

As the insurance pool grew, so did my circle of acquaintances, especially after the Moss Landing boat owners enthusiastically embraced it. Moss Landing, tucked in a cove halfway between Monterey and Santa Cruz, was entirely oriented toward the fishing industry, and the boats there were owned by longtime professionals as affected by current conditions as anyone in the fleet. Several of the men there served with Ty on the board of directors for the insurance pool, and I become well acquainted with their families.

"Great! If I had known when you started fishing that all this fun was coming, I wouldn't have made such a fuss," I admitted, thinking of our two trips to Hawaii in conjunction with the Professional Fishermen's Association annual conferences.

They had been rollicking great fun. The rationale behind choosing such an exotic locale was that probably the best way to get enough members together for finishing important work in the PFA was to make the task an "event." Choosing a destination like Hawaii and putting it at the end of the season, when everyone still had a few dollars to spend, proved to be a very good idea.

I giggled, thinking of the PFA's first conference in Honolulu. "Remember what a fuss those fishermen made when they discovered that all the resort rooms had nothing but twin beds?"

Ty laughed ruefully. "Men who spend months away from their wives didn't think much of that arrangement, did they?" We both smiled, recalling how quickly the hotel had remedied the situation.

"I wouldn't be surprised if twin beds in Hawaiian resorts disappear altogether," Ty laughed.

Such working vacations were a welcome respite from the busy whirl of my life, and lolling on warm sands or swimming in clear Hawaiian waters affirmed that I had lost nothing in Ty's decision to buy the *River Run.*

These were good years despite the drain of keeping up with Ty, helping the last of my fledglings leave the nest, and dealing with the decline and passing of my parents. Most troubling was Kayla and the loss of my nephew Jake, who had succumbed to a drug overdose. One of the far too many victims of the hippie era's drug culture, his tragic death dramatically increased Kayla's hysterical inability to cope with the existing and long-standing problems in her personal life, let alone this emotionally insupportable loss. She sank deeper into depression and increasing isolation, refusing to be helped by anyone. I knew I had to accept this hard truth— there was nothing more to be done for my unhappy sister until she could allow it.

With Chance home and off again to explore New Zealand, Jenny settled at university, Cole alternating between college and working summers, Cord and Chase still with the navy, and Carlos paired up with the veteran owner of the *Anchors Aweigh,* the old demands of home disappeared. What responsibilities remained were those shared with Ty. It was a happy morning when I awoke to sunshine and the realization that my life was now my own. But what in the world was I to do with it?

Once again, I decided to throw in with Ty and the *River Run*.

39

DYNAMITE AND HAMMERHEADS

Only a day out, we were chugging up the coast nearer shore than usual. Ty steered from the flying bridge as I sat next to him, enjoying the view. We had reached a spot somewhere below San Francisco when I excitedly grabbed his arm. "Look! Look at those balloons, Ty, hundreds of them!"

He picked up the binoculars and peered ahead. "Windsurfers. It must be a competition with all those pylons set out. A pretty sight, isn't it?"

"More than pretty. It's breathtaking!" I continued to enjoy the spectacle, marveling at the brilliantly colored skimmers soaring over and through the blue water. Only half seriously, I ventured, "It really is so beautiful that it must forebode good luck, don't you think?"

Ty smiled indulgently.

A day or so later we were tied up in a little cove, sheltering from a nasty wind, when something bumped heavily against the boat. In sudden alarm, Ty scrambled to the deck, muttering darkly, "What's going on? We were anchored solid."

Lulled by the proximity to land, secure and resting comfortably, I sat still and jokingly called out, "What is it? Are we sinking?"

"We aren't sinking—yet. It might not be long before we are. Come have a look."

I hurried to the boat rail and was stunned at the sight of a battle-scarred behemoth crowding the boat. Ty stared in clear concern as a whale rubbed against the hull of the *River Run* while the sun glinted on its barnacled back etched here and there with evidence of forgotten injuries. It was one of the few times I saw Ty look nervous at sea, but he characteristically made light of the situation.

"I think our friend here has fallen in love with the *River Run*. I hope he's a gentle lover."

Uneasily, I clutched at Ty's arm as we watched the creature swim from one side of the boat to the other, pushing and bumping, seeming to nuzzle and cuddle. I found the suggestion of romance appealing but soon realized that the creature was quite unromantically trying to rid itself of irritating parasites. Motive aside, it was a large whale, an uneven match for the boat, and its pounding and slapping was unnerving.

We endured several hours of this unwanted company, waiting in tense anticipation of our visitor's leave-taking. We tried to hurry it, to no avail. Yelling and slapping the boat's hull caused not even a flick of its tail.

Eventually, the wind died down enough to allow us to be on the move, although Ty was uncertain that it would solve the problem.

"If we move, there's a chance of cutting our big boy with the propeller. I just won't run the risk of wounding him. Besides, he might go berserk and damage the boat."

As it turned out, there was no need to worry. The whale seemed to know our plans. As we prepared to leave, it moved out into the open, then followed beside the boat for a few miles. I felt a twinge of sadness when an empty horizon was our only companion.

Although the whale was, as I insisted to my skeptical husband, another omen of good, it was not my favorite, though it confirmed my conviction that there was something powerfully appealing about the *River Run*. I had noticed from the first that anytime we ran a steady course, we were sure to have a pod of porpoise with us. I often perched on the bow for minutes on end to watch those lucky talismans play in the rise and fall of the bow break's white-water spray. I loved the porpoise best of all.

Despite the beauty and the sense of adventure, the days and weeks began to meld into an unrelenting routine of grindingly hard work. In my opinion, Ty's drive to achieve sometimes went beyond sense. At the first hint of a slackening catch, he was off and away, seeking better opportunity, while others were content to stay, doggedly pulling every last fish. More often than not, his instincts paid off in new hot spots. Our deliveries were as fast as possible, many times within a single day's turnaround.

"Why can't we stay ashore long enough for me to get my hair done?" I begged. "Nobody else is in such a hurry, and I hear there's wind out there."

"There's always wind out there," Ty countered. "Anyway, we've got to go because I just talked to the Professor, and he hinted that things are really shaping up off Washington. You know he doesn't hint unless it's a pretty sure thing."

"Washington? But you said we'd go south! Heck, I was planning to get home to check on the house. Why must you keep changing your mind the way you do?"

"What do you mean, changing my mind?" As always, he laughed at me before adding his usual tag line. "That's 'flexible determination' we're talking about."

Flexible determination: He had plenty of it. Determined to catch every albacore within range of the West Coast, he was willing to flex just about anything in his determination. I decided it didn't really matter. I was along for the ride. Ty was happy in what he was doing, and life at sea did have its rewards.

Fishing had slacked off after more than a week of good numbers. Sometime in midmorning of the second day of this lull, Ty leaned out the cabin door, flashing a big grin.

"Hey, Bailey, how about a party? Wally just called to say he's got a couple of steaks, a couple of kids, and a barrel of ice cream that need attention. Are you on?"

"Really?" I knew that the *Mariner* was in the general area, and that Cole and Jeff had taken summer jobs with Wally, but supposed that personal contact was as likely as it would be if they were on the moon. Doubtfully, I looked around at the unusually calm water surrounding us and wistfully wished for a patio.

"Where's this party going to be? Does Wally know of some magical island?"

"Yeah, he thinks the deck of the *River Run* is just the ticket. Wally doesn't have a grill, and besides, there's no room on his deck because it's so loaded with extra fuel barrels. Maybe you'll want to whip up something special, but for sure you should get a couple of steaks out to thaw."

Hoping this event was actually going to take place, I got the steaks out of the freezer, tossed some potatoes in the oven to bake, and chopped up lettuce and tomatoes for a salad. Before the potatoes were halfway done, the *Mariner* hove into sight, Jeff and Cole waving wildly from the deck. I waved excitedly back, marveling at the happy self-assurance radiating from the two cousins, something I hadn't seen in Jeff since the death of Jake.

When the *Mariner* drew close, I watched, tense and nervous, as Ty and Wally maneuvered the two boats bow to bow. Even more anxiously, I watched the boys jump from bobbing boat to bobbing boat, in the process gaily tossing steaks and ice cream from deck to deck. Wally jumped last, and Ty moved the *River Run* a safe distance away from the *Mariner*. Both captains stood watching for several minutes until sure of tide and wind.

In the meantime, the boys, now aboard the *River Run,* noisily demanded and offered news. At last Wally joined us as Ty devoted himself to getting the coals just right, and we all relaxed, chatting in the balmy sunshine. It was a welcome change after weeks of sameness.

The steaks, barbecued to perfection on Ty's little grill, disappeared in short order along with potatoes, salad, and the rare treat of abundant ice cream. I had almost forgotten about the voracious appetites of growing boys. It felt good to be reminded.

Most of the family and fishing news was well chewed by the time we scattered ourselves over the deck in various states of sated ease, enjoying an after-dinner coffee.

"There's nothing to beat a good barbecue, is there?" Ty observed. We all grunted our agreement, and Wally began to chuckle.

"I remember the time my boat puller, a new kid, went grocery shopping with me just so he could pick out the biggest, fattest chicken he could find—that boy loved barbecued chicken. We were saving it to cap off a really good day of fishing, just to celebrate, you know." Wally held out his coffee cup for a refill, assessing his audience as he did so. Reviewing our rapt faces, he sipped his fresh coffee, nodded approvingly, and continued.

"Well, we finally had a pretty good day, big numbers definitely worth celebrating. Naturally, the weather was snarling nasty, but I'd made up my mind that we were going to celebrate that night with barbecued chicken come hell or high water."

Wally described how he had lined up the coals and matches in readiness, sheltering the grill in the most protected corner of the deck he could find, and then started the coals. The wind was bitter and the seas more than choppy, but Wally stuck with it. The coals had burned down to the point they were ready to take the chicken, when an unexpectedly rough swell crashed water over everything, dousing the grill as it did so.

Undaunted, Wally started over, only to have the little grill swamped a second time—and a third. The fourth attempt was the charm, however, and by the time the bird was cooked, Wally and his boat puller's mouths were watering as much because of the late hour as the tantalizing smell of barbecued chicken.

"At that point we could have each eaten a dozen barbecued birds," Wally said. "We bit into that chicken like we hadn't eaten for weeks—and just about broke our teeth!" he chortled. "No matter how hard we tried, we could barely gnaw a sliver off that thing. I'll never forget the sight of that poor kid sitting there staring at the miserable chunk of meat in his hand, looking purely heartbroken."

It turned out that the fat, tender chicken the boat puller had envisioned and selected so carefully at the grocery store, the very bird that Wally babied over storm-tossed seas through four attempts on a thrice-doused barbecue grill, had been nothing more than an ancient stewing hen.

"That old, plucked hunk of tire rubber probably brooded a thousand chicks in her prime," Wally shouted gleefully above our hoots of laughter. "I'll bet even the sharks couldn't eat it after we tossed it overside!"

"Speaking of sharks," Ty said after the laughter died down, "I recall the time Chance decided to go swimming in the middle of the Pacific."

It was on a rare day of windless sunshine on a glassy sea. Chance, apparently eager to wash off a few weeks' worth of sweat, had asked his dad if it was okay to take a swim.

"I looked around and saw nothing alarming on the horizon, so I gave him the go-ahead," Ty said, coyly looking sideways at me, knowing I had never heard this story.

"He'd been splashing around for a few minutes when I thought to climb up on the flying bridge for a better view. It's a lucky thing, too."

From the bridge, Ty recognized the chillingly distinct profile of a huge hammerhead shark easing its way toward the boat, and immediately began shouting at Chance to get his butt back to the boat *now*! Something in the tone of Ty's voice apparently communicated more to Chance than the mere words.

"Let me tell you, that boy sure is a good swimmer," Ty recalled, laughing. "He got onto the boat lickety-split, eyes big as saucers, wondering what I was yelling about but knowing it must be pretty serious. I pointed out his swimming companion, and that kid turned as white as a sheet. Those hammerheads are nothing to be cavalier about—it spooked him so bad that he had to lean against the wheel for support."

Catching my horrified expression, Ty addressed his next words to me, trying his best to be soothing.

"I didn't want to make too much of it, but I didn't want to make too little of it, either," he explained. "I was actually relieved when I saw how scared he was. He's got sense. He didn't need any lecture from me—he knew exactly the danger he'd been in."

To Ty's delight, once he got over being spooked, Chance looked him square in the eye and said, "Next time I go swimming three hundred miles out, I carry a rifle!"

Trying to keep my tone light to hide how much this tale disturbed me, I only half smiled as I admonished Cole and Jeff. "You heard that, I hope!" I shook my finger at them. "Don't you dare go swimming without a good lookout on deck. Better yet, stay on the boat."

After a few joking protests and a couple of "Aw, Moms," the afternoon drifted back into its lazy pattern of idle talk, some serious, some nonsensical.

"Did you ever hear about Jamison Hayes on the *Wilma Blaze*?" The query was purely rhetorical, for Wally launched into his tale without waiting for a response. "He was a little different than most of us, but always a nice fellow, ambitious, and he liked to fish alone; a wiry little guy with a nice-looking, seaworthy boat, though it wasn't very big, and it was a poor fisher. Drove Jamison crazy! Especially so, since he dreamed of becoming a top albacore fisherman.

"Poor fellow, no matter what size the school, he could never seem to catch more than a few fish, where other boats could sail through the same patch and pick up half a load. He was purely bothered when in midday he passed some guy signaling that he'd already decked a hump."

This term stumped me on my first trip, but I now knew that a hump meant one hundred fish, and its signal was shown by lifting both arms in a circle around the head. A series of five such signals represented five hundred boated fish, or a unit. With this crude representation of Roman numerals, various arm, hand, and finger movements conveyed in relative privacy exact fish tallies to specific boats. In the competitive environment we worked, radio communication offered no privacy and could invite too many boats for safe or productive work on a hot spot. Wally demonstrated these signals frequently and with great artistry as he continued his tale.

"Now, Jamison was a great one for jumpers. He went out of his way to look for them, always trying to figure how to get them aboard. Unhappily, he had no better luck catching jumping albacore than he had in hooking them before they took to the air. Then one day he hit on a surefire plan. He bought a case of dynamite sticks with waterproof fuses, and the biggest dip net he could find."

Jeff interrupted excitedly. "I bet I know what he did! I read about how South Sea island folks used old war ammo in their lagoons to stun the fish enough to float them to the surface and then picked them out of the water! Right?"

Ty and Wally exchanged amused glances before Wally continued.

"Well, Jamison sailed off and found a school of jumpers, got his big dip net ready, and dropped a stick of dynamite where the fish boil was the biggest. Then he throttled up to full speed and ran from danger.

"There wasn't much of an explosion, but he was sure he'd find some albacore floating at the spot. He went back—to nothing. He figured it was only that he needed more firepower. With the next patch of jumpers, he dropped two sticks of dynamite, then more quickly returned to the spot with net at the ready for the expected harvest, but again found only unsullied ocean. On the third try, he upped the ante to four sticks—skunked again, not a single albacore to show for the effort.

"Undiscouraged, he decided to go for broke. He lit one dynamite stick, dropped it back into the case with the remainder, tossed the whole thing into the drink from the stern of the *Wilma Blaze*, and started on a run for the wheelhouse. Unfortunately, when he looked back, he saw that the box of dynamite, smoking fuse and all, was caught on a line just a few feet from the stern.

"He knew there was no chance of making a Mayday call, so he did the only thing he could. He ran as far forward as the bow allowed and hung on tight, knowing that his future might well be his past."

"This time, Wally said, the explosion was spectacular. A great gush of sea shot skyward, the stern of the boat lifted as though a giant hand had swatted it like a fly. Jamison was thrown flat, facedown on the bow, dead sure that he and the *Wilma Blaze* were on the way to the bottom."

Wally paused theatrically, offering the thrill of suspense before continuing, "It was a while before he realized that the sound of the engine and the boat rocking peacefully with the swell bod-ed no ill for man or vessel. When he managed to right himself and stumble aft, he found that the boat, miraculously enough, was undamaged. And how many floating albacore do you sup-pose he saw?"

Wally scanned our expectant faces. "Not a single one!" Then he leaned back, clearly pleased with his performance. "The moral of the story, boys, is that hook and line catch more fish than dynamite."

Cole and Jeff stared, clearly disappointed.

"Aw, come on, Cap," Cole protested. "Your lies usually have a point. So the guy wasted a lot of dynamite and scared himself half to death. So what?"

Grinning like a Cheshire cat, Wally eyed the boys. "Albacore aren't like other fish. They don't float because they don't have an air bladder!"

This was news to me and apparently to Cole and Jeff as well. Wally was smugly pleased by their demands for an explanation, which he gave with gleefully measured patience.

"Albacore must swim constantly to stay alive. Most fish capture the oxygen they need through their gills and store it in a bladder, or air sac—that's why most fish float when they're stunned or hurt. Albacore use the same basic process but without the storage cham-ber. They need to keep moving to get a constant flow of oxygen-ated water through their gills. And I'll bet both you college boys knew these things but didn't put two and two together."

Cole remained dubious—not about the albacore's need to remain constantly on the move, but about Jamison Hayes's trying to fish with dynamite.

"Is that really a true story, Wally?" he asked.

"Cross my heart." Wally made the motions of childhood avowal with his big work-worn hands. "But, fortunately for fish everywhere, Jamison swore off dynamite forever. So did anyone else who heard his story. It's illegal, I guess most places, now."

"Well, that's a good thing," Jeff ventured. "There must have been a lot of crab bait on the bottom after that experiment. I know nothing goes to waste down there, but I'd rather have those fish still alive and swimming around where we could catch them fair and square."

The talk turned to serious analysis of what might cause the *Wilma Blaze,* an apparently viable boat, to have such problems with catch numbers. Debating the pros and cons of a variety of keel shapes and structure and how fish react to each, the possibility of electrolysis driving fish away, and how poor line rigging could have the same effect, took up the next hour.

I left them to the discussion, which was of little interest to me, and quietly went back into the cabin to wash the last of the dirty dishes.

It was hard to muster a cheerful smile when Wally stuck his head through the door with thanks and the announcement that he wanted to take my boys back to their boat to be in a safe drift before nightfall. The sun was surprisingly low on the horizon when I looked; how the hours had flown! Soon Ty powered up and headed toward the *Mariner* off at a distance. I hurried out to again nervously watch my guests, with their empty ice cream barrel, scramble back onto the *Mariner*'s deck.

Feeling a bit foolish, I fought tears as they disappeared into the distance. Unfazed, Ty lashed his cooled and clean fire pit in its usual stowage locker.

40

BAILEY HITS THE JACKPOT

One day in late September, the weather was beautiful as we worked about 150 miles offshore. Albacore had shown up over a wide expanse and in good numbers, but the hot spots weren't localized, and fishing was slow. Ty was getting restless.

"Take the binoculars up on the flying bridge, Bailey, and have a look around. You might see some birds working."

"Sure." As bored with the lull as Ty, I welcomed the diversion. Grabbing a light jacket, I climbed the topside ladder and almost immediately was excitedly hollering, "Jumpers! Over there, to the northeast!"

The next few hours were spectacularly exciting. It seemed we zigzagged over half the Pacific while I spotted jumpers. Each time, Ty drove the boat to the spot and pulled in fish until that particular minischool disappeared. Like a drunken gambler hitting a jackpot in Las Vegas, I felt an indescribable thrill each time I saw a new patch, then had the traditional after urge to keep trying for another win. I didn't notice when the sun began to edge toward the horizon.

It must have been the same for Ty because he was grinning happily when he at last found time to look up at me. Instantly the grin faded. "Get down from there, Bailey! Now! Why, you're shivering so hard you can hardly sit."

It was almost more than I could do to move, and, to my surprise, getting down the ladder was an ordeal. With chattering teeth, I begged, "Help me down, Ty. My feet don't want to stay on the steps."

"Haven't you heard of hypothermia?" Worriedly, he half carried me into the cabin, lecturing the whole time. "You should know better. What were you thinking?"

The truth is that I wasn't thinking at all. I was having a perfectly wonderful time, so involved that, impossible as it sounds, I didn't feel uncomfortable until the damage was pointed out to me.

Heat and hot coffee soon worked their remedy, but most important, I learned two things—appropriately warm dress was essential, even in the mildest of sea breezes, and that the view from the flying bridge was a view into a different world. From then on, I spent every idle moment there.

"Look, Ty, look! They're everywhere!" It was another rare day of a sea gone smooth, but today we were sailing through masses of gossamer creatures floating throughout the crystalline depths, their long, radiating tentacles swaying in rhythm with mysterious underwater tides that had turned the water an iridescent green.

"Jellyfish! Can you believe the size of those things? They're as big as platters! There must be a billion of them!"

"Oh crap!" Ty, drawn from his electronics, was unimpressed. "Be careful not to get any of the gear near your mouth when we hit fish again. Jellyfish poison really sticks to the lines when we run through these things. If that stuff touches skin, it stings like the devil."

"Oh. But they *are* beautiful! They look like huge flowers blowing in a meadow."

"Yeah, well, they'd be a lot prettier about fifty miles from here."

I stuck my tongue out at him as he turned away, and continued to relish the sight of my underwater garden until we ran out of blossoms.

Later on the same day, I spotted what must be the ugliest beast in any ocean, but perhaps that opinion is only because of the animal's contrast to the beautiful, flowerlike jellyfish we'd seen earlier. We were so many miles from land that when I first spotted something large and black floating in the distance, I thought it was debris. But as we drew near, I saw it was an animal that watched us closely, turning as we turned.

"What the heck is that thing, Ty?"

With a chuckle, he answered, "A real beauty, isn't he? In common language, it's a sea elephant. They belong to the manatee family, I'm told. Out here, you never see more than one at a time."

"No wonder. Even a mother could turn her back on a thing that ugly."

"Yeah, she must have been horrified when he was born."

This whiskered ton of black blubber boasted a pair of beady eyes hidden in obscene folds of fat that vaguely resembled a lop-sided version of a scarred, wrinkled, and unmanageable elephant's trunk. It was a revolting sight, hinting of something unclean. My prevailing thought was that it ought to blow its nose.

While seeming to remain stationary, the grotesque creature kept its eyes steadily on us as it effortlessly turned its massive body to match our circle. We eyed one another for perhaps ten or fifteen minutes, after which, with a sudden signal snort, the creature disappeared without a ripple, or a single regret from me.

Far more entertaining were the albatross. These largest of the North Pacific seabirds were wonderfully graceful, with long, streamlined wingspans sometimes skimming inches above the waves. We did not often see them, but when we did, it was impossible not to stop work long enough to admire their soaring beauty, and it was pure fun to watch their antics if they decided the albacore jigs we trailed were a likely snack. Not equipped for an easy launch, once down, they were comically inept at getting back into the air. They were also notoriously dim-witted.

"Quick, help him, Ty! He caught one of the jigs!" The poor bird was no longer a thing of beauty, or even a clown, as it struggled to free itself.

Instantly Ty throttled down to a crawl, creeping forward only fast enough to keep the lines from the propeller as we pulled the struggling thing within reach. After gently removing the hook, Ty tossed the bird into the air and watched it glide away. "We escaped some bad luck, Bailey. Killing an albatross is strictly taboo for a sailor."

On the move again, we cheered the bedraggled creature winging upward to become its usual thing of beauty. Imagine our consternation when it immediately dove again on the jigs! I now understood why, during World War II, on many of the Pacific Islands' jury-rigged airfields, they were called "gooney birds," and not always affectionately.

Not everything I saw from the flying bridge was entirely entertaining. This event took place on an autumn day near the end of the season as we made our way home after a delivery in San Pedro. While running through the Santa Barbara Channel, not far from one of the islands, I lolled contentedly on the flying bridge, tending the wheel while Ty worked belowdecks. The sun felt good on my back as I watched a contingent of porpoise play in the bow break, though my job meant keeping an eye out for hazards. As always, I vaguely hoped to see something unusual in the search, and on this day, I was not disappointed.

Off in the distance, perhaps three or four miles from the island we passed, I spotted what at first looked like a large patch of jumpers. Grabbing the binoculars, I stared, then started yelling, "Ty, come look at this. Tell me what it is."

When he didn't respond, I went searching and found him down in the engine room, sweating over some new problem. At my excited insistence, he reluctantly put down his tools and came topside. With the binoculars, he watched for some time, muttering his bewilderment, but at last handed the glasses back to me, saying, "Looks like orcas, killer whales, but I've never seen them swarming and jumping like that before. Beats me what they're up to."

He started back to his recalcitrant machinery, turning to me only long enough to give a nod toward a ship off in the distance. "Hey! You need to get back to the watch." He was back in the throbbing engine room before I reached my topside post.

Settling back into position, I noticed that our porpoise convoy, a fixture anytime we were in the channel, was gone from the bow wake and moving swiftly away from the black mass boiling in the distance. As the porpoise disappeared, I felt an odd ripple of misgiving.

I went back to watching the seeming hundreds of orcas leap and splash. Whether they were mating, playing, or feeding, I am not sure, but most likely they were making a particularly large kill on a blue or gray whale. Ty seemed to have immediately forgotten the incident, and I never mentioned that strange sight to others, being too cowardly to risk receiving a blank stare, or worse, a look of suspicious doubt. Orcas are generally perceived as benign and playful, but I sensed neither in that turbulent tangle of black and white. On the contrary, I felt almost as if I had witnessed some horrible secret ritual.

Later that same autumn, in nearly the same location, we were running in to make a delivery. It was early dusk, and I'd washed the dishes and then stepped outside the cabin door to toss a pan of water over the side, when I was arrested by a sound I'd not heard before. Above engine noise and radios was a strong, steady swish, much like a fast-running river. Curious, I peered across the water and was startled to see, not more than five to ten feet away, two orcas, one on each side of the stern. The pair were eyeing me intently.

My heart began to bang as their pointed scrutiny suddenly made me realize how truly vulnerable I was. These were not the whimsical, graceful creatures of SeaWorld. These huge beasts were in hunting mode, cruelly threatening as they rose and fell in synchronized rhythm, their oddly intelligent eyes following my every move. Instinctively, I froze against the cabin wall, too frightened even to call for Ty. How long I waited, I have no idea, but I know I hardly took a breath until they swerved off in tandem, swishing their way toward a spot in the distance where birds worked and baitfish jumped.

Thoroughly shaken, I fled into the cabin and fell down at the table with a moan. "Now I know how a rabbit feels when it comes face-to-face with a bobcat!"

Ty's response was an offhand, "You have too much imagination."

41

TOLEDO SPEAKS

As the days and weeks passed, I became more and more comfortable in my job, to the point that it seemed impossible I had questioned Ty's decision to change careers. With every trip confidence increased, and enjoyment of my small adventures, even of the impossibly hard work and eighteen-hour days, increased; it felt perfectly natural to be a working partner sharing in the highs and lows of this largely masculine lifestyle.

We were holed up at Crescent City, a tiny, isolated port town just at the Oregon border, having been driven off the grounds by a vicious Pacific storm. The harbor was jammed with boats waiting it out, and as always, time weighed heavily for these men whose livelihood depended on the number of days that the fish remained within range and the number of those days that gear could be kept in the water. That great bane, alcohol, has been the celebration, comfort, and crutch of sailors since time immemorial, so it was not surprising that I found myself one among bored fishermen fighting loneliness and anxiety by spending hours of idle time in the local tavern.

With Ty and perhaps half a dozen other men, I sat nursing a beer at a bar table boasting a sizeable collection of empty glasses.

It had been a particularly anxious day because the weather ashore was beautifully calm, at odds with the reality of high winds and wicked seas just a few miles outside. The angst created in minds unwilling to accept this disparity between the visible and the invisible had taken its toll. Conversation had already progressed through the usual gamut of fish scores, engine trouble, and near misses with disaster. We were now at a state of maudlin.

"I don't know why in the hell anyone would want to go into this business." Toby was a man in his midfifties with laugh lines creased around eyes set deep in skin burnt the color of singed toast. He sat in gloom, head down, with fingers clutching a half-filled glass. "I've never in my life tried any other line of work but fishing, the same as my dad and his dad. I guess I didn't figure I had a choice." He mused for a moment or two and then looked up with a sudden grin. "What's your excuse, Doc?"

We all looked over at Doc, a medical doctor who had abandoned his practice for a life at sea. He lifted mild eyes to Toby. "It must be because I'd rather lose a fish than a patient. Or maybe eyes begging for what I couldn't give got to me. Too many folks looking to me to fix the unfixable. Then again, sometimes a man can be successful enough to believe he can do the impossible. Maybe I didn't want to be that man." With a wry grin, he glanced over at his neighbor. "Now, if I was a lawyer, like Fritz here, it might be different."

Fritz leaned back in his chair, cupped his hands behind his head, and looked at the ceiling. "Lawyering got a little nerve-wracking. I left the firm when I started confusing the cops with the criminals. And that's not mentioning the judges!" He shook his head ruefully. "Even a lawyer can hit a moment when he wants peace, quiet, and solitude." He thumped his chair down, picked up his drink, and gave a little salute. "Besides, what red-blooded man doesn't want to go fishing?"

We all laughed and were sinking back into our personal webs of woe, when from a shadowed corner of the table, a man called Toledo began to speak so softly that we all leaned forward to hear him.

"I was heading for upper New York State, feeling desperate. I heard there might be work up there." He scanned us with seeking eyes, explaining, "The Depression, you know. I was riding the rails. A lot of us did back then, always trying to stay out of the way of the trainmen who were hired to roust us off. January, it was, and bitter, bitter cold."

Slowly and poignantly, Toledo described a time when most trains were still steam run, taking on water every few miles from big cisterns, a messy, wet business that left water dripping between the cars at the couplings where transients who hadn't been thrown off were huddled together for what heat they could generate against the merciless cold.

"One day I was on the rails a pretty long time, pushed up with others, sleeping standing up, hanging on, and trying to keep what little warmth there was. Here and there, the fellows who got too cold, hungry, or tired dropped off. Maybe they hoped to find a meal and shelter—who knows—but I just had to get to where I'd made up my mind to go.

"By the time I got so miserable I knew I had to jump, there was only one man left beside me. I reached out to rouse him, figuring he was probably ready to make the leap, too."

Toledo looked down at his hands and flexed the gnarled fingers. "I thought I was touching stone," he said. "Like as not, water dripping from the tank above was the cause, but that poor fellow was froze solid right where he stood."

I must have gasped, or made some sort of noise, because Toledo turned to me. His eyes held a peculiar, near-smiling glint of optimism in odd contrast to his tale and the general mood.

"Don't fret, little lady," he said kindly. "The fellow was freed of his troubles, and it set me running fast as I could in the opposite direction. I didn't stop until I found warm work shoveling merchant steamer coal up and down the Sunshine Coast. The way I see it, that poor fellow got me a start on a good life."

Ty and I left shortly after, both lost in private thoughts as we made our silent way back to the boat.

Once the fleet was able to get back out to the grounds, Toledo was one of the first through the jaws of the harbor. He gave me a respectful little wave as he passed our berth. I answered with one of my own and then watched until his boat disappeared in ocean mist.

42

No Two Street Drunk

It was necessary for me to leave the boat for a few weeks to deal with the finalities of my parents' estate, and Ty was making noises about being without a boat puller.

"Wouldn't you know none of our boys are available when I need them? How about Jenny? Do you think she might make herself useful?"

He was making his little joke. Not only was Jenny away at college, but she had long ago made it clear that she was not interested in sailing with her dad. The boys were all off and busy with new lives or exploring the world, each with his father's explicit blessing.

I smiled. "I thought Danny Cabales was looking for temporary work."

"Yeah, he is. He's hit a bad patch—this might be good timing. After his wife left, he started hitting the bottle big-time, but he's a hard worker and reliable. I don't allow liquor at sea, so he should be okay. At any rate, he claims he's ready to clean up his act."

Danny hired on happily. Always a favorite with me because of his carefree attitude and sunny smile, I rejoiced to see him waving cheerfully as the boat left the harbor.

Back in my childhood home, I found myself in renewed discovery of the hazards of working with my deeply disturbed sister while distributing what remained of our parents' lives. Despite my graceless, even desperate, protests, Kayla had emerged from her self-imposed exile to help sort through Mom's and Dad's treasures.

"I don't know why they made you their executor, Bailey. I'm the oldest. I should have the say about these things."

"Kayla, you can have any special item you want. You should have what's important to you, but there's nothing we can do about the will. The lawyer says their wishes are clear and legal. Really, I think it's a wonderfully fair and generous document for all of us. Everything is so beautifully planned."

"Of course you'd think that," Kayla snapped in retort. "You have five kids, and I have only one. Add that up! I should be getting equal. I need it more than you or your kids do."

"For heaven's sake, Kayla, Mom and Dad gave you an equal share. Besides that, you have everything you could possibly need, with your beautiful home and the huge settlement Wes gave you in the divorce. What more do you want?"

Kayla straightened with an angry look and then sagged down on my shoulder, weeping helplessly. I gently stroked her hair until she could gasp out between sobs, "It isn't fair. It just isn't! Everyone is so mean, especially, Jeff. He's cruel, absolutely rotten, not to come home to live with me. He knows how unhappy I am!"

She continued wailing until exhaustion and the satisfaction of one last barb quieted her. "You can't possibly understand, Bailey. Nothing ever goes my way, and everything always goes just the way you want. You are so lucky, it makes me sick."

I kept my thoughts to myself; trying to reason with my miserable sister was useless. I even refrained from reminding her that no one ever said life is fair, and that luck is usually what you make for yourself.

We managed to get through those pain-filled weeks, even selling the home where we had grown up. I was increasingly exhausted by Kayla's constant wrestling with our parents' wishes, and my obligation to see that they were carried out, but the day finally came when the end of this frustrating chore was in sight.

I was due to sign off on the last document within the hour when Ty called from Eureka. It was 11:00 a.m., and he was furious.

"Has Danny been in touch with you?" Disappointment and anger rang in his voice.

"Why on earth would Danny be in touch with me? He's with you!"

"No, he's not! We docked at about nine o'clock last night and went up to the Whisky del Mar for a bite to eat. I went back to the boat around ten and left him flirting with some blonde at the bar. I haven't seen him since. I know he likes to talk to you, so I thought he might have called. I can't believe this! He went off and left me flat, to unload alone."

Here Ty went into a tirade about irresponsibility and a man who couldn't stay away from liquor or women long enough to finish a job.

When I could finally get in a word, I said, "That doesn't sound like Danny. You know he has a reputation for being really conscientious about a job. When it comes to work, I've never heard anything but good about him."

"Yeah, well that reputation just blew to hell. He must have gone off with that babe. Damn! I'm so tired I could drop, but the boat still has to be scrubbed, and I'll have to do it alone. I have half a mind to dock his pay for my time."

Half amused and half sympathetic, I hung up and went on about my business, knowing that Danny would get his full share and that this escapade would be a matter of amusement within days. Ty called back that evening in a slightly better mood but no less perplexed.

"Still no sign of Danny," he said. "All I can say is that gal must be pretty good. I'll have to leave without him if he doesn't show up before tomorrow morning. It looks like the fish are showing up down below. I should be home to pick you up in two or three days."

"Are you sure about doing that, Ty? You can't go off with Danny's personal belongings, and you know he's broke."

"I bundled up his gear along with his payout. I've turned the whole thing over to Mel, the bartender at the Whisky del Mar. It'll be in good hands until he shows himself, but the blasted fool is going to get an earful when I catch up with him."

The next afternoon, Kayla and I said a last good-bye to our childhood home and waved each other off as we returned to our respective lives—she to an empty house with nothing to wait for, and I to an empty house where I waited for Ty's arrival and our immediate departure on yet another fishing trip.

It was months before we got back to Eureka. The first place we visited was the Vista del Mar, and Ty was grinning as he went up to shake hands with Mel. "How's it going? Danny got his stuff all right? What kind of line did he give you?"

Mel paled as he laid aside his bar towel. "Oh, hell's bells! You don't know! I'm sorry, Ty, but his body was fished up out of the bay a couple of weeks after you left."

Ty's face turned ashen as he sank down onto a barstool. "What happened?"

Mel shrugged sadly. "Don't know. He was taken to the local morgue. There was no secret about it."

"That's all? Why didn't the cops call me? You would think they might be interested in the guy he was sailing with."

Mel offered only a wry little smile in answer before volunteering, "Danny's brother showed up a couple of days after you left, asking about him. He was concerned because Danny called him on the night you guys got in and made plans to be at his place next day. I had the feeling that when Danny didn't show up, he thought he'd be rescuing him from a royal bender. We hunted up the blonde, who said she'd left him at the bar that night. That's when we called in the law."

Mel explained that he'd told the police about Ty and shown them Danny's belongings and the paycheck that Ty left for him. When the police heard Danny's brother admit that he figured Danny had tied one on and needed to be bailed out, their general attitude had been, reasonably enough, that Danny was holed up with a bottle somewhere and would reappear when sober. Sadly, the law didn't show much further interest, even after Danny's barely recognizable body was retrieved from the harbor.

"Not knowing Danny they probably figured they were wasting their time on a Two Street drunk," Mel ventured grimly.

Ty was silent for some time. There was little comfort I could give other than to offer a sympathetic hand.

"You know, yours was one of the boats tied up at that bad section of the dock," Mel said, his tone gentle. "I figure he was trying to get back to the boat when a plank caved, or maybe the dock ladder was more rotten than it looked and gave way. Danny must have been hurt or unconscious when he hit the water. Otherwise he'd have swum to shore or grabbed a bumper buoy. They couldn't tell much by the time they found him."

"Danny was no Two Street drunk," Ty choked, half in grief, half in anger. "I should have stayed with him that night. But I didn't figure he needed a sitter."

"He didn't need a sitter, Ty," Mel said firmly. "He was no kid, and he was okay last time I spoke to him that night." He picked up his bar towel and began absently rubbing the bar. "I turned everything over to his brother—strange he didn't get in touch with you."

Ty shook his head. "Well, I hope Danny's share of the catch covered the wake." He said it gamely, and I had the sense that he said it for Danny's listening spirit as much as anything. Danny, always sunny and filled with humor, would have laughed.

We spent a quiet couple of days in Eureka, grieving. In something of a memorial mood, we stood together listening to the Salvation Army band that was, as always, working its good in front of the many bars on Two Street. Ty contacted the disinterested police but heard nothing further. As for me, I found myself thinking of Toledo's admonishment not to fret, to remember instead that the "fellow was freed of his troubles."

43

DEATH WATCHES

After Danny's death it seemed I heard of nothing but sadness and disaster. First was news of Chap and Nora. This hardworking couple were some 150 miles offshore when their boat, the *Angela C,* had an electrical fire that got out of hand, and though there was help in the area, it arrived too late. The fast-moving flames fanned by a brisk breeze quickly consumed the boat, leaving no survivors. There was not a soul in the fleet who didn't shiver at this terrible reminder of a boatman's ultimate nightmare—being surrounded by water means nothing to those dealing with a drifting inferno and no way to bring up enough of the salvation beneath to squelch the flames.

Rough weather is often a factor in trouble at sea, but sometimes disaster takes a different turn. We had just experienced a period of unusual calm combined with a record run of albacore close to the Southern California shore, a welcome boon to some, downfall for others. Lured by flat water, short distance, big fish, and fast catches, boats and owners often unfitted for the job swarmed to the hoped-for bonanza.

One boat, its captain and crew unknown to us, was among the hopefuls. The skipper made several calls to others on his run to shore, celebrating success while reporting that he would be late getting in as he'd needed to cut his travel speed. Wash was regularly covering the deck where fish, too many for the hold, were stacked. The overloaded boat was now so heavy in the water that there was dangerously little freeboard.

Now at the Channel Islands, it was this dangerously overloaded boat whose desperate Mayday call electrified all hearers.

Unlike most such calls, nearly always given calmly and clearly, this SOS was little more than a series of panicked screams and was on the air for a few seconds only. Every boatman within earshot immediately ran for the spot where the boat was known to be. When it wasn't found, searchers spent days, and covered many miles of surrounding sea, but found no sign of the lost boat nor a trace of flotsam.

No explanation for this mystery was ever given, though speculation was huge and lasted for months. In the mix of ideas, it was noted that great white sharks were plentiful in the channel and that there were current reports of an unusually high number of orcas in the area. I listened to it all, but kept to myself the recollection of a parade of sharks circling in response to fish blood draining after a night on the *River Run*'s deck. And more recently, being scrutinized by a pair of orcas in hunting mode, as well as watching a horde of sleek black-and-white bodies boil in the distance while my convoy of porpoise streaked off in the opposite direction.

Soon after that, word came that our friend Joe had met with disaster when his boat was swamped and capsized at the harbor mouth while bringing the *Sarah Ann II* in from a regular rockfish trip. His puller survived; Joe did not.

"How can this be, Ty?" Desperate to make sense of it, I begged for answers. "Joe knew that entrance as well as any man alive! He was in and out of the bay a thousand times, the most careful boat-man anywhere. Why Joe?"

Ty dejectedly studied his hands clasped atop the galley table. "It had to be a freak breaker. His puller was at the wheel while Joe was belowdecks in the engine room. He would never have gone below if the entrance looked tricky. It had to be that a big one snuuked up from behind and flipped the boat. His man made it into the water, but Joe was trapped below. He couldn't get out. Simple as that."

"Poor Bess. Oh, Ty, how is she going to stand this?"

He didn't answer, only continued to ponder his clenched fists.

Soon after that, Ty received a call from the offices of the insurance pool. Not meeting my eyes, he reported, "One of our boats had trouble outside the Columbia River, the *Shamrock*, the boat bought by that young fellow you thought looked like an Irish elf."

"Colin! What happened?"

Ty hesitated. "No one knows. Word is that he left harbor with his wife aboard. The boat was discovered just outside the bar, running in a slow circle. There was a dog on deck, no one else. They searched as long as there was hope." We both knew that survival beyond minutes in those cold waters was impossible.

"Oh no," I moaned. "He was married only a few months ago." For some reason, the loss of that happy-go-lucky Irish elf, with his sparkling dark eyes and black curls, filled me with as much grief as had the loss of Joe. "They were so young, Ty. Kids, really, their whole lives ahead."

We grieved for them all—for the lost and for those left behind, just as countless seafaring generations had grieved before.

AT SEA

44

SUPERSTITION, THY NAME IS FISHERMAN

Each time there was a tragedy at sea, we began hearing age-old lore from the superstitious. And "superstition" is surely the definition of "fisherman."

From my first days of sailing with Ty, I heard plenty about women aboard bringing bad luck. The belief was widespread among the elders of the fleet, less so among younger generations. It certainly failed to register with Elmer, the young puller who was shipwrecked with Joe a few years earlier, now the proud owner of a boat of his own. When he began looking for a shipmate, the word went out in the usual way: ships' radio and dock gossip.

His quest took place during the earliest days of the flower children's descent on San Francisco, and it was there he began his search. He was besieged with unqualified applicants, mostly unbathed and smelling it, or "stoned" beyond usefulness.

"I was just about to give it up and go out alone, when a miracle walked out on the pier," Elmer told us. "I was down on my knees scrubbing up a spill on the back deck when this pretty voice floated down to me from way up high, asking, 'Excuse me, but are you the one looking for help?'"

Elmer looked up to see an "angel" standing on the dock, calling down to him. With the sun behind her, she was bathed in light, and her hair was a shimmering halo, he claimed.

"That was it," Elmer said. "I knew she was sent just to me. I don't remember another thing about that day except for thanking the fate that brought her."

His angel stayed aboard as his helper for a year or two, then at their home ashore, as a wife and mother. From that point on, whenever I heard a belittling remark about a woman jinxing a boat, I thought of Elmer, a sailor who had laughed at superstition and won.

An especially exasperating fishermen's superstition was the deeply rooted belief that disaster was a certainty for any boat beginning a trip on Friday.

That this was a serious matter hit home for me one Friday afternoon as we were preparing to leave northern Washington's Port Angeles. Groceries were aboard and stowed, and all was ready for an immediate departure with a group of other boats. However, necessity kept us tied to the dock after startup told Ty's discerning ear that we had a troubled engine. After a brief assessment of the problem, he rushed off to find replacement parts, promising to be right back, but it was nearly dark before he returned and dropped down into the engine room.

Soon, he was hollering over the noise of the repaired machinery, "Enoch on the *Belle Anne* is ready to leave, and he wants to partner up. Get things tied down as fast as you can so we don't hold him up."

I scurried around finishing my chores and was soon ready to go. Ty finished his job within the hour.

When the *Belle Anne* still hadn't powered up by seven o'clock, Ty went over to find out what was wrong. He was back a few minutes later wearing an expression of half amusement, half exasperation, picked up a deck of cards lying on the table, and began idly to shuffle them.

"What's wrong? Why aren't we moving?" I demanded.

"We're not leaving before midnight," he said as the cards chattered beneath his fingers.

"What? I thought you said Enoch was ready to go."

"He is. But he's not starting a trip on a Friday, and that's that! One minute after midnight and we'll be on our way."

"That's ridiculous! Nobody believes that stuff."

"Enoch does. His two brothers started a trip on a Friday and were both lost the next day. He's a believer, all right."

"Then we should go without him. There must be somebody else ready to go now."

"No. I told Enoch I would wait. It's probably a good idea anyhow. This time of year and this far north, we want a reliable partner. Anyway, it's always better not to leave in a rush, like we were doing. We can have a nice dinner, get a couple hours of sleep, and be ready and rested at midnight."

And that's how it went. It was a particularly good trip—but that's just luck.

Seabirds have long been a particular focus of superstition among seamen—even the bold and pestiferous wharf-side gulls and pelicans are protected by it.

Pelicans are big birds with a wingspan of four to five feet, beautiful in the air, ungainly on land, and they have beaks ending in a wickedly sharp, curved hook for snagging prey. The distensible pouch hanging from the lower bill is designed to store the small fish that make up their diet. Eerily reminiscent of pterodactyls from the age of dinosaurs, pelicans ordinarily eat small fish and are always ready for a handout of leftovers at piers frequented by pleasure boaters, fish cleaners, and dock fishermen.

On one memorable occasion, the *River Run* was delivering a large catch in San Pedro with Chaco and a dock helper in the hold loading frozen albacore into hoist buckets. As was always the case at the unloading docks, a squadron of pelicans perched disinterestedly on roofs and wharf poles or waddled aimlessly across the dock. What triggered their interest in the *River Run* this day, no one could tell, unless it was that a pelican mistook sun glint for bait as the silver fish moved from the hold into sunlight. If so, the bird was in for disappointment; albacore are much too large and heavy for a pelican's manner of dining.

Whatever the attraction, about halfway through the unloading process Chaco's yells brought me running. A quick peek through the hatch revealed two pelicans, Chaco, and the helper battling in a space roughly the size of an ordinary living room. It was uncertain who was winning, but powerful wings knocked the men against the bulkhead, and the treacherous hooks that capped sharp beaks threatened. The combined noise of squawking birds, the helper's yells, Chaco's swearing, and a flurry of drifting feathers quickly drew an audience of hooting onlookers.

Finally, one of the hapless birds was caught and tossed to the deck, where it haughtily glared at the throng before padding its way to safety. Loud squawks and the sound of flapping wings continued to erupt from the hold until the helper's triumphant shout announced a successful capture, only to be followed by Chaco's profanity-laced blast as he ordered, "You got him too tight! Let go! I'll bust your gut if you hurt that bird."

Strings of expletives filled the air until Chaco's brooding face and the pinned pelican, gently cradled in his muscled arms, appeared in the hatchway opening. The fascinated audience, now including Ty and the scale master, watched as the irate bird was lifted up and released on the dock, where it stared balefully at the onlookers, shook its feathers into place, waddled to the edge of the wharf, and made an effortless launch into the breeze.

Chaco saw the pelican off with darkly serious watchfulness, then spoke directly to Ty. "Don't worry, Cap'n. We didn't lose our luck. That old bird's doing just fine."

As I said, superstition is fisherman.

One of Wally's favorite tales is of a time when he went clamming with a cousin, also a fisherman. After the pair collected their limits and were cleaning the catch, they were besieged by seagulls determined to steal the entire lot as fast as it was removed from the shell. In a rage, the cousin grabbed his twenty-two rifle, while Wally tried frantically to stop him.

"I told him! 'Don't ever shoot a seabird—it's bad luck!'" Wally never failed to glower at this point in his story. "That danged fool went ahead and shot anyway, and that gull dropped dead right in front of us. The other birds backed off, but they didn't leave. They just hunched down and watched every move we made. I knew they meant no good."

I could never tell if Wally really believed the superstition, because it was always at this point that his usual grin returned.

"Sure enough, next day my cousin sailed out in perfect calm, and his boat just plain sank under him. He got ashore all right, but when I went to pick him up, there were seagulls everywhere, flying overhead, in colonies eyeing him from beach benches, phone wires, car tops—you couldn't look in any direction without seeing two dozen seagulls. He swore that the whole congregation was on hand cheering, laughing at him while the boat went down." Here Wally invariably shook his head and solemnly pronounced, "He never shot another seagull, you betcha!"

Another of Wally's "superstition" stories was not so amusing. He had a new hand aboard, a kid who enjoyed target practice at sea. For much of the fleet, this was a pastime that took place on long, boring runs from one location to another. The usual targets were floats or empty cans, but on this day, the boy was taking potshots at dolphins. Wally was horrified.

"When I called the idiot on it, he claimed there was no way he could hit one, considering the playfulness of the dolphins along with the screwy bounce of the boat in a chop. Well, first thing you know, there was one of those fine creatures bleeding its life away. I was so mad I couldn't talk to him for the rest of the day."

Despite the tension this caused, the pair continued in their usual travel routine; Wally bedded down for his regular two-hour nap while the hand was on wheel watch. When he wakened, the man was nowhere to be found.

"I nearly went crazy looking through the boat for him before I heard this pitiful cry from way in the distance, off the stern. I'm switched if it wasn't my man, hooked and dragging on the whisky line!"

He was, Wally said with a chuckle, the "biggest fish I ever pulled in, and mighty hard to land, being too tired to help." Apparently he was at the rail, relieving himself, when a rogue breaker hit, knocking him over the side. It was pure luck that he was able to grab the whisky line and somehow wrap it around his body. There was very little chance otherwise that Wally could have found him.

"That poor kid was half drowned," Wally concluded. "We were both so done in by the time he was back aboard that I had to break the trip. He stayed ashore, and I doubt he ever went to sea again.

Last thing he said to me was, 'That dolphin sure turned my luck bad, Cap'n. I ain't never going to shoot at nothing again. I didn't mean to kill it! Honest I didn't!'"

Frankly, I always thought it was pretty *good* luck that the kid didn't drown!

45

CHANGE ON THE HORIZON

Ty began to talk about buying a bigger boat. In a near repeat of our history before he bought the *River Run,* the idea was first broached while I worked in the kitchen. My response was no better than it was when he announced that he'd found the *River Run.*

"Are you crazy? We don't want a bigger boat. Even if we are in pretty good financial shape, with the expense of Jenny still in college and costs going up every day on boat improvements, it's too much gamble. Why in the world would you want to do a thing like that?"

"I don't believe this." Ty rolled his eyes before letting loose his exasperation. "You know as well as I do that we've gone as far as we can with the *River Run.* If we plan to stay in the business, we've got to upgrade."

"Not now, Ty. Things are going along just fine. Why can't we sit tight and wait to see how it looks next year?"

I might as well have petitioned the tides. By the time spring rolled around, he was talking to the owners of a big steel boat that would soon be for sale. Worse, Chance, home from roaming around New Zealand, and Cole, back from a long, experimental albacore hunting trip across the Pacific to Guam with Tiny on his big new boat, *Lila*, were temporarily at home between adventures and excitedly discussing the possibility of taking over the *River Run*. Even Jenny brought me no solace.

"Forget it, Mom. You should know Dad wouldn't quit pushing for more. Hasn't he always?"

"Oh, I guess so, but I don't see why he has to encourage your brothers. They should be finishing school. Both of them have wasted so much time."

"Don't be silly, Mom. They can go back to school when they're ready. Not everyone needs to go to college. There are plenty of people who don't."

"I know. That's what I'm worried about."

What I couldn't admit to was unease in another direction. Where would I be if Ty bought the boat he was considering? It was a lot bigger, and it had a bait tank. That bait tank meant adding another job to those I already had. The extra work would require a degree of stamina and agility that I wasn't sure I could sustain. Worse, bait meant that rack and pole fishing might well be in the offing, and I knew that the system basically required hoisting fighters that could weigh as much as thirty or forty pounds up and on deck with handheld "jack poles." Moreover, it would need a crew of two or three.

Endless discussion on the subject, replete with my objections, filled the rest of that year and continued into the one after it. Ty talked but made no move to commit. By the time the second year was well in place, the plan had changed.

"I don't want to take on redoing someone else's boat, Bailey. I think I'll have one built. That way, I'll have exactly what I want."

I breathed a sigh of relief. This decision assured at least one more year of grace.

46

CASPER'S PHILOSOPHY

Our life went on in its routine of hard working months at sea broken by months at home no less demanding. The house, inhabited sporadically by our adventuring and not-too domestically inclined children, needed maintenance no matter the season, and I was always happy when it was necessary to pull into home port for any reason at all. On this occasion, we were there for a few days while Ty collared Casper long enough to debug one of the electronic systems.

For the first time, Casper and I found ourselves in one-on-one discussion. Lugging a sizeable box, he made his way down the ramp and jumped aboard the *River Run*, where I was checking the galley supplies; Ty was off on an errand at the marine store.

"You won't mind my waiting for Ty to get back, will you?" Casper asked after a light greeting. "I have some ideas about installing this new unit. Go ahead with what you're doing. I promise to stay out of your way."

"Here's a better idea, Casper. Let's have a cup of coffee, and you can tell me how Clara is doing."

He grinned in his slow way, nodded, and sat down. "She'll be glad to know you asked after her, Bailey. She took quite a fancy to you and misses your talks since you went off with Ty."

Surprised, I blurted, "I didn't spend enough time with her for that." Then, ashamed of the dismissive tone, I hurried to add, "How sweet of her! She is such a nice lady."

With a devilish twinkle, he said, "Yes, she is a nice, sweet lady, and you are right; she doesn't have enough friends."

To cover my embarrassment, I hurried on. "She spoke of having lots of friends before you came to California. I had the feeling she was lonely for them."

"So she is. My poor Clara can't leave her Arkansas roots long enough to look for the contentment at hand." He sat sipping his coffee. "She needs a little of your get-up-and-go."

"I'm no model for anyone, Casper. Besides, we all see through different eyes."

He laughed in his lazy way. "So we do. Anyway, she's going to have her wish soon enough, I'm happy to say. I've decided to go back to Arkansas. I have farm property there, and it's in a nice countryside." He took a swallow of coffee. "It's not my idea of an interesting life, but I guess I'll have to put what I've been preaching to Clara into practice."

"What's that, Casper?"

"Folks have to learn to be happy without happiness!"

In some strange way, this paradoxical pronouncement made utter sense.

47

ON THE HOME FRONT

During each stay at home, I took advantage of the opportunity to wash mountains of boat laundry in my own machine and to clear the main rooms of layers of dust. This time, Jenny, blooming with first womanhood, took a break from her books to join me.

"Mom, when was the last time you had a decent haircut? And just look at your hands and nails!"

Quickly hiding my scarred hands and shattered nails, I defended myself. "I haven't had time. Besides, it's not important."

Jenny gave a snort. "You taught me that appearances are first impressions and that you never know which first impression will be the important one." She looked me up and down. "I hope you don't have to make a first impression anytime soon."

"Okay, okay! I'll make an appointment tomorrow. I know I've gotten careless." Hoping to change the subject and to discover what might be new in her life, I casually asked, "Are you dating anyone in particular?"

"No. I'm too busy to be worried about that."

"Just wondering." At her pointed scrutiny of my hands, I relented. "Okay, I promise to do better with my appearance. I'll even have my nails done while I'm fishing." Then, slyly, "Oh, by the way, we met the nicest young man up north. He was working with Enoch on the *Belle Anne.*"

With rolling eyes, she shot back, "Forget it, Mom!" Our eyes met in companionable amusement, and we giggled together for a moment before going on to other things. It was always good to be at home with my baby.

We heard little of Kayla. According to Jeff, now working for his master's degree, his mother was a complete recluse, refusing to leave her house, refusing to see anyone, and using the telephone only for grocery orders.

Glumly, he reported, "When Dad remarried, she got even more impossible. I know she is lonely, but everybody she ever knew is sick of her ranting. The house is a mess, and I hate going there; she keeps it dark, with all the shades down."

I clucked sympathetically, pained to imagine this in my normally fastidious sister and pained even more by the look of near desperation in my nephew's eyes.

"I am so sorry, Jeff. I've tried to reach her. She refuses to see me and won't answer her phone."

Jeff sighed. "I know. It's hard to watch. She claws at my arms when I leave, begging me to stay, but when I visit, she hardly says a word. When she does, it's a torrent of spiteful crap. The doctors say she's depressed and mentally unstable, but not incompetent. Making everything worse, she refuses to take any prescribed medication." He shook his head, half in anger and half in anguish. "She was never a really bad person, Aunt Bailey. She was just so busy trying to control things that were out of her hands that she finally went nuts. She drove people away—who in their right mind would stay?" He sat staring vaguely into space for several minutes before earnestly asking, "Do you think she'll ever come to her senses?"

I could give no hopeful answer.

48

TRAGEDY

Chance returned and was working temporarily with Wally before leaving on his next adventure, while the twins finished the final year in their navy stint. Cole was off on a sailboat with Carlos, no doubt hoping to find a pirate's cache on some deserted island, and Jenny was in her last semester of studies, looking forward to new adventures of her own. At sea, I continued to work hard and tried to remember my daughter's admonition regarding appearance. Ty remained oblivious to anything unrelated to the industry. It was life as usual.

The albacore were showing up in early abundance, and the season was well under way with promise of good profit. The weather was beautiful, and we were fishing somewhere off Northern California where the bite was hottest. It seemed as though everyone with a boat that would float was there. We must have made an impressive sight, though I doubt anyone took time from pulling fish to look. Howard was there with a big new boat. Wally was there with Chance, and Virgil with Karl. The atmosphere was one of celebration. For a week the radios were in a constant buzz of shared information, camaraderie, and good catch numbers. Ty gloated every day at the speed with which the hold was filling. I was happy, relishing my place in it all.

About three-quarters of the way to a full load, I was busy pulling fish, little interested in much beyond hooks and lines. When I
finally did chance to look around, it was intriguing to notice that
the unusual number of scattered boats were visible only occasionally, appearing and disappearing behind silken-smooth mountains
of water that we slowly climbed and then slid down. It wasn't until
Ty beckoned me in to answer a radio call that I comprehended the
meaning of the sea change.

"Hey, Bailey, how's it going? We heard you were in the area,
and I wanted to say hello." It was Sal, cheerful as ever. "It looks like
we're in for some weather, so we'll beat it for shore. We're heading
for Noyo. You think you guys will hole up there? We can catch up
on the gossip if you do."

Sal and I agreed to meet in port if Ty decided to head in. I put
the radio microphone in its holder and turned to Ty. "Sal says a
storm is brewing."

"There is a big one outside, pushing up the swell, but it's predicted to hit above us. Another front is moving in, too, but pretty
far out. It shouldn't be a problem for a while yet." He paused,
scratching his head. "I sure hate to leave this kind of fishing."

Satisfied, and hoping with Ty to catch a few more fish, I went
back to work thinking of Sal and the possibility of seeing her
soon.

No one in the fleet was prepared for the storm's speed or in-
tensity. It was on us within hours, blowing a furious gale. Even Sal
and Jim, running early, were caught outside the harbor and had

hard sailing before they crossed the bar. We stayed where we were, along with our partner boats.

"Don't you think we should go in, Ty? It's pretty rough." The wind was howling now, and the smooth swells were no longer benign. There was white water everywhere.

"No, I've been talking it over with the others. We all agree we'll be better off setting the boats adrift, and we won't have the long run back out when the storm's over. It'll be rough, and we'll bob around like corks, but we'll be okay."

"Are you sure that's a good idea?"

"We'll be fine. Most trouble comes from running against the seas with winds driving down. No, the best thing is to cut loose." At my look of doubt, he explained, "Glass floats and drifting crates make it all the way across the Pacific in every conceivable kind of weather without breaking up. It's the same principle." He glanced out at the cresting waves and then said with a grin at the irony of his joke, "Why don't you pull in a few more fish while the weather's good?"

The boat continued at troll speed, despite the increasing winds. Decked out in foul-weather gear, I went back to pulling fish and kept at it until Ty broke away from the radios long enough to look back and see me standing waist deep in cockpit water, clinging to a cable. Luckily, I had looked up in time to see a monstrous tower of water higher than the mast, drenching me in its spray while the bouncing, nearly vertical boat rose up and over the massive swell.

Ty came on a run, talking in no gentle terms about the dangers of washing overboard, especially while wearing boots and heavy foul-weather gear. Within minutes he had the lines brought in, loose gear secured, and the engine shut down. We were adrift, both of us relieved that all possibility of work was at an end.

Once safely in the cabin, wet, shaking with cold and the memory of those tons of water looming overhead, I made my sheepish admission. "I thought I was a goner with that one."

Ty was curt. "Yes, you damned fool! Don't you know when it's time to come in from the rain?" Then, with a lopsided smile, he turned and pulled me close.

His response comforted me, and in the warmth of the cabin, we settled down while the radios clattered around us. Feeling secure there, I let fear sleep, coiled quietly around my heart.

Later, the Mickey Mouse was rattling away with the light chatter of men keeping track of one another. Ty and I were laughing together at Howard's current tale, when the single sideband radio capable of long-distance transmission suddenly boomed out a distress call.

"Mayday, Mayday. This is the *Lark*. Mayday! Is anyone picking this up?"

At the first Mayday, Ty jumped to the direction finder, and in the instant silence of radio chatter, I knew that everyone in hearing distance had done the same. Before the first transmission from the boat in distress was complete, the coast guard had responded and was under way. As quickly, Ty had our engine roaring, and we, too, were on a run for the trouble spot, as was everyone else.

"That boat is awfully far away, Ty. Can we get there in time?"

He shook his head. "I don't think so, but we have to try. The more boats that reach their location, late or not, the more chance there is of picking people out of the water."

This drama lasted through the longest day of my life. The endangered boat was a small one, and the new owner, lured by reports of fine weather and good fishing, had his wife and two small children with him. Boats everywhere were running to them. We all well knew that there was no help for the skipper of the *Lark*, sailing without a partner boat, until someone reached him. The nearest hope was hours away in heavy seas.

Heard through storm and static, the voice that came to us remained steady and cool. "We're going down. Boat sprung a plank below the waterline. My pumps can't keep up, and water's up to the engine base now. I'll keep trying to slow the leak." The radio silenced with this word.

It seemed an age before we heard from the *Lark* again. The transmission was calm, though terse. "My wife has her hands full with the kids. She can't handle the radio, too. I'll come back when I can." It was clear that he spoke only because of the urgency of the coast guard demand for response; radio contact was necessary for their cutter's direction finder to keep the location as it also ran for the distressed boat.

For some time after that, there was only static and the regular coast guard check. When the *Lark*'s skipper came back, his voice was still steadily matter-of-fact.

"I had to leave the engine room. Water is too high. I can't get at the leak anymore, but I slowed it as best I could with mattresses and bedding. The batteries are still above water. The radio should be okay for a while. We're listing hard to starboard, and the skiff is wedged tight. I'm going to try again to hack it loose." Once more, we were left to listen to crackle.

When the last message from the *Lark* reached us, its heart-wrenching report was unbelievably clear and unemotional.

"I can't get the skiff loose. Too much pressure against it. Just no way to get at it. My wife's got the baby. I've got my boy. We'll stay with the boat as long as we can. The radio will be gone in a few minutes." We listened, hardly breathing, until the steady voice was lost with the *Lark*'s batteries.

During all this, we had a series of crises of our own as we battered our way toward the stricken craft. The instant we began to move, the boat became a whale amok, and misery quickly became companion to fully awakened fear. Tons of black water smashed us from all angles as the boat pitched, bucked, and rolled, throwing everything, including Ty and me, against the bulwarks. I was certain that we, too, would sink. Ty seemed unaffected. Despite the effort of clinging to grab bars, he stood glued to his electronics, intent on our dials and gauges and the vessel in distress. I wept, not sure if my tears were for myself or for the innocents aboard the *Lark*.

We were listening to one of the regular coast guard reports when the engine room alarm bell shattered my brooding. Ty started, and after a quick look at the gauge panel, turned urgently to me. "It's the oil alarm. It looks like pressure is falling. You'd better get up here at the wheel, Bailey. Watch that we don't get knocked too far off course while I find out about this."

Too stunned to protest, I wrestled the bruising wheel while Ty went below to check the engines. It seemed an eternity before he came back. With every fluming smash against the hull, I'd been certain that he was thrown into hot, moving engine parts, convinced that my worst fears of disaster were realized.

Teary eyed with relief, I watched him calmly climb through the engine hatch. "The roll of the boat is messing up the oil levels. The gauge can't get a consistent read—nothing to worry about." Hardly were the words out of his mouth before a second alarm began to scream, this time the bilge pump. Back down into the engine room he went, and once again my terrors matched the slam of waves until he emerged safely to report, "Same thing. We're bouncing around so much that none of the gauges are registering properly."

Despite the churning of my heart, his calm eased me from panic, letting me hang on in the savage ride with some little degree of confidence while waiting for the next call from the *Lark*. It was as I listened, white knuckled, to the message about the jammed skiff that a terrifying shower of blue sparks exploded above Ty's head.

My instinctive scream was quickly squelched by Ty's black glower and his order, "Cut that out, Bailey! Quick, take over here."

There was no time for hysterics. The world ceased to exist beyond this moment's threat, and I did as bid while Ty methodically went after the cause of the trouble. Before long, he found a trickle of water following a radio antenna connection through the bulkhead. With a wry grin, he observed that a mix of electricity and water often did cause fireworks.

It seemed to take forever for Ty to plug the leak, make essential repairs, and ensure that all the necessary electronics were back in working order. When he was at last able to relieve me of my battering duty at the wheel, I collapsed on the plunging and heaving bunk, beaten and miserable. I wasn't there for more than two minutes before I realized that my nose was filled with smoke.

Wildly, I leaped up screaming, "I smell smoke! We're on fire."

Ty wasted no time with niceties. He grabbed my jacket and threw me aside while he tore the mattress from the bunk in what seemed like one motion. Grimly, he threw open the machinery cover below our bunk, allowing acrid smoke to pour out. "Watch the wheel," was all he said before reaching for the glow that smoldered in the depths of the housing for the radar power pack and voltage converter.

Once again I found myself struggling with the wheel, this time choking on smoke while praying sincerely, much too conscious of the horror of a fire at sea. As I watched through a haze of dread and smoke, Ty quickly and efficiently snuffed the beginning flames. Even in my state of near panic, I was struck by his calm steadiness, the same kind that came through so clearly in the voice from the *Lark*. As he worked, he reassuringly explained that the cause of this emergency was the same as the previous one: smashing waves had widened an aperture enough to allow water to trickle down a cable, creating more fireworks.

Once repairs were made and order restored, I sat paralyzed, my heart shaking my bones, and was there still when we heard the last call from the *Lark*. We continued to buck our way toward the doomed vessel until word came that a rescue boat had reached it. It arrived just ten minutes after the survivors went into the water, too late for the baby. Caught in rigging, she was carried down to rest with the *Lark* in the depths of that wickedly tumultuous sea.

When word of the rescue came through, Ty set a landward course with no more talk of drifting. The change in direction lessened the sea's brutality, making the long trip to shore only miserably bruising. We made our way through the narrow channel into the Noyo boat basin, too drained to wonder at the sight of hundreds of refugee boats rafted the full width of the river. With comfort and security in sight, I sent up a little prayer of gratitude, certain that even the most determined atheists in the fleet had done the same.

Sal waited on the dock. Our hugs were subdued.

"I can't quit thinking about that poor little mama, Bailey." Sal's face was contorted with grief. "The guys who got there first said she tried to fight them off. She was still trying to find her baby, wanting to get down deeper in that awful water. That must be worse than never having a kid at all, like Jim and me." Her eyes were filled with sorrow as they searched for mine, and for an instant I think we mourned two babies, one lost at sea, the other never to be.

Other dramas took place during that storm, though, mercifully, we knew nothing of them until later. Altogether, three boats went down, but the situation I was most grateful to miss involved Chance, sailing with Wally. With several others, including Howard, they went back adrift after the rescue of the survivors of the *Lark* and were pushed by wind and tide far south of us.

It was long hours into the storm when a man on one of the drifting boats suffered a heart attack. He was lashing down deck gear loosened during the worst of the weather and was washed over the side before his boat mates could reach him. There was no question of leaving the man; if humanly possible, he would be brought ashore for his family. Wally and Chance were the unlucky pair to find the floating body. Chance told us what little there was to learn.

"It was bad, Mom. He never did sink. Wally said air in his lungs kept him afloat and that it was proof that he died before he went into the water. Anyway, we caught his oilskins with a gaff hook, but together we couldn't lift him up to the deck. The dead weight was too much, and the seas were knocking us all over the place. We had to hold him in the water until we could bring in a boat with more men to help. It was bad."

My overriding thought was, *This is my child! He's too young to deal with death and tragedy.*

Ty patted him on the back and pronounced him a man to be proud of.

49

Life Celebrated

It's been said that man is the only animal with a sense of its mortality, and I believe it is true. Perhaps other creatures gather in grateful celebration of escape from mortal threat, though I know of none. Sal and I were standing together, still mourning the terrible losses, when word reached us that a great party was in the making.

Startled, I asked, "Is a party the right thing after all that happened?"

Sal lifted her eyes to mine, and we stared at each other for a moment. Suddenly her garish Clara Bow lips widened in a grin.

"It must be. I feel real good about getting to shore in time, and I sure was glad to see you and Ty. If Jim and me stayed out another half day in our little old lady, we might not have made it, either. Yeah, I feel like a party would be just dandy!"

At her words, pure exhilaration lit my whole being. "So do I! For a while there I thought I would never see land again, but here I am, and grateful for it. Why shouldn't we want to celebrate?"

Sal flung an arm out. "Can't change what's already happened; might's well get on with today and be happy we can!"

So it was that we accepted the unchangeable, as humans always have. We began to make plans for the party that was causing excitement all over the docks. Soon we were on our way to Fort Bragg, the small town only a quarter of a mile from the Noyo boat basin. Mindful of my promise to Jenny, I looked for a manicure and a decent haircut. Sal wanted a new pair of shoes.

Philosophy could not be said to have entered into any previous conversation between Sal and me. That day we came as close to it as we ever would. I noticed that she studied her own feet as we walked toward town, so wasn't surprised when in a wistful voice she said, "I sure hope I can find some pretty shoes." At my casual nod, she hesitantly offered, "Did you know I used to model shoes, before Jim?"

A bit taken aback at the unfamiliar tone and softened look, I did little more than shake my head as I glanced at her feet. I had never before noticed how surprisingly small, nicely shaped, and delicately arched they were, even in colored tennis shoes.

"For catalogs," she elaborated, smiling. "Jim was so proud of me. Sometimes I wonder if I should have quit modeling, but he needed me with him." We were several more steps along before she added in an odd half whisper, "I liked that."

A lump rose in my throat as I pushed my rough hands with their ragged nails deep in my pockets. Did Ty need me in that way, I wondered. Was the reason I stayed on the boat because *I* felt needed? Had I changed as Sal had changed?

The party that night was a once-in-a-lifetime event. Sal found her shoes. My hair was clean and styled, I had my manicure, and there was dancing in the streets. Where a live band was found on such short notice in that little town is beyond me, but there it was. The sense of celebration permeating that softly moonlit night was unsullied despite the abundance of alcohol. There was no drunkenness, no unhappy disruption, only a deep sense of camaraderie in that crowd of seagoing refugees.

Sal was the essence of the party, raucously assuring everyone, "It's a helluva good life, ain't it?"

Maybe she said it all.

50

TIGHT BOOTS

B ack at sea, I worked as hard as ever but no longer felt the zest for it that I once did. I told myself that nothing was changed, and believed it until the day Ty asked, "Something wrong, Bailey? You aren't up on the bridge as often as you used to be."

I smiled, denying a problem, but the question haunted my sleep.

Then, one morning, as we stopped for coffee during a lull in fishing, I found myself spilling out doubts only recently recognized, and adding a new discovery.

"I'm not scared all the time, the way I was before the storm. I don't think I ever will be again. What bothers me is more important. Ty, have you wondered what would happen in a real emergency where you needed someone who knew what they were doing?"

At Ty's perplexed expression, I elaborated.

"That storm told me how inadequate I am for anything more than pulling fish and cooking. You would do so much better, and probably be safer, with a puller who had more strength, more stamina, more knowledge of machinery and electronics." I hated to go on but knew I must. "And I've been thinking about things I've always wanted to try. Things that have nothing to do with fishing."

Ty wordlessly heard me out. In the end, he nodded and said only, "Okay."

Nothing more was said, and we continued on as before until another day when we sat together in the cabin. Gazing off into the distance, my man quietly and carefully said, "I've been thinking about everything you said, Bailey, and I appreciate that you told me. It's good that you're past being afraid, but it was bound to happen with or without the storm. I'm glad that isn't the reason you're thinking of staying home." He hesitated for several moments before adding softly, "You looked good at the party—nice, and even prettier than usual."

Then with an air of determination, he went on. "Ever since the storm, I've been backing off when things get a little rough. I think it's because I don't want to put you through anything like that again, and there's no room for that kind of thinking in this business."

Near tears, I answered, "Not if you want to be successful, and you do."

It was time for him to move on to a bigger boat, and I suddenly knew that it was okay. Every bit of it was okay with me, and I said as much.

"I've fought the idea because for a long time I've known that there's no way I could do the work a puller on a bigger boat would have to do. Besides, you might need another man or two, and that wouldn't do, would it?"

"No, it wouldn't. I've been thinking about it for quite a while, too. I just didn't want you to think I wasn't happy having you aboard, because it's been great."

"For me, too, Ty, and I love you for it. Greater minds than ours have said there are times and tides in every life. Why would ours be any different? The tide has changed, and it's time to move on."

My relief was twofold; I could release the tangle of indecision in my gut, and I could do it knowing that the timing was exactly right.

Our new direction was settled, but there remained fish to be caught before we could "hang it up" for the year. Life at sea returned to established routine, this time with less tension and far more comfort.

One tragedy at sea in a season is enough. That year, there were many. Heartbreaking word came that Tiny and the *Lila* had disappeared without trace on another long Pacific haul. The boat was known to be in a specific area, and Tiny was in regular radio exchange with others, when all contact ended without trace or explanation.

Cole was devastated, insisting, "I should have gone along like he wanted, Mom. Maybe it would have made a difference if I had."

It was with difficulty that I kept my own selfish gratitude hidden, allowing only grief to show.

The final, almost unbearable sorrow came on a late fall day of crisply blue skies. Ty and I were sitting in leisure on the flying bridge, watching a school of porpoise rise and fall in the opalescent water below, when the radio came on with another Mayday. It was Jim on the *Pisces*, fishing nearby.

When we reached the scene, we found Jim gone berserk, running crazily from radio to deck rail and back, staring down into the clear sea while the boat slowly circled.

Sal, taking advantage of the mild weather and slow fishing to wash down the boat, had garbed herself in foul-weather gear and the tall seaboots that she always wore too tight. In some misstep, she had toppled over the side. The heavy boots filled instantly with water, pulling her quickly down into the depths. Jim heard her yell when she went over. He reached the railing just soon enough to see her yellow slicker flared around her as she sank relentlessly out of sight. She was smiling, he insisted through his tears, and reaching up to him. His effort to catch her hand was useless. She went too fast.

51

FACING REALITY

Together, Ty and I finished out the year, but it was time for me to go. There was no lingering doubt; a seagoing life was not for me, as it could not be for most women. Sal's end haunted me, sapping me of both energy and enthusiasm, but Ty remained unchanged.

I am sure that we females deal with our realities in a different way than our men do, depending on emotion and instinct to lead us, resorting to analytical reason only for confirmation of decisions made. My time on the *River Run* convinced me that the basic male is, first and foremost, a reasoning creature. He can remain stoic when confronting very real danger because all of his being is submerged in thinking out the best way to survive. There is no room for emotion; that luxury can come after danger is past.

Perhaps these male and female differences are not arbitrary, but fixed and intrinsic, the result of eons of response to separate instincts in the long march of human survival. Maybe the choices Ty and I each made were only the demands of our separate natures. I yearned for the warmth of home and the comfort of security, while he required freedom to challenge convention and to explore new possibilities.

When the next year's season began, I stood again at the end of the breakwater as Ty proudly skippered his newly built big steel boat, *Typhoon Too*, through the jaws of the harbor. Close behind came the little old *River Run* with Chance grinning happily as he steered from the flying bridge while Cole danced on deck.

Calmly, I waved my men over the horizon.

EPILOGUE

Great change marked the lives of those who laughed, loved, and sweated at the crest of an industry. My nephew Jeff returned to the home and haunts of his youth after several years out of the country, unchanged, though now exuding confidence and an air of prosperity. With the smile I remembered from his boyhood, he surprised me one day with unexpected news and an invitation.

"Aunt Bailey, my mom would like to see you. Will you go home with me?"

"She doesn't want to see me, Jeff."

He shook his head. "No, it's all different. She's been seeing a doctor for quite a while and even goes to church. Please come."

Jeff walked me through her home, open and sunny, and out into the yard, where the sister I thought lost knelt to tend a colorful bed of flowers. When she looked up, her eyes were clear and happy.

"Hello, Bailey. How wonderful to see you. Shall we have tea here in my lovely garden?"

Jim walked away from the *Pisces* within weeks of Sal's death and joined her before a year was out. Virgil is long since gone, as are both Wally and Martha. Karl lived only a bit longer, and I lost track of Bess when she went back to her Oregon roots. Howard, ever seeking the new and challenging, bought a still bigger boat and joined the long-distance albacore fishery working across the Pacific from California to Okinawa and points between.

Paul continued to fish his boat, *Faith*, for several years after Amanda left. He did not remarry. He did eventually buy a larger boat, though I think he continued to yearn for his comfortable little *Faith*. We visited often over the span of years, and he always had wildly unbelievable tales of his numerous amours. Unbelievable, that is, until a certain concert and its secret is remembered. He was one who kept to the business long after it became less viable, and left his boat home only for the hospitalization that foreshadowed death.

None of our boys measured up to their mother's expectation that they would stun the world with accomplishment, but they are all good, steady family men. Despite the evidence of young manhood, neither Chance nor Cole continued to fish, but found other careers. Once out of the navy, both Cord and Chase returned to school long enough to strengthen the skills first learned among their waterfront mentors. Jenny remained true to promise. She did not marry a fisherman—she married a pilot. Carlos is with us still, a loyal member of the family, with beautiful children who call us grandparents.

Change is, we know, the one inevitability. Still, it can surprise us, as I was surprised on another blustery April day, years after I left the *River Run*. It was the day that Ty came stomping home from the docks and tossed his white cap up to its peg, saying, "I think I'll hang it up, Bailey."

Laughing, I turned to face him. "What is it this time?"

"No, I'm serious. They cut back on the length of salmon season again and are now talking about even more drastic restrictions on where we can fish. We're being regulated out of the business."

"Does it matter that much? You've been quitting salmon fishing early, and it never was your main fishery." Seeing how dejected he looked, slumped at the kitchen table, I dropped what I was doing and sat down with him. "You aren't serious about this, are you?"

"Yeah, I guess I am. There's no fun in the business anymore. It used to be that we were all in it together, but not now. Cooperation and sharing information on the grounds is a thing of the past. Just today, the men were talking about setting up another radio code for our bunch. What I hate is that they're right. With so many new boats on less and less unrestricted grounds, and with the number of new, efficient electronics, it gets so crowded on a spot that we're literally running over each other. It isn't just the overregulation and everything that goes with it. What it comes down to is that the future of the industry is unpromising on too many levels."

I reached for his hand. "Can't your organizations get a campaign going to at least fight some of the regulation?"

He shook his head. "We've tried, but there are powerful forces against us. Look at what happened to the abalone industry. We all knew what was going on, even a lot of the fish and game experts knew, but a million-dollar industry was sacrificed to the otters. Hundreds of jobs were lost, along with a satisfying way of life and seafood second to none. How can any of us fight government interference and radical environmentalism when an uninformed public supports it? Where there is need for some restrictions—well, I guess it's just hard to draw a line between hysteria and common sense. No, it won't be long before there isn't much of the commercial fishing business left. Inevitable, I think."

"I can't believe that."

Ty patted my hand. "The young ones going in don't know what the old days were, and some of the old-timers will adapt and find ways to stay with it, but for me, this is my last year."

And so it was. He stepped away from all his industry obligations, turning them over to younger blood. In believing the future of the business compromised, he was justified. Even Chance and Cole, ever their father's sons, chafed at the restrictive changes and sold out. Today, the industry as we knew it is all but gone. Few small boats remain.

At home now with piano and books, Ty and I are staid old landlubbers, sharing memories. Only yesterday we were laughing together over some now ancient photos, discussing those times and changes, when I casually asked, "If you could live life over, Ty, would you make the same choice?"

He eyed me incredulously. "You bet! What wouldn't I give to live it again, mistakes and all? I wouldn't change a thing. We had it good, Bailey. We had it the best."

I smiled as Sal's jubilant words reached from the heavens, straight to my heart: Men!

You just gotta love 'em.

GLOSSARY

bilge pump: Constantly pumps out water that inevitably collects in the bottom of the boat

bilge: All the water, flotsam, and jetsam that ends up in the bottom of the boat

boat puller: Crewman on a fishing boat (also, "puller")

breakwater: A long, narrow strip of boulders piled high in the water to act as a sea break

bumper tires: Old car tires hung on boats' sides to act as buffers

charts: Navigational sea maps with water depths, hazard markings, and more

cockpit: Stepped-down area at the back of the boat where pullers stand to pull in fish

dry dock: When boat is out of the water for maintenance

electrolysis-dampening zinc bars: Used to retard fish-repelling properties of boats' electronics

embarcadero: Business/public/commercial waterfront area of a town

fish gurry: Glue-like slime and guck from fish

flying bridge: Watch and steering area on the cabin roof, with compass and ship's wheel

Friscos: Frisco brand black denim stovepipe jeans

galley: Kitchen

girdies: Spools girdled by fishing line, used to winch in hooked fish

hang it up: To quit

hatch: Covered opening on deck accessing a belowdecks compartment

haul out: To put the boat in dry dock

head: Shipboard toilet

hoochies: Fishing lures

inclinator: Gadget that measures the boat's degree of list

iron mike: Automatic pilot

jigs: Fishing lures

Jimmy diesel: A GMC diesel engine

Mickey Mouse: Short-distance citizens band radio

moorage docks: Where the boat is tied up during the off-season

nippers: Hand/knuckle gloves cut from inner tube rubber to protect against hazards

Norwegian Stetson: Flat snap-brim white cotton cap, similar to a sports car cap

peanut anchor: Lightweight anchor used by small craft such as sailboats

port: The left side of the boat; also, a harbor

puller: Crewman on a fishing boat (also, "boat puller")

skunked: No fish

starboard: The right side of the boat

stern lines: Fishing lines strung from the back of the boat

tag lines: Fishing lines strung from the poles

the bends: Debilitating physical effect to undersea divers if they come up too fast

the grounds: Where the fish are

the jaws: Narrow entrance of a harbor when confined within two jetties of blasted stone

trawler: A fishing boat that drags nets

troller: A fishing boat that drags lines with lures through the water

ways: The structure that supports a boat when hoisted out of the water for maintenance

weasel pee: WD-40

wind chop: Action of the water with various winds, not severe

ABOUT THE AUTHOR

Photo by Gaelle

M. J. Munro is a fourth-generation San Luis Obispo County native. She lives on California's Central Coast, next to the sea and within eyeshot of land her great-grandparents cleared.

Munro has worked as a reporter and writer for a local weekly newspaper. In addition to Porpoise in Quicksilver, she has published the novel O'Halloran Land and the short story collection Tracks on the Big Sur. Both books are fictional accounts inspired by the stories of old-timers in the area surrounding San Simeon, Cambria, and Big Sur.

Porpoise in Quicksilver is loosely based on personal experience. When their lives in agriculture became problematic, Munro and her husband turned to commercial fishing.

Made in the USA
San Bernardino, CA
19 January 2016